C
M2/00

✓ S0-BRK-205

MacDonald, John D.

Slam the big door

SEP 1 4 1987

DATE DUE

8/95
H 1/98

SLAM THE BIG DOOR

Also by JOHN D. MacDONALD
In Thorndike Large Print

ONE MORE SUNDAY
THE LONELY SILVER RAIN

SLAM THE BIG DOOR

JOHN D. MacDONALD

THORNDIKE PRESS · THORNDIKE, MAINE

Library of Congress Cataloging in Publication Data:

MacDonald, John D. (John Dann), 1916-
  Slam the big door.

  1. Large type books. I. Title.
[PS3563.A28S6 1987b]   813'.54   87-11256
ISBN 0-89621-819-8 (lg. print : alk. paper)

SEP 1 4 1987

Large Print edition available in North America by
arrangement with John D. MacDonald Publishing, Inc.
c/o George Diskant & Associates.

Large Print edition available in the British Commonwealth
by arrangement with John Farquharson Ltd., London.

Cover design by James B. Murray.

SLAM THE BIG DOOR

one

The big house — the home of Troy and Mary Jamison — was of stone and slate and glass and redwood — with contrived tiltings and flarings of its egret-white roof. It stood on the bay side of the north end of Riley Key, over-looking the Florida Gulf, partially screened from occasional slow traffic on the lumpy sand-and-shell road that ran the seven-mile length of the key by a grove of ancient live oaks, so gnarled and twisted, so picturesquely hung with fright-wigs of Spanish moss that Mike Rodenska, walkng across to the Gulf Beach in the sunlight of an early April Sunday morning, had the pleasant fancy that the oaks had been designed by the same architect who had contributed the light and spaciousness and a certain indefinable self-consciousness to the Jamison home. The architect had drawn the trees and subcontracted them to an artistic oak-gnarler.

There was a shell path leading from the

sleeping house to the road edge where a big rural-delivery box, lacquered pale blue, stood solidly on a redwood post. Aluminum letters, slotted along the top of the box, spelled out D. Troy Jamison.

All these years of knowing the guy, Rodenska thought, seventeen years of war and peace, and I never knew about that "D" until it popped up on a baby-blue mailbox.

The dulled edges of the broken white shell bit into the tender soles of his feet, and he walked gingerly. He wore dark blue swim trunks with a wide white stripe down the side, carried a big white beach towel, a cigar case and tarnished lighter.

He was a sturdy man, Mike Rodenska, who couldn't stop lying a little bit about his height, and felt disappointed in himself whenever he caught himself in the lie, because he despised all forms of deceit. He was half-bald, with a fleshy nose and a solid thrust of jaw. There was a wryness and a gentleness about him, particularly evident in the brown eyes, deeply set under a grizzle of brow. He had been Troy and Mary Jamison's house-guest for the past five days of perfect Florida weather, and he had used the beach opposite the house with such diligence that the new deep red-brown tan over a natural swarthiness disguised the softness of all his years of newspaper work.

Beyond the road there was a path through small creeping plants and taller sea oats down to the wide beach. The path curved and he started to walk across the plants, winced and hobbled back to the path, sat down, pulled his left foot up onto his knee and picked three sand spurs from the sole of his foot.

A very bright man, he said to himself. You learn easy, Rodenska. Before, you wore shoes. These are the things that stuck to your socks yesterday, boy. They have a place, a destiny. They stick to you, they get farther from mother, then they settle down and raise baby sand spurs. Nature's devices.

He got up and followed the path down to the beach. The morning sun was low behind him, so the Gulf was not yet a vivid blue. It was gray and there was a silence about it, a long slow wait between the small lazy nibblings of immature waves against the flat wet sand left by the outgoing tide.

A flock of short-legged sandpipers ran south along the beach, pausing to stab needle bills into the wet sand, eating things too small to be seen, their legs a comic and frantic blur — a batch of tiny men grabbing breakfast on the way to work.

"Eat well," he said. "Be my guest."

He spread his white towel. Nine pelicans in single file flew north, a hundred feet off the beach, beating slow wings in unison, stopping at the same moment to glide long and sure, an inch above the grayness of the water, full of a banker's dignity and memories of prehistory.

"The loan committee," said Mike Rodenska. "Renew my note, hey?"

The Jamison cabaña, of enduring tidewater cypress, weathered to a silver gray, stood on thick stubby pilings just above the three-foot drop where the big storms had cut into the beach far above the high-tide line. He could see glasses standing on the porch railing, glinting in sunlight, a few with an inch of amber in the bottom, stale forgotten liquor from last night's party.

He walked along the beach, wet sand cool on the soles of his feet, and came suddenly upon a line of footprints that led directly into the water — narrow feet with high arches. Feminine. He looked up and down the beach and saw no evidence of her return, and he suddenly felt very alert and apprehensive about the whole thing. Some of the ladies last night could have . . . but logic came quickly. Wet sand. Outgoing tide. And with the last footprint so close to the lethargic suds it had to be a recent thing. He looked up and saw a towel and beach bag on the cabaña steps, then he stared out and at last spotted, at an angle to the south, the tiny white dot of a swim cap over a half mile out.

He waded in and swam, making a great splashing and snorting, losing his wind with a quickness that hurt his pride. He floated on his back, gasping, and as his breathing became easier he was pleasantly conscious of the almost imperceptible lift and fall of the swell. He winded himself again in a grim sprint toward the beach, and had a fit of coughing as he walked up to his towel. When he looked for her again he saw her about two hundred yards out, coming in, using a slow and effortless crawl, rolling on the beat for air, snaking her brown arms into the water. He took pleasure in watching her. She stood up and waded ashore, and he admired the width of shoulder and slenderness of waist before — as she took off her white cap and fluffed that coarse black, white-streaked hair — he realized it was Mary Jamison. She wore a gray sheath swim suit with some pale blue here and there, and as she walked up to him the sun touched droplets on her thighs and face and shoulders, turning them to mercury.

"Good morning, Mike."

"What year was it you won the Olympics?"

11

"Oh, pooh! What would you expect? I could swim as soon as I could walk. That makes forty-one years of practice."

"You do this every morning?"

"When it gets too cold I use the pool."

"You looked so alone 'way out there, Mary."

"That's the good part of it," she said, and added quickly, "How does coffee sound?"

"Hot and black? Like a special miracle, but you shouldn't go all the way back . . . "

"Just to the cabaña."

"Oh. I keep forgetting the conveniences around here."

"Sugar?"

"Maybe half a teaspoon, thanks," he said: "Help you?"

"Stay in the sun, Mike."

He watched her walk up to the cabaña. A little heaviness in hips and thighs. A little softness in upper arms and shoulders. Otherwise, a girl's body. Make them all swim, he thought. For forty-one years. What if I'd had that routine? With me it would be forty. Thirty-nine, starting at one year. Rodenska — beach boy. Flat belly. Good wind. All I needed was money. Does swimming keep your hair? Are there any bald beach boys? In Hawaii, no.

Troy's letter hadn't said much. But the inference was he had landed neatly on his feet in this marriage. "Mary and I want you to come down, Mike. We've got a beach place with plenty of room. We built it three years ago. You can stay just as long as you want."

And so, Mike had been prepared for a younger Mary, a second-marriage type, golden and loaded. Not this gracious woman who had greeted him with genuine warmth when they arrived, after Troy had driven all the way up to Tampa in the big Chrysler to pick him up and bring him to Riley Key. She was obviously the same age as Troy or a little older, with strong features — a hawk nose, flat cheeks, wide mouth, dark eyes that held yours steadily, rosettes of white in her curly black hair. She had such a special poise and dignity that, after the first ten minutes with her, Mike could not imagine her doing any crude or unkind thing. He found himself thinking — not without a twinge of guilt for the implied disloyalty — that Troy had received better than he deserved.

She came down from the cabaña with a tin tray, quilted in the Mexican manner, with fat white beanwagon mugs of steaming coffee, a battered pewter bowl full of Triscuits, and big soft paper napkins weighted down with her cigarettes and lighter. She had brushed her hair, put on lipstick and sunglasses with red frames.

As she put the tray on the sand in front of the towel and sat beside him, she said, "I took a chance you might share one of my vices. There's just a dash of Irish in the coffee, Mike."

He grinned at her. "I'll force myself."

"What did you think of the party?"

"I was supposed to bring it up first and say thanks. Thanks. I got names and faces all screwed up. I got sorting to do."

"The party was too big."

"No, Mary. I like a big party. You know, you get a sort of privacy in a big party. You can do more looking. I'm a people-watcher. Like a hobby. No binoculars, like with birds. I got an hour to kill, I sit in a bus station."

"Maybe I can help you do some sorting."

"A pink-faced joker, sixtyish, in Bermuda shorts, with a political voice. Taps you — or at least me — on the chest to make his point. Soon as he found out I was newspaper — or ex-newspaper, or whatever the hell I am — he cornered me and made oratory."

"That one is easy. Jack Connorly." He saw her make a face.

"No like?"

"I guess you could say he's trying to be

Mister Republican in the county, but he's about fifth or sixth in line, I'd say. He's been after Troy to run for the County Commission."

"Troy!"

She giggled "That's my reaction too."

"My God, will he?"

"Honestly, Mike, I don't know. He won't say yes and he won't say no."

"So that's why Connorly was bugging me about the duty of the citizen and all that jazz. I'll have to have a little chat with our boy."

"Jack's wife is the little dark jumpy-looking one. He's in real estate."

"Now how about the blonde on the aluminum crutches?"

"Beth Jordan. She chopped herself to ribbons last year. She ran her Porsche under the back of a truck. They didn't expect her to live, but now they think she'll be off the crutches in a few more months. Did you notice the scars?"

"It was too dark."

"They've spent thousands on plastic surgery."

"Just one more for now, Mary. The kid with your daughter."

"With Debbie Ann? Oh, that was Rob Raines, a local lawyer. They practically grew up together."

"You notice lawyers get younger every year? Doctors too. You want old guys, full of dignity and wisdom. So you get a kid looks like a bat boy, and how can he have had time to learn enough? There was one guy who treated Buttons. . . . "

A familiar bitter twisting of his heart stopped him, and he sipped the coffee, chewed savagely on a Triscuit, and outstared an optimistic gull who was walking back and forth ten feet away with all the assurance of a city pigeon, staring at him with alternate eyes.

"You try to be casual and it doesn't work," she said gently.

He could not look at her. "Also," he said, "you don't expect anybody to understand at all. And when they do, just a little, you resent them, maybe. The special arrogance of grief, Mary. You know. I hurt worse than anybody ever did."

"Mike, I wanted you to come down, very much. Troy and I talked it over. There was never any question. But I don't want you to think that I expect that you have to . . . sing for your supper by talking about private things. But if you ever want to talk . . . "

He overrode her with a heavy insistence. "I was talking about the one guy that treated her. A kid, you would think. But old around

16

the eyes in the special way the good ones have. And he leveled with me. I appreciated that. None of that mighty-mystery-of-medicine jazz. He gave me time to brace myself by saying — no hope. And I never could lie to her and get away with it, so she got the message too, and had time to brace herself, so toward the end in that hospital — well, like a big airline terminal where the flight is a couple weeks late and you got time for ways to say good-by in all the little ways, and nobody is too surprised when they announce the flight."

"Mike," she said.

He could look at her then, and see tears standing in her fine dark eyes and manufacture a fake Hemingway grin and say, "Knock it off, lady."

"Mike, it fades. It really does. Oh, it always comes back, but not as sharp."

"They keep telling me that. How long ago was it for you?"

"Seven years. 1952. I was thirty-five and Debbie Ann was sixteen. Haven't you got a boy about that age?"

"Close. Micky is seventeen and Tommy is fifteen. And three years later you married Troy?"

"Yes. And we've had four wonderful years."

He stared at her until her chin came up a lit-

17

tle, in a small motion of pride and defiance, and then he said, "Until when?"

"I don't know what you mean."

"Mary, Mary. I know the guy. Five years I didn't see him. Does he turn into somebody else? I'm not so wrapped up in my own sorrow I suddenly get dense about people."

"It has nothing to do with you. Excuse me, but it has nothing to do with you. You're here because you're Troy's best friend. And because it's good for you to be here at this time."

"You said to me if I ever want to talk . . . Okay, I give you the same deal."

She looked angry for a moment, then suddenly smiled. "All right, Mike." Just then an old car came clanking and chattering up the key from the south and turned into the Jamison drive. Mary stood up and shaded her eyes against the sun. "That's Durelda already. Oscar brings her. She works a half day on Sunday. I should go up and get her straightened away on the food. Sunday is a vague day around here, Mike. People come and go, and pick their own indoor and outdoor sports. I do absolutely no hostessing. The only standard item is a big brunch-lunch-buffet deal by the patio pool, from noon to three. Eat what you please and make your own drinks. Introduce yourself to anybody who looks interesting. When you're finished would you put the tray in the cottage?"

"Sure."

She walked toward the house, pausing to pick up her towel and beach bag from the cabaña steps.

Mike was left alone in the morning sun, thinking about Troy's second wife, and Troy's first wife, and how you always knew when the flavor of marriage was not just right. This one was not just right, and it could be permanent wrong or temporary wrong. He hoped it was temporary. They can't fool you. Not with the love words and the affectionate gestures, because there's always that bitter aura, that little stink of coldness, the tension-edge of love gone awry.

A hundred feet offshore a black monster, flat as a plate, burst high out of the water, seemed to pause at the top of the leap, then fell back with a resonant crack of leathery wings against the water. Taken completely by surprise, Mike's first thought was, I'll tell Buttons about that.

And he knew immediately that Buttons had been in the ground since the second day of March. Something happened inside him that was like tumbling down stairs, and he caught up a fistful of sand and squeezed it until his knuckles popped.

Who do you tell?

The coffee was gone. He carried the tray into the cabaña and placed it on the countertop beside the sink and rinsed the cups.

He went out and swam again, then lay prone in the sun on the white towel, his eyes clenched against the dazzle, while he walked back through the corridors of memory to the time when he had first met Troy Jamison.

It had been late in 1942, and he could well remember the completeness of the miracle of being clean, of being between coarse white sheets in a hospital bed, and hearing the voices of women after too many lifetimes on the island. He was twenty-three and he had all his hair, a permanent ring of quinine in his ears (they had atabrine but in limited supply), the gray pallor of island warfare (as opposed to the cinema bronze of Errol Flynn in Burma), some ugly ulcers on his legs, and a peach-sized piece of meat missing from his left thigh — high and on the outside not affecting important mechanical parts — but bitching up the muscle just enough so the slight limp lasted three years.

He was twenty-three, and he had felt he couldn't ever get any older or any wiser, and

Micky had been in the world almost a month but the news hadn't caught up. And he couldn't seem to get enough sleep.

As one of the combat correspondents assigned to the First Marines, Rodenska had rated officer accommodations in the hospital just outside Melbourne, one bed in a twenty-bed ward, with windows to let in morning sun. It seemed appropriate that near the end of the year it was spring in south Australia. The whole world was screwed up that year.

There were all kinds in the ward, and some of them were very bad off, and on the third day when the major on his left died of his head injury without ever regaining consciousness, Second Lieutenant Troy Jamison was put in that bed. Nobody felt conversational. It was a kind of wariness. The dialogue, what there was of it, was inadvertent Hemingway. You really didn't want anybody to detect how perfectly, wonderfully, overwhelmingly, goddamn glad you were to get off that island.

But when they were awake at the same time they picked up the essential information about each other. They were both twenty-three. Jamison was with the First. He'd got his field commission on the island. He felt uneasy about being an officer. He'd graduated from Syracuse University, and he'd been

21

working in an advertising agency in Rochester when the war came along. He had a smashed shoulder. He was a big underweight blond, sallow skin pulled tight across high hard cheekbones, green eyes set slanty in his head.

Mike couldn't remember seeing him on the island, but he had spent twelve days with Baker company of Jamison's battalion, and that made a link. And he had spent six months on the *Times-Union*, so that made him familiar enough with Rochester to make a second link.

But Troy didn't warm to him. Mike found he liked Jamison, and he knew the reason for the reserve. He knew he could break it down, but he didn't want to sound like a horse's ass while doing so. Finally, when he had his chance, he said, "I belong to the club, Lieutenant."

"What do you mean?"

"I didn't drop a typewriter on my foot. I had seventy-one days on that island, and the morning banzai meant work for everybody."

So Troy had studied him and then given him a slow grin and said, "That's against the Geneva Convention, boy."

"They didn't give me a copy written in Jap. You're not trade school anyhow. At heart you're a crummy copy writer."

So Troy had loosened up some and a little

later, when Captain Irely arrived with a foot missing, and full of noisy lies about Fearless Rodenska, the poor man's Pegler, Troy loosened up the rest of the way.

By the time they were permitted to draw a vehicle from the hospital pool for visits to Melbourne, they had become very close. They had both spent too much time with brave men who, if you tried to talk about a play, a book, a painting or a philosophy, would look at you with utter blankness which would crystallize to contempt. They told each other how many times they had come close to cracking. It took a little time before they could talk about the island. They got steaming drunk on Australian ale. Mike told Troy all about Buttons and how he met her and how she got her name. "It was kid stuff. Bring your hobby to school. She was maybe eight, and she collected buttons and brought them, hundreds of them, in a box to school and the bottom fell out of the box. Buttons all over hell. And the name stuck." Troy admired the pictures of big-eyed Buttons and seemed to take almost as much pleasure in the pictures of Micky as Mike did.

Troy had a girl in Rochester. Her name was Bonita Chandler, called Bunny. They wrote faithfully. Troy said he was going to marry her, and he called himself a damn fool for not marrying her before he left, in spite of her parents' opposition.

They talked about women in wartime, and how being unfaithful to girl or wife was so damn easy it was really a unique accomplishment to be true. Certainly unique in the Corps. But all that talk of virtue was before running into Marty and Liz. They were hearty, wholesome sisters of twenty-five and twenty-seven, with the typical buoyancy and easy laughter and sturdy bodies and bad teeth of most young Australian women. They were both from Broken Hill, and their men were in the African desert, and their kids — one belonging to Marty and two to Liz — were in Broken Hill with their parents while the girls did war work in Melbourne, clerical work connected with the port. They lived in a small apartment, and, on one Sunday afternoon, on their way to a date, they were energetically annoyed by two tipsy Marines in a small park. Troy put the fear of God into the Marines, and then the four of them sat in the park for a little while and talked, and then the Henderson sisters decided not to show up for their date and they all went back to the apartment.

They were two good-tempered healthy women lonely for their men, and they were

24

two lonely men with more islands in their future. The arrangement lasted through the remainder of the hospital time, and through the rest of camp time, right up until they re-tuned to duty, Mike first and, as he found out later, Troy two weeks later.

It was an indication of their special rapport that after the involvement with Marty and Liz had begun they did not talk with each other about either faithfulness or guilt. They accepted the situation. Troy had more time with the girls. Mike was by then writing color pieces on the Melbourne scene and wangling them through censorship, while Troy jeered at him, calling him a beaver.

On the night before Mike was returned to duty Marty's tears dropped hot on his throat in the bedroom darkness, but not many and not for long. She cried without making a sound. He was back in Melbourne eight months later, but somebody else was in the apartment. They knew the girls had gone back to Broken Hill. The husband of one of them had been killed, but the couple in the apartment did not know which one.

In 1943, Mike got back to the States for three weeks, and when Tommy was born he was back in the islands, but that was 1944 and it was a different kind of war because by then you knew how it would end. You couldn't be certain you'd live to see the end of it, but you did know how it would end. He knew he'd very probably see the end of it, barring some air-transport foulup, because it was no longer necessary for him to prove to himself the things it had been important to prove in the beginning. He had learned that he could react adequately, though not brilliantly, to utter and desperate emergency. He had been to the well. And there was always a sameness about the well. And so he was able, without feeling any self-contempt, to start taking better care of the pitcher. And he had long since gotten over the juvenile affectation of trying to look like a combat type despite the correspondent insignia. It was the newcomers who had something to prove — more to themselves than to others. So he could prop up a bar, as neat as if he were on Pentagon duty, and be mildly and not unkindly amused by the hairy affectations of the new ones.

But he could not keep himself from taking childish pleasure in moments of inadvertent revelation.

Like at Naha, a couple of weeks before Hiroshima. He'd been at the officers'-club bar talking with two of them. He'd listened while they were being very profound about kamikazis and island warfare. One was from a little string of Texas papers, the other from a slick magazine.

"You been out here long, son?" the fat one asked him.

"Quite a while."

The thin one looked him over and said, "You'll learn it's a hell of a lot different than Stateside."

"I guess it is," Mike said. They wore helmet liners, canteens and trench knives.

And just then Colonel Billy Brice, the Corps artillery specialist, wearing only the important bits of fruit salad, came barreling up, scowling like thunder, and gave Mike a punishing smack on the biceps and said, "If I'd known what you were going to send off Saipan, you son of a bitch, I'd have shot you myself."

"Always a pleasure to write up one of my heroes, Colonel, sir."

Brice gave him a tight grin. "Or maybe you could have saved me the trouble on the Canal, zigging instead of zagging. Say, I got an old drinking buddy of yours on my staff. Jamison. I took him off the line three months ago. He'd had his share."

"Where is he?"

"Stick around. He should show." Brice strode off.

"Isn't that Billy Brice?" the fat one said.

"Yes."

"I don't think I caught your name," the thin one said hesitantly.

"Mike Rodenska."

"Bell Syndicate?"

"Yes."

"Jesus Christ!" the fat one said. "I thought you'd be older. You been out here since the Crusades. Was I telling you all about island warfare? Jesus Christ."

It was one of the pleasurable moments in a long war.

Captain Troy Jamison arrived about twenty minutes later. By then the club had gotten too noisy for coherent conversation. They walked down and sat on the docks in the chilly night, with a bottle to keep the chill off. They talked half the night. Troy had seen more than his share. He was no longer ill at ease about being an officer. He had lost a lot of his people. It had rarely been his fault. And he had protected and saved a lot of his people, and that had always been his design, within the range of his orders.

It was, Mike thought, a narrow maturity, an encapsulated and forced version which left the eyes old and the mouth still young. He had seen a lot of it, and seen it in death when the eyes were merely empty, and the mouth forever young.

"One last island," Troy said in the night, "the biggest one of all, and that ends it. I feel so goddamn remote. Once upon a time I wrote a hell of a lot of copy about a new shopping center. And kissed a girl named Bunny. Hell, Mike, I've got to go back into that and it's got to become important again. That's the deal. Is it going to become important?"

"For nearly everybody."

Troy offered the bottle, then killed it and hurled it into Naha Bay. "I wanted a lot. But in a dreamy half-assed way. Now I'm going to want a lot — more than my share. And one damn way or another, I'm going to get it. What do you want?"

"I didn't have the same war you did, Cap."

"What the hell do you want?"

"Mom's apple pie."

"Screw you, Rodenska."

"Twice on Tuesdays. I'm a newspaper bum. All I want is my byline. And Buttons. And beer. Alliteration."

"Now without drama, Mike. Listen. Some of the guys I had, they'll never even begin to find their way back. And there are some who'll have no trouble at all. I can see them, but I can't see me. I'd just like to know how

I'm going to be."

"You're going to be fine."

They were on the same dock with another bottle early in the evening when word came that it was over. Within a half hour the six hundred ships in the area and most of the shore installations were hurling bright hardware into the sky. By then they had a bottle apiece and they crawled under a Navy warehouse. Twenty-one men died that night when the fragments of celebration fell out of the sky and down on their joyous heads. There were a million men on the island, all suddenly technologically unemployed.

"You seem to be breathing," the girl said. Mike, startled, rolled up onto one elbow and stared at her. She sat cross-legged in the sand beside his towel, wearing a yellow swim suit. He had been so far away it took him several sun-bleared moments to remember where he was and identify her as Debbie Ann, Mary's pretty daughter.

"Hello. Slow reaction time. I was fighting an old war."

"That's where you and Troy got to know each other?"

"That's right." He could not avoid an instinctive wariness where Debbie Ann was

30

concerned. He knew she was twenty-three, but she managed to look fifteen. Her voice was thin and high and childish, and he suspected that the effect was intentional. She had been Deborah Ann Dow, and then she had, without adequate warning to her mother or step-father, left Wellesley to become Mrs. Dacey Hunter of Clewiston, Virginia, for two years. Troy had told Mike about her on the drive down from Tampa. Debbie Ann had her own money from Bernard Dow's estate. Last August she had come back to stay with them and, six months later, in accordance with the Florida divorce laws, she had become Mrs. Deborah Dow Hunter.

But she looked fifteen, and she was very pretty, and she looked like trouble. She was a little girl, with rusty-blonde hair and delicate, rather pointed features. She had a flavor of wanton mockery about her, of sexual cynicism. She gave an erroneous impression of plumpness, despite her obvious — at a distance — slenderness.

On the way back from Tampa, Troy had said, "I don't know how long she'll stay, but Mary is happy to have her home again. The two of them stopped off with us for a week in fifty-seven when they were on a four-month honeymoon. Mary was sick about it. Hunter was about thirty-five then. Big red-faced type. Traveled with a lot of expensive gear. Bottle-a-day man. Called up friends all over the country. Gave Debbie Ann a belt across the fanny every time she got within reach. Then he took her back to his horse farm to live."

"Why did they break up?"

"She never said. I'd guess that after sex wore a little thin, he bored her. She gets good alimony until she marries again. The closest she came to telling us why it went sour was when she said she got sick of being cooped up in the old homestead with a lot of Hunter women around clucking over her narrow pelvis while Dacey went galloping cross country tipping over all his old girlfriends in box stalls."

Debbie Ann slowly scratched a bug welt on a perfect shin and said, frowningly, "I get the scoop that Daddy Troy was on the heroic side. Or is that a new family legend?"

"He was good. He had a squad and then a platoon and then a company, and he earned it every time."

"Somehow it doesn't fit."

"He was twenty-three when I met him, Debbie Ann."

"Oh, I don't mean age. I'm not stupid,

Mike. Anyhow, after my own father, Troy seems more like my generation. It made Mary a little jumpy at first, marrying Troy, worrying about what her friends would think, I guess. Daddy'd been dead two years, and he was nearly sixty when he died. More like my grandfather, I guess. I never did get to know him real well."

"I didn't know there was such a big difference in Mary's age and your own father's age."

"He married her when she was eighteen, and she had me when she was nineteen. He was a business associate of my grandfather. And he fell in love with Mary. He'd never been married. There was a lot of opposition. But it worked out. It was a good marriage, and Mother told me once she didn't really fall in love with him until after she had me. Anyway, I wasn't thinking about age, talking about Troy."

"About what, then?"

"Skip it. I can't explain it. How long did the party go on after I left with Rob? You met him, didn't you? Rob Raines, the earnest attorney. I've known him forever."

"I remember meeting him. When I folded at one, the party was still going on."

"Rob brought me back about three. I was afraid he woke you up, the fuss he made. Did he?"

"Didn't hear a thing."

She sighed. "We left here and went to a damn beach party. A couple of miles down the key. I used to adore them when I was young and gaudy. But I've outgrown them, I guess. Charred meat and drinks that taste of paper cup, and a zillion bugs and somebody who can't quite play a guitar, and dirty songs and somebody throwing up and then the inevitable routine — a prolonged interval of skinny-dipping in the romantical moonlight. I feel all over fingerprints. I swear to God I thought at one point Rob was making a sincere effort to drown me, but all he had on his mind was some sort of amphibious love-making. He was a good kid, but he certainly has turned out pretty self-important and dull."

"Mary says you practically grew up with him."

"Now there's an apt phrase," she said, and smirked. He could see that she did resemble her mother, but in some strange way the character and passion and strength in Mary's face became weakness and self-love and indulgence in the girl's. "Want to hear about my reckless past?"

"Not so much I'm panting," he said.

She moistened her lips. "I like you, Mike. Here's how it was with me and Robert Raines.

34

I was fifteen and he was nineteen, and he had a dandy little Thistle named Dizzy and I crewed on her in the yacht-club races. We necked when we had a chance and that was all. And one summer day — that was while Daddy was dying — it took him a long time to die — we snitched a bottle of white rum and bought two fried chickens and took Dizzy down the bay and out through Horseshoe Pass and down the outside — this key wasn't built up the way it is now — and beached Dizzy in a very deserted place and had a picnic which turned into necking and, with some help from the rum, I suddenly found myself right in the middle of a fate worse than death. It scared hell out of both of us. I kept him handy until the calendar let me off the hook, and then I called him up and told him I never wanted to see him again. I was squeamish about boys for a year. Yes, we practically grew up together. And now he's the promising young attorney and he can't understand why I'm not in a fever to jump back into the sack with him. He hasn't got marriage on his mind and neither, may I add, have I, and I can also add that I'm not what you'd call dead set against fun and games from time to time, but damn if I'm going to let him get away with assuming all he has to do is snap his fingers, just because

35

he was the very first. He was actually indignant about my not letting him into our cozy little guest wing last night. And when he left he roared off like a jet, wheels spinning and gravel flying."

"I dimly remember that kind of a sound."

She rose lithely to her feet and smiled down at him. "The first dramatic chapter in the life of Deborah Ann, Girl Failure. Be good and I'll tell you more."

"The script will never sell."

"Why not, sir?"

"I got the feeling it would be monotonous, I mean hearing all of it."

Her eyes narrowed for a moment before she regained her composure and made a face at him. She walked down toward the water. He watched the swing of her hips, the honey-brown of her shoulders, the narrowness of waist, the flex of calves. Sensing that she would look back at him when she reached the water's edge, he lay back to deny her the satisfaction.

A bald old guy, he thought. But it doesn't matter to her. It's her kind of narrowness. There are businessmen and doctors and such — very dull guys who have no interest at all outside their work. So with her it's sex. Vocation, avocation and hobby. Intentional and unintentional provocation. I wear pants so I'm am audience. Legitimate. Somebody to practice on. The girlish confession was provocation. So is the way she leaves the guest bath we share. Full of steam and perfume and soppy towels. Poor Rob. She's a bad type, Rodenska. Don't sleepwalk. Don't get too hungry. And subtle rebuffs aren't going to work, because she is really pretty stupid.

He thought of a way to give her a message. He liked it. So he got up, picked up towel, cigar case and lighter and, without a glance toward the Gulf, trudged back to the guest wing for his shower.

two

The large patio on the bay side of the Jamison house was half-roofed and completely screened. A small swimming pool, about eighteen feet by thirty, took up a third of the available space. There was a lushness about the inevitable planting areas, tree ferns, jasmine, Jatropha. A big broad-leaf Monstera dreamed in a fat cedar tub, nursing its fibrous fruit. Part of the floor area was of compacted concrete block stained dark blue, and there were other areas of slab concrete broken by cypress strips into random rectangles, with broken beach shell set into the cement to give a pleasing texture. There was deck furniture of redwood with wide arms, chairs of tubular bronze, and small, unmatched, glass-top tables.

In the warmth of the April noon the glass doors that separated the living room from the patio had been rolled back on their aluminum tracks into the recesses in the walls on either side. There were bright cushions, sun-faded, on the apron of the pool.

There was a long table near the pool, with a white cloth, stacks of paper plates, and a pattern of sunlight and narrow shadows across the chrome and copper and ceramic tureens under which blue alcohol flames burned, paled by sunlight.

There was no sea wall along the bay shore. Mangroves grew there, and some had been cut away to provide vistas of quiet water and the mile-distant mainland shore speckled with pastel block houses. Just to the north of the house there was a sea wall and a boat basin where the Jamison cruiser, a thirty-eight-foot Huckins, sat hot and white at her moorings, glinting in the sun.

There was quiet music on the high-fidelity system, from speakers hidden in living room and patio.

Mike Rodenska, ravenous after showering and changing to slacks and sport shirt, ladled himself a plate so generous he felt guilty about it, walked over and sat in one of the big redwood chairs in an empty corner, and began to eat.

Two minutes later a round brown woman wearing orange shorts, a red shirt, straw slippers and a clattering jangle of junk jewelry came over to him, carrying half a large Bloody Mary.

"Now don't try to get up, Mr. Rodensky. I'm Marg Laybourne. A neighbor. We live just down the key. The pink house. I'm terribly sorry we couldn't make the party last night. I'm one of Mary's very closest friends." She pulled a straight chair close and sat down. She had a breathless way of speaking. He had seen dark brown eyes like those before, and in a moment he remembered where. In the chimp cage at the zoo — an intent and liquid curiosity, full of malice and mischief. "Don't you think these Sundays are a wonderful custom, Mr. Rodensky?"

"Rodenska. Mike."

"Oh. Rodenska. Is this your first visit to Florida, Mike?"

"The first."

"Please keep eating. Everything looks delicious. We've been down here five years now, nearly six. Charlie, that's my husband, was in banking and he had a coronary and retired, but you wouldn't know it to look at him now, but he does have to be a little careful, but not as careful as he should be, I keep telling him. Are you on a vacation, Mike? Oh, I'm sorry. That was a stupid question. Mary told me you lost your wife a little while ago and they'd asked you down here for a change. Mary said you're in the newspaper business."

"I was."

"You and Troy got to know each other in the army."

"Marine Corps."

"Well, in the war anyway. Charlie was in the Navy in Washington on a sort of civilian thing. I guess this must be a really total change for you, Mike, coming to Riley Key."

"After what I'm used to?"

"It is unusual here, don't you think? I call it the last outpost of gracious living, and yet we're not formal at all. I mean the homes along here, it's more like a club. This whole north end of the key. The Jamisons and Laybournes and Claytons and Tomleys and Carstairs and Thatchers. Gus Thatcher, and he *is* an old darling, bought up most of this land in the beginning and he's been careful to sell it to the right people. And the Key Club is so handy. We usually all end up there Sunday evenings."

"We do?"

"Haven't you seen it yet? It's a rickety old place, full of stuffed fish, but the food is divine, really."

"It's all like one big happy family."

"What? Oh, yes. Exactly. There are a few

who don't . . . participate very much, but we don't have any of the wrong sort."

"This old darling-type fellow, this Gus somebody, you figure he'd sell me a hunk of land?"

She seemed startled. "Well . . . the best pieces are gone and it's really gotten terribly dear. The last piece sold, to a perfectly darling couple named Crown, well, it went at a hundred and sixty a foot, Gulf to bay, so they had to pay thirty-two thousand for their two hundred feet, and they're going to start to build soon."

"I wouldn't need so much, Marg. Just to park a trailer on."

"A trailer!"

"We call them mobile homes now. It sounds more deluxe."

"You couldn't do that! This is all zoned A-1 residential. My goodness, you'd never . . . you're joking, aren't you?"

"Yes. I'm pulling your leg, Marg. Actually I'm loaded."

"What?"

"Loaded. Up to here in money."

"Really?"

"What you call *nouveau riche*. I'm a diamond in the rough. Heart of gold. I really come on for dogs and kids. I'd be an asset to the Key."

She had become very uncertain. "Are you really thinking of staying here?"

"I'm looking around, kiddo. Put it that way. Of course, I move into a place like this, I'd change my name to Rodens."

"Are you being rude?"

"I don't want to make you sore. I figure you could tip me off on something good down here to get into. Or that Charlie of yours could. Got to put money to work, you know."

"Did you . . . sell your newspaper?"

"I never owned one. No, it was like this, Marg. My old man was a real slob. Ran a sheet metal shop in Buffalo, New York. He was so dumb and crude and ignorant people couldn't stand him. I couldn't. I never saw him one time since I was sixteen. But he had one hobby. He bought little chunks of stock and put them away. I never knew about that. Not until he died. Crazy stocks like Polaroid and Electric Boat and Reynolds Metals. The timing is interesting. Last October my wife gets a diagnosis of cancer, one of the fast hopeless kinds. By the end of November I am entirely out of money. By middle December the lawyers in Buffalo find me, ten days after the old man is buried, and suddenly I'm worth a few hundred thousand bucks. I could draw against it right away, but I didn't get it all until two weeks after my wife died. Now my kids are in Melford School in Vermont, and I'm loaded, kiddo."

She stared at him. He noted that her hand shook a little when she hoisted the drink to her mouth.

She got up and said, "I hope you'll have a very nice visit here, Mr. Rodenska."

"Thanks, Mrs. Laybourne."

She started to turn away and then turned back with a small and social laugh, and a special gleam of malice. "You'd better be careful about putting any of your great wealth in Troy's project. My Charlie would tell you the same thing."

She walked away. Rodenska forked up the last piece of cucumber and spoke to himself sharply. Down, boy. You're too shaky to play games. Even with a target like that.

At one point he had felt close to tears. With no reason. Not about Buttons. Tears, maybe, from a kind of helpless frustration at finding himself mauling the woman without cause. She couldn't help what she was. Of the two of them, he had been the vicious one. (Except for that crack about Troy.) She was merely empty, in a way that seemed to comfort her. He had been writing dirty words on the sidewalk, out of a kind of compulsion. As if, when

44

Buttons had died, patience had died with her. The world was crummy, and they came at you from all angles lately. Have to watch it.

He changed the subject by focusing his specialized attention on a couple by the pool — a man, dry and brown as a corpse left too long in the sun, sitting angularly on a poolside cushion talking privately to a rounded blonde in a pink suit who lay on a chaise lounge with her face upturned toward the sun. He soon realized they were quarreling, slowly, quietly, viciously, with long silences between the unforgiveable things they were saying to each other. He did not change expression and barely moved his lips when he spoke to her. When she answered her face would change. She had prettiness, marred by too small a mouth and a piggy little nose. She looked spoiled, petulant, bored, and bitter when she answered him. The lines would go away when she again composed her face for the beat of the sun.

Married, he decided. And he's twenty years older, and it's probably a second one, and he was so charged up about those tits he didn't stop to think of what they'd find to do outside of bed, and now she's started fooling around a little, and he can't prove anything but he's suspicious as hell. She was twenty-five when she married him and now she's thirty — five years older and fifteen pounds heavier — and afraid he's going to live forever.

The last outpost of gracious living. But informal.

He went over to the bar and found gin and collins mix and made himself a tall strong drink.

As he started to turn away from the bar Troy said, "Party pooper."

Mike turned and looked up at the taller man. Troy had grown a lot heavier in five years. The hair was thin and blonde-gray. There were dark pouches under his eyes.

"I couldn't keep my eyes open. Don't kid me. I wasn't missed."

Troy started to build himself an Old Fashioned. "I should have folded when you did. How are you coming along?"

"Adequate. I just ate like a pig."

"Mary says you were swimming early."

"You know how it is with us athletes. What the hell does the 'D' stand for?"

"What? Oh, 'D' for 'Dexter.' "

"Dexter Troy Jamison. My, my!"

"Looks juicy on that blue mailbox, doesn't it?"

"Real rich. I'll call you Dex, like I was a friend."

"Try it. One time."

They took their drinks over and sat on a bench on the far side of the pool.

"The Sunday routine," Troy said. "If I recover fast enough maybe we'll take the boat out, but probably no. There'll be a group on the beach. There'll be some ways you can lose money. Or you can play tennis at the Laybournes or the Key Club. Or just drink."

"I won't be playing tennis at the Laybournes."

"No?"

"Marg Laybourne tried to work me over. But she wasn't used to a counterpuncher."

"Same old Mike. Same old war against the phonies. Surprised you bothered with her."

"So am I. It was too easy. No challenge."

"In a little while I'm going to see if I can make it all the way to the Gulf."

"Say, are you used to a counterpuncher, old Troy?"

"Am I a phony?"

"How can I tell?"

"What do you mean by that, Mike?"

"Let me put it this way. I got here Monday. You got a fine place. And, let me add, a dandy wife. I like Mary. But I get the polite, gracious, impersonal routine from you, boy. I'm maybe somebody you met in a club car and in-

47

vited down here to this last outpost of gracious living. We met seventeen years ago, Troy. Remember me? Chrissake, I don't want hugs and kisses, but I don't like you being on guard."

"On guard?"

"That's the impression you give. Damn if it isn't. Are you self-conscious about all this? It's what you wanted, isn't it? And you were on your way to making it one way, and you goofed yourself out of that, so you married it. All right. I've got nothing against you marrying it."

"That's nice to know. I needed your approval."

"Get nasty. At least it's a change."

"It's been five years. People change."

"Not this much."

"I guess I've got a lot on my mind."

"All of it none of my business, eh?"

"Relax, Mike. You're down here to relax. Soak up the sun. Have some laughs. Get drunk. But stay off my back."

"You've got bad nerves, Troy. Worse than mine."

"There isn't any rule says you've got to know everything about everything."

"With me it's a habit. Like finding out this big Horseshoe Bay Estates of yours is sour."

Troy stared at him. "Who says so!"

"Nobody did. It was a shot in the dark. You just confirmed it, boy."

"Maybe a week is long enough. Maybe that's all the rest you needed."

"I'll stick around a while, thanks."

"Goddamn it, Mike!"

"Let's drop it. When you get off this remote kick you're on, and realize I might have some ideas — maybe even good ideas — about what's chewing on you, look me up. I'll probably be on the beach. Let's drop it for now. Brief me on that pair over there."

Troy scowled at him for a few seconds, and then shrugged. "That's the Claytons. Rex and Tracey."

"A very loving couple."

"He loves her and she loves anybody. I got to go find some aspirin."

During the next hour Mike had some dull talk with some dull people. When he was free he built a third drink and took it back to his pleasant guest room. He stretched out on the bed and thought about Troy. Friendship was one of the great variables. Like everybody is in their own little rowboat, with no oars, and the currents move you around. With some people it's worth paddling with your hands to keep the rowboats side by side. With others

49

neither of you have to work because you're caught in the same current anyway. It had been like that with Troy. And he suspected it still was, if Troy would stop being remote. With Troy it wasn't like other interrupted friendships — where you get back together again with great expectations and find out you're a couple of strangers. Either you grew in different directions, or one stood still and the other one grew.

He was cynic enough to know that Troy could never entirely forgive him for that New York mess. Nobody can conquer all the sub-conscious resentment against a man who sees him at his hopeless, helpless worst, and drives off the dogs and gets him back on his feet.

He remembered how it was in New York. New York had to be put into historical per-spective, because it was a part of a lot of things that had gone before.

After the war Mike had tried to continue with the column. It meant good money. But a lot of things went wrong. The syndicate was small and couldn't afford to invest in a promo-tion to make Mike Rodenska a peacetime suc-cess. The bookings began to dwindle. A bunch of the best wartime columns were pub-lished in book form, and didn't sell enough to make the advance. And the labor of tapping out the columns had become more than labor. It was misery. Mauldin and Hargrove were having the same problem — and probably Pyle wouldn't have found it too easy either had he managed to miss his rendezvous on Iwo Jima. Actually Mike hungered to be back as a member of the working press. Doing a column seemed too remote — almost phony. Buttons wanted him to do what would make him happiest.

And so, by the middle of 1946, Mike and Buttons and Micky and Tommy moved into an elderly rented house in West Hudson, unpacked the cartons with gypsy efficiency, and Mike went to work at Guild minimum for the ancient, honorable and somewhat self-important West Hudson *Leader*, covering City Hall, County Courthouse and police, doing assigned Sunday features and a three-a-week op. ed. column on purely local matters, happy as a flea on a large hairy dog.

Three months later, quite by accident, he heard of a good opening in the largest local advertising agency, and on a hunch he wrote to Troy in Rochester, then tore up the letter and phoned him. For Troy it had come at exactly the right time. Troy was getting very tired of taking directions from a very young and very stupid man who happened to be the only son of the senior partner in the Rochester agency. And he was getting fed up with most of his pregnant Bonita's Rochester relatives.

Two weeks later Troy and Bunny were installed in a pleasant apartment Buttons had found for them. The first little girl, Lycia, was born on Christmas day, 1946, and the second Jamison baby, Cindy, was born on New Year's Day, 1948.

Those were the best years, Mike recalled. Buttons and Bunny got along perfectly. They were both smallish, talkative, excitable women, Bunny as dark as Buttons was blonde. The four of them spent a lot of time together. And had fun. But to Troy, fun was secondary during those years. He had a lot of drive and intensity, taste and talent and a kind of ruthlessness that was too veiled to be disturbing. Mike remembered how Troy had said, "I want more than my share."

There was an inevitability about the way he went after it. And an inevitability about the way his work eventually came to the attention of one of the big New York agencies. Both wives wept when the Jamisons moved on to New York, toward Troy's big golden future.

Mike well remembered a curious thing that happened about a week after Troy and Bunny and Lycia and the baby were gone. He had been in the kitchen, talking to Buttons. And he had said, casually, and perhaps with a little twinge of envy, "Here you are stuck with a newspaper bum, while Bunny gets to lead the fat life."

Without warning, and only half playfully, Buttons had given him a smack in the chops that made his eyes water and shocked him. "Don't you ever say that! You're worth — fifty of Troy Jamison!"

"Hey! I thought you liked the guy."

"I do, I guess. But he's weak."

"Weak? Troy? I don't understand. . . . "

"He's pressing too hard, darling. He's pushing too hard, without really knowing what he wants. And when he starts to get what he's after, and finds out it isn't as important as he thought, something is going to give. He's going to come apart. Bunny is going to be hurt, and maybe you'll be hurt too, if I let you get dragged into it."

"But he . . . "

She had come sweetly into his arms. "Hey, I busted you a good one. It left marks."

"I'll get you a bout in the Garden with Sugar Ray."

"I love you, Mike, and don't let me ever hear that kind of talk about the fat life. We live that fat life, honey. I couldn't imagine being married to anybody but you."

He had thought her wrong, about Troy. But four years later, in 1953, when he was thirty-four, that clever, promising, driving, and demonstrably courageous young man, Troy Jamison, a thirty-five-thousand-dollar-a-year man with Kelfer, Sorensen and Ryan, owner of a lot of house in Larchmont and a pocketful of credit cards, blew up in everybody's face. And they were astonished.

Bunny had phoned Buttons long distance, incoherent with tears, pleading for help. So Mike had taken time off — by then he was Assistant to the Managing Editor, a promotion that had come about when he had gotten wistful about the Korea thing. They had stashed the boys with a close friend and neighbor and had driven down through soiled sleet to Larchmont, to a big house and a soul-sick woman who bore the bruises of the cruel and drunken beating she had been given, and a situation beyond repair. Bonita Jamison was under control, long enough to give them the facts. It had taken three months for it to go entirely sour — starting with a restlessness on Troy's part, a compulsion to make savage comments to their friends, a growing indifference to both her and the children. Apparently things were still all right at the agency. But their personal life had gone to hell. There was a woman in the city, from all reports a cheap, amoral type named Jerranna Rowley. Troy had a hotel room, but most of the time he was living with the Rowley woman. He had made no secret of the relationship — in fact he used it as a club. Bunny was sorry she had bothered them. She was going to leave the girls with her people in Rochester and get a Nevada divorce. It was all over. She said there was no point in Mike going into the city to talk to Troy. It had ended.

But he went anyway, the next morning, a grubby gray Saturday morning. He checked the hotel from Grand Central, but Troy's room didn't answer. Bunny had said the Rowley woman was listed in the Manhattan book, so he phoned there. Just as he was about to hang up a fuzzy, sleep-thickened, querulous voice answered.

"I'd like to speak to Troy Jamison," he said.

"Oh, God! What time is it anyhow?"

"Quarter of ten. Are you Miss Rowley?"

"Who the hell are you?"

"I'm an old friend of Troy's. Mike Rodenska."

"Oh, sure. I heard him say that name, I think. Mike, you got a bad habit. Phoning people at dawn. You oughta break that habit."

"Can I speak to Troy?"

"Lover-boy didn't come home to Jerranna last night. Jerranna got drunky with friends. I don't know where the hell he is. Try the Hotel Terr . . ."

"There's no answer there."

"Then check the old manse out Larchmont way. Maybe he crawled back to wifey."

"He isn't out there either."

"Then I can't help you, old buddy."

"Could I come and talk to you?"

"About Troy? I don't think you got the scoop, Mike. I can give you a message. You'd be wasting time."

"I've got a little time to waste."

"Okay," she said listlessly, "but don't show up in no half hour. Make it about eleven-thirty, hey? And look, they drunk me out of goodies, so you be a pal and show up with a jug of Gordons and a jug of Early Times, okay? It'll save me going out on such a stinky-looking day."

The apartment was a third floor walk-up a few doors from Second Avenue on East Fifty-First. It was in a defeated building and the enclosed air was both musty and sharply antiseptic. When he rang she buzzed the latch from above and he climbed the stairs to 3G,

56

wondering how many times Troy had climbed those stairs. And why.

When she opened the door, took the brown paper sack from him and thanked him absently, and turned toward the kitchen with long strides, saying, over her shoulder, "Siddown and make like it was home, Mike," he had even more cause to wonder why Troy climbed those stairs.

She was younger than she had sounded over the phone. Nineteen or twenty, he guessed. She had a round, rather doughy face, a careless mop of pale brown hair worn long, a rather small head, a very long neck, and narrow shoulders. She was thin, but it wasn't the kind of leanness that can be called slenderness. This was actually scrawniness, accentuated by knobby joints and a sort of shambling looseness in her gait.

"Want I should fix you something?" she called from the kitchenette.

"Bourbon and water. A weak one, please."

He sat down in a sagging, overstuffed chair with a torn slip cover and unidentifiable stains. No sun would ever come into this room. Aside from the furniture that had obviously come with the apartment, any additional touches seemed to be added by things won at carnival booths. There was a classic collection of liquor rings and cigarette burns. A broken spring prodded him in the left ham.

He got up and thanked her when she brought his drink.

"Manners, huh?" she said, and grinned at him, and sat in a chair that half-faced his and threw one leg over the arm of the chair. She wore black denim slacks and a burgundy cardigan. The rudimentary breasts under the cardigan, pointed and wide-set, seemed almost anachronistic compared with the rest of her figure.

She had a tall glass of orange juice which he suspected contained plenty of gin. "Here's lookin' up your address," she said and drained a third of it. "I was thinking I could get back to sleep maybe, but you cooked it for me."

"I'm sorry about that."

"Sleeping is the best thing I do. I can damn near fall asleep standing up, like a horse."

"It can come in handy."

"I suppose you're going to sit there lookin' at me like the cat brought me in, wondering where the hell to start saying what you came to say. So I'll save you the trouble. He's got a big career and a fine wife and a fine home and two darling little girls and it's a damn shame he has to get mixed up with somebody like me, so I should give him up and go away quietly or something. That's where you have the wrong message, Mike. He can take off any time. I don't give a damn. I can get along. I have before and I will again, without him paying the freight. I don't love him and he don't love me. Now that's all over, what'll we talk about?" She grinned at him.

He stared at her. Her mouth was wide and heavy, her lips habitually parted, her teeth large and strong and yellow-white, ridged. He had seen her before, when the state cops had picked her up off the highway. Seen her in the hospital after a gang rape, still bitter, arrogant, undefeated. What in the name of God could attract Troy to this? A will to destroy himself completely?

"Where did you meet Troy, Jerry?"

She frowned "Jerranna. I always use the whole thing. It's my whole name and I don't like nicknames. I met him at a hockey game at the Garden. The boyfriend I was with, he slipped on those damn steep steps and hit his head, and they took him away, and Troy was with some out-of-town guys, all a little high, and we went here and there and to and fro for kicks, me and those three guys, and Troy was the one lasted the distance and brought me home. That was . . . oh . . . months ago. I'm not so good on keeping track of time.

"Do you have a job?"

"Not right now. I gave it up. It was a cafeteria on Broadway up near Eighty-sixth. But I'm not sweating. I can go get a job any time. I always have and I always will. Since I was thirteen, picking beans out in the Valley. And I'll always have boyfriends too. Not so big shot like Jamison maybe, but ready and eager to take care — you know how I mean."

"I guess so."

"We're all of us just here for kicks, I always say, so get all you can."

He asked her more questions. She answered frankly, acted slightly bored, smiled easily, combed her hair back with long fingers, joggled her foot in time to imaginary music, and made them a pair of fresh drinks. And in some entirely inexplicable way she seemed to change slowly, in front of his eyes, as they talked. He knew it was not the drinks. She had made his weak, as he had requested. In the beginning he had thought her entirely unattractive — so much so that he had thought her boast about boyfriends rather pathetic.

But gradually he was becoming more and more aware of her in a physical-sexual way. The thick contours of her mouth, the girdle line along the top of the careless thigh, a knowing, self-confident look of mockery in her bland gray eyes. Yes, even the careless tangle of the brown hair, the thinness of a slightly soiled ankle, the bawdy and knowing tilt of the sharp, immature breasts.

Awareness increased until he wondered how he could have been so unaware in the beginning. Feature by feature, line by line, she was unattractive — almost, in fact, a grotesque. But there was now evident an unmistakable aura, an amiable pungency, about her that was beginning to make his heart beat more quickly and heavily. He suddenly became aware of a silence that had lasted for some time.

"Say it, old buddy," she said. "What you're thinking."

"Could you ... would you want to ... send him on his way?"

She shrugged. "Why the hell should I? Anyway, I couldn't. He'd be coming back."

"So how does it end?"

"The way it always has. He'll get on my nerves. You know. Giving orders like he owns me. You can do this and you can't do that. No other boyfriends. No ramming around town. Stay right here. Hell with that noise. That's when I quit."

"How?"

"How big is this town? I move four blocks and he can't find me. He can walk the streets howling like a dog, but he can't find me."

"How much longer do you give him?"

"You're pretty sharp, Mike. Oh, maybe a month."

"This has happened before?"

"Oh, sure. A thousand times. But not with a fella so rich like Troy."

"Why does it happen?"

She smirked. "You mean like whadda they see in me? Nothing you can't see right now, Mike. I'm not pretty. But I could always get fellas hanging around. I used to wonder. My God, how women hate the hell out of me! I'm the way I am. That's all. I like kicks. And I don't feel a damn bit shameful about the way I am. Like that song, doin' what comes natcherly." She swung the dangling leg.

Mike put his empty glass aside. "I better be on my way."

She didn't get up. She looked blandly up at him. The gray eyes were slightly protuberant. In the dim light he could see a slow pulse in her throat. "You in a big fat rush?" she asked.

"I've got to be getting along."

"You're a cute guy, specially when you look nervous like now. I could tell you what you were wondering about. I can always tell.

Don't you want to find out?"

"But Troy might . . . "

"I told you I do anything I want to do. I wouldn't answer the door or the phone. I'd have no reason to tell anybody, and you sure wouldn't want to. Like a bonus, for trying to help your pal."

He looked at her and felt actually, physically dizzy. Her gray eyes seemed to grow big enough to fill her half of the room. Her voice had been like fingernails being drawn sharp and slow down his spine. It was a persuasive, evil magic — a spell cast by a contemporary witch, a soiled, scrawny, decadent witch.

He shook himself like a wet and weary dog, and made his voice flat and hard and said, "No thanks."

"Suit yourself," she said and got up and went to the door with him.

When he was in the hall, safe, like the swimmer caught in an undertow who climbs out onto a sand bar, he turned and said, "It's messed Troy's life up, Jerranna."

"So I'm bleeding? It wasn't me, Mike. He was ready to be messed up. He was looking for it."

"What makes you say that?"

She lifted one narrow shoulder. "I just know. I can tell. I knew others like that. They

63

get hooked on me, like on a drug, on account of — like a drug — I can stop them from thinking about anybody else or anything else in the world. I can keep then from even knowing who the hell they are, and maybe that's what they want me for. But they got to be ready for me. So don't blame me."

"You've got it all figured out."

"I've been here and there," she said, and winked with great solemnity and closed the door, opened it immediately and said, "Thanks for the jugs," and closed it again.

After he had gone down one flight he leaned against the wall for a few moments, his eyes closed. His body felt sticky and there was a bad taste in his mouth and a dull headache behind his eyes. Though not a superstitious man, he felt that he had been in the presence of evil. Not contrived evil, full of plots and connivings, but a curiously innocent and implacable evil. He knew that Buttons should never know how close he had come to an act that would have irreparably changed his own inner image of himself, made it forever hard for him to have looked deep into his own mirrored eyes.

As he reached the sidewalk he saw Troy paying off a cab driver a hundred feet away. As the cab pulled away, Troy turned and saw him. Troy looked lean and pallid, unpressed, unsteady on his feet. Mike wondered what in hell he could say to Troy. Troy whirled and went around the corner onto Second Avenue, almost running. When Mike reached the corner, Troy was halfway down the block. Mike did not follow him.

A month later, while Bunny was in Reno and her girls were with her people in Rochester, Mike got a phone call one evening from a man in New York named Grady. After he hung up Buttons stared at him, frowning, and said, "Who was that? What about Troy? When do you have to go to New York?"

"It's a man named Grady. Troy's at his place, in bad shape. I either go get him, now, or Grady calls Bellevue and has him picked up."

"So let him call Bellevue!"

Mike looked at her with a fond and crooked smile. "Grady said he had resigned so that left just one friend of Jamison's. Okay. I'll call back and tell Grady I can't bring a mess like that into my home."

"Darn you anyway," Buttons said. "I'm going to feel awfully disloyal toward Bunny, but go get him."

"Bunny would understand how it is."

It took three and a half hours to drive to

New York and another twenty minutes to locate John Grady's bachelor apartment in the Village, so it was nearly one in the morning when Grady, a tall young man with big glasses and a harried expression, let him in.

"Mr. Rodenska? Good. He's in the bedroom. I got worried after I called you, so I got hold of a doctor. He charged me fifteen bucks for a house call."

"I'll pay you back."

"Hell with that. Call it my last contribution to Troy Jamison, thank God. I better brief you. Sit down. Drink?"

"No thanks. What did the doctor say?"

"Alcoholism. Malnutrition. He gave him some shots."

"Can he be moved?"

"Not tonight, damn it. In the morning, when he wakes up. Which will be about ten. If he has the shakes too bad to travel, he can have a two-ounce shot in the morning. I won't be here. I've got to go to work."

"He's out of work?"

"Man, he's about as far out of work as you can get. He left in a big way almost a month ago. I'm with K. F. and S. too. He hired me, as a matter of fact. There's been talk about him for months, around the shop. His marriage busting up. And when he was coming in

66

at all, he was coming in half-loaded. And he didn't seem to give a damn. I think they were trying to talk him into a leave of absence. When you get as high up as Troy was, there's a sort of rule you don't fire a man. They took Walther Electric away from him. It had always been his baby, a very tender account. They bill three million five. They took it away two months ago. Just about three weeks ago Mueller was giving a presentation to a flock of Walther executives. Jamison came walking in, boiled. Before they could hustle him out he yelled that the new program was tired old crap, that Walther would be better off with somebody else. He busted Mueller a beaut right in the eye and knocked him down. He knocked the projection machine off the stand, then turned and told the executives of Walther he was glad he didn't have to deal with such lint-heads any more. About then they got him out, too late. Walther canceled out. And they didn't even let Troy clean out his desk. They sent his stuff to the hotel by messenger. It's a damn shame, Mr. Rodenska. He was as sharp as they come. But he's dead in this industry forever. There isn't anybody connected with it from coast to coast who doesn't know the story by now. He'll never get back in, and I guess he knows it."

"Where do you fit in, Grady?"

"Good question. He hired me. I felt some obligation, even though I hope everybody forgets I was hired originally by Jamison. So I've been taking care. I got him out twice when he was charged with D and D. After he got tossed out of the hotel he slept here a few times. I've loaned him money."

"He can't be broke!"

"He gives a good imitation if he isn't. Lately I've been thinking it isn't going to do me any good at the agency if people find out I'm helping him. Anyhow, he's been getting worse. And I figure I've paid off any obligation. Tonight was the end. He knocked. I opened the door. He staggered in, fell down, threw up on my rug and passed out. He'd told me about you. So I phoned you. I told you what I was going to do if you didn't feel like taking over. Want to look at him? If you haven't seen him lately, it'll be a shock. He looks like any skid row bum."

Troy woke up at eleven the next morning. He didn't seem either surprised or grateful to see Mike, or particularly interested in the plan of going up to West Hudson. Mike could detect neither shame nor remorse. Just a dullness, an impenetrable apathy. Grady had donated some elderly but clean clothing to the cause. He had said it wasn't necessary to have them back. After the hot bath and the permissible two ounces, Troy was steady enough to shave himself.

Mike made a few futile attempts to start casual conversations on the way north, and then gave up. He did not take Troy home. He took him to the office of a friend who was a doctor. After the examination, Troy was taken directly to a rest home fifteen miles from town, a place which specialized in such problems. Three weeks later Mike brought him back to the house on Killian Street. Buttons received him politely, and with a measured amount of warmth.

"When you want to talk," Mike said. "I'll listen. In the meantime you can stay here until you're well."

"It's a lot for you people to do."

"Don't worry about that."

"One thing you may be glad to know. They told me out there. I'm not a genuine, honest-to-God alcoholic. This was more like a nervous breakdown. So you don't have to lock up the liquor. I thought you'd like to know that. They said I can drink socially again, if I feel like it. But not this year. It won't matter a damn to me to see other people drinking."

"Okay."

"I'll stay out of your way as much as I can. Don't figure on trying to pull me into social things. I'm not ready."

"All right."

"I'll go to work soon as I can."

"Don't try to rush it."

"Maybe you could do one more thing. I don't know where the hell I stand. I don't even know if the house was sold. That goes into the settlement. You could check with George Broman, 114 East Forty-third. He's my lawyer and tax guy. It'll be interesting to find out if there's anything left."

"How about alimony?"

"It's being set up on the basis of a percentage of earnings. That's lucky for me, and tough on Bunny. She's got people to help her, though. She gets it until she marries again. And I've been wondering about mail, Mike. I didn't . . ."

"I fixed that up. They were saving a bunch of stuff at the hotel. It's here now. I changed your mailing address to here. They didn't want you getting mail out there. Do you want to see it now?"

"No. Not now. I'll look at it later on."

He slept a great deal in those first weeks, and as the spring days grew warmer he would sun himself in the backyard. Later he began to take long walks. Buttons took pride in putting the pounds back on him. He spoke little and seldom smiled, though he was not irritable or sullen. He was good with the boys. As his strength came back he began to do minor repairs around the house — fixing doors that stuck, ripping up and replacing asphalt tile in the store room. He was good with his hands, neat and quick.

The divorce became final. George Broman ascertained that, after income tax refunds had come in, and after Bunny's settlement, Troy Jamison had a balance of nearly thirteen thousand dollars. After it was transferred to a savings account at West Hudson National, Troy insisted, despite Mike's protests, on paying the medical expenses Mike had incurred on his behalf.

In late June of 1953, Mike and Buttons got a letter from Bunny, postmarked Colorado Springs.

Dearest Ones,

You may cluck and shake your heads wisely as my entire family did, and you can feel hurt and left out, just as they did, and about all I can do is apologize and say it was all terribly sudden.

But not too sudden, believe me. I'm Mrs. Robert Parker Linder, and I've been married four whole days. Bob's ranch is twenty miles from the Springs, and it's half dude and half working ranch. We met in Reno — both there on the same mission. We've gone through all the necessary soul-searching and we're confident that it isn't purely rebound. I'm very happy. The country here is glorious. Bob is forty, a big, slow, sweet guy with the world's best disposition and a grin that can turn me to butter. My gals adore him, and his son, Jaimie, age sixteen, seems to think I am a wondrous thing. You can judge how messy his situation was and how blameless he was by the fact he divorced her, and he got total custody of their only child.

Buttons, I haven't heard from you for almost a month so I do not know whether Troy is still there with you. I hope not. You've had more than your share of giving and forgiving. I feel sort of queer about writing this news to him. So if he is there would you please tell him, or, if not, drop him a note. He will probably be relieved to know he is off the alimony hook. I don't want to wish problems on you but I would rather he heard that way than more indirectly.

As I wrote you before, Troy has court permission to see the girls at his request, but not oftener than six times a year, and for not longer than eight hours at a time. You could give him this address amd tell him that when he gets back on his feet and wants to see them, he can write to me and we can make arrangements.

All my love to both of you,
Bunny

The letter arrived at lunch time. After Buttons read it she gave Mike an odd look, and then handed it to Troy to read. He was halfway through his lunch. He read it quickly, got up without a word and left the house. Mike then read it. Troy was not back by the time they went to bed. He had his own key.

At three in the morning Buttons shook Mike awake and said, "I think he just came in, honey. He may be dreadfully drunk. You better go check."

He put on his robe and met Troy in the upstairs hallway. Troy was not drunk. He whispered to avoid waking the boys.

"Sorry I took off like that, Mike. It was rude."

"Where have you been?"

"Walking. Thinking. A hell of a long walk."

As Mike looked at him he sensed that Troy had changed during that walk. There was more alertness in his expression. The brooding look was hidden. Not entirely gone. But not as obvious.

"I had to get used to her being married to somebody else," Troy whispered.

"Sure. I know. Well . . . good night."

He went back to bed and told Buttons. As he was going back to sleep he realized that Troy would soon be gone.

Two days later, on a Sunday afternoon, Troy told Mike his plans. "I know I can't get back into advertising. Maybe I could get some crummy little job with a small-town agency, but I don't want that. My father was a builder. Not a big one. Small houses, and I don't think he ever had more than eight men working for him at one time. I worked for him for four straight summers. I've got a tiny bit of capital. That's what I'm going to do. It's the only thing I can think of."

"Here in West Hudson?"

"No. I've decided on Florida. The west coast. I'm going to go down there and hire out to a contractor down there and learn what's new in the field, and what special local problems they have. When I'm ready, I'll try it on my own."

"All cured?"

"Thanks to you, Mike. And Buttons. I'll never forget it. It's not . . . a total cure, I guess. But the best I can manage."

"What happened, Troy? Is that a fair question?"

"It's a fair question. I just wish I could give you an answer. I don't know what the hell happened. Everything was fine. Overnight everything went sour for me. I hated the work and the city and myself. I just plain stopped giving a damn. Like a motor stopping. Running down. I don't know."

"I saw that woman."

"I know you did. I remember seeing you in front of her place. Memory of that period is all . . . misty. And I don't get things in the right order. But I remember seeing you there. Running away from you. But she didn't do it. Everything had slipped a long, long way before I found her. She just helped me find bottom — slide all the way down." He managed a faint smile. "It was easy."

"Grady told me about your farewell performance in the office."

"I can just barely remember that. I did a

great job. It was just a few days after she disappeared. I don't know how many."

"Strange girl."

Troy stared into space. "There should be a better word than that. I think about how it was. And sometimes it makes me want to throw up. It couldn't have been me. But I've got this fear, Mike. That if I ever saw her again . . . I'd either kill her, or it would be the same thing all over again. But this time . . . there's not as much to lose. You can only lose your career and your wife one time."

"Maybe it will be easier . . . in one sense, not having so much to lose."

"It's a big comfort to me. Sorry. I didn't mean to sound snotty. I'm dead, Mike. In a special way. Walking, breathing, eating, but dead. You've been swell. And there's nothing more to say about the whole thing."

"Delayed combat fatigue?"

"That's a wild idea."

"Is it? Take it this way. They didn't kill you. They just twisted you a little. New values. But the values didn't fit you, Troy. And it took you a long time to find out. Then the roof fell in."

Troy studied him. "Interesting. You know, if I was anxious to find an excuse for myself, boy, I'd be hanging on every word. But some-

76

how I don't give a damn about the reasons. I know what happened. It happened. I didn't dream it. Keep your psychiatrics."

"You must be better, you're so much nastier."

For the first months after Troy left he wrote at dutiful intervals, and his letters had somewhat the flavor of those a boy might write home from army training. He had decided on Ravenna, Florida. Big opportunities for growth. He was working for Brail Brothers Construction, living in a used house-trailer he bought, doing a lot of weekend fishing. The letters became less frequent and had a more distant tone. In August of 1954, he started his own small firm, doing foundation work on subcontract. Troy Jamison, Builder. They got a card at Christmas, with a short note. He was busy and prospering, had made a small investment in land and was putting up three low-cost spec houses.

In late March he wrote them that he had married Mrs. Mary Dow, a widow. The next communication was a Christmas card, without note, from Troy and Mary Jamison. It looked elegant and expensive. And others in 1956 and 1957 and 1958, except that in 1958 he knew about Buttons and no cards went out.

About two weeks before the whole thing was over, after Buttons was back in the hospital again, a letter came to the house for her from Bonita Linder, and Mike opened it. It was a warm, amusing, chatty letter, and she sounded a little bit cross about not hearing from Buttons in months.

It made Mike realize that it wasn't entirely fair to leave Bunny, who after all the years was still Buttons' best friend, completely out of it. By then, through that sardonic miracle, there was enough money, and he had quit the paper in order to spend more time with her. And he was trying desperately to be steady and dependable and reliable and unhysterical about the whole thing. So that evening he had placed a call to her in Colorado, and tried to tell her how things were with Buttons. But in the middle of it something broke, and she arrived two days later, leaving the girls and her three-year-old son on the ranch, and moved in and took over with a compassionate efficiency that made things a little easier than they had been. The two women had some chances to talk, and it seemed to make Buttons a little less scared of the blackness dead ahead of her — not that she had ever whined or even come close to it, but you could tell about the being scared.

So he thought he had been prepared for it, that he was braced for it. But when it happened it was worse than he had been able to imagine. It was like being struck blind and sick and dumb, and left in a world of strangers.

There were plenty of friends to try to help, but Bunny helped the most. She organized the routines of death, and got him and the boys through it somehow, and stayed until he could talk to her about the future — a word that had always had a nice ring to it, but now had an ironic connotation. Bunny had wisdom. She sensed that if he tried to hold the family unit together it would be an artificial thing, and bad on the three of them. If the boys were younger they would need that security, but at fifteen and seventeen, it would be like three men forever aware of the empty chair, the empty room, the silences where her voice had been. So, in addition to getting rid of Buttons' things, instinctively knowing the things he would want to keep, she made the arrangements to get the boys into the Melford School, and through the subtle uses of propaganda, got them into a frame of mind where they were looking forward to it.

She talked with Mike about the money, and she said she felt that old wheeze about hard work effecting a cure was largely nonsense. The thing to do was get away, go somewhere with no obligations, and sit and mend — and told him he was lucky he could afford it.

She wanted him to come to the ranch, but he said maybe later. He had written to all the faraway friends about Buttons, and all of them had answered. But Troy hadn't, and that was a special hurt, combined with indignation.

After they drove the boys up and got them settled, Bunny went back to her kids and husband. He had promised her he would go away. Close the house for an indefinite time and go away. But after she was gone he couldn't seem to make the move. He lived in the emptiness of the house, and often he would not answer the phone or the door, and he did not eat very well. He could not seem to get enough sleep.

And then the letter came from Troy. It was a good letter. He explained they had been on a cruise, hadn't had their mail forwarded, had come back and tried to reach him by phone. He insisted Mike take time off from work and come down and stay as long as he could. Mary Jamison had written her warm invitation at the bottom of the letter. It was the stimulus he had needed. So he had made the arrangements and gone down, and been met by Troy in a shining car a half block long, and been driven down through St. Pete, and over a bridge, and down through Bradenton and Sarasota to Ravenna and on down to Riley Key to a home so beautiful, a wife so gracious, in a setting so sun-and-sea spectacular that Troy Jamison was obviously fighting to keep from showing understandable pride.

He had explained to Troy about the money, but had concealed that the fact of his unemployment was largely the result of Bunny's instinctive wisdom about him and the shattering extent of his loss. Left to his own devices, he would have gone back to work, would have tried to dull mind and memory by knocking himself out on the job and trying to keep up a shallow imitation of a family unit.

On the second day of his visit, on Tuesday, alone on the beach, he had suddenly lost all reservations and knew that Bunny had been right. He wasn't the kind of man who could make an adjustment to loss by turning away from it. He had to be alone where he could look at it squarely and brace himself solidly, and then open himself up to the realization of the total significance of it. It was his only hope of mending, and Bunny had sensed it.

He sat on the side of his bed and drained the drink and sighed again, then went to the small desk to write to his sons. They did not like joint letters. They wanted one apiece.

"Dear Micky, There is a curious phenomenon down here called sunshine. I will try to explain it to you. Every day this big round yellow thing comes up out of the east, surrounded by a sky which is an abnormal blue instead of the grubby gray we're used to. Exposure to this yellow thing turns people bright red instead of the infinitely more pleasing fish-belly white, but the natives down here seem to feel this ugly red is a desirable. . . ."

The "o" on the old portable was printing solid. He opened the lid, picked the goo out of the "o" with a match stick, lit a cigar and continued the letter, typing with four fingers, working — in a special sense — at his trade, taking comfort in the familiar sound, the cigar angled well to port to keep the smoke out of his eyes, a stocky man — very much alone.

three

On the nineteenth day of April, on that sleepy Sunday afternoon while the residents and their guests on the north end of Riley Key used the beach and each other's houses and cabañas, with a customary stop at the Jamison's, and drank, and played bridge and tennis, and did a little surf-casting and went out in their boats, and discussed the weather, property values, segregation, the Vice-President, local sexual intrigues, diets, investments, and where to go in Nassau and Varadero, and while they made their vague arrangements about ending up in one group or another at the Key Club, later on, four men, thirty-five miles away in another county, were deciding the financial future of Troy Jamison.

They had met, by prearrangement, at Purdy Elmarr's ranch, twelve hundred acres, part of it bordering the upper Myaka River. The old frame ranch house was set back about three hundred feet from State Road 982, at the end of a straight sand road bordered by squat elderly oaks. The infrequent tourist who braved the potholes of 982 could look at the old house with the oak hammock beyond it, and the old trucks and implements corroding away in the side yard, and the gray, soiled-looking Brahma cattle feeding in the flat pasture-lands between the scrub pine lands and the over-grown irrigation ditches, and see a certain picturesqueness in a down-at-the-heel ranch with rickety sheds, sway-backed roofs, weather-worn paint. If they jolted by shortly after the rual delivery truck, they might see Purdy Elmarr himself trudging out to his roadside box, a wiry old man in dusty work clothing, with a big shapeless black felt hat, steel-rimmed glasses — and feel that pleasant pity which is born of a sure knowledge of superiority. Poor old fella.

They could have no way of knowing that Purdy lived exactly the way he wanted to live, that no matter how frequent his visits to his bank in Sarasota, wearing his drab city-suit and an old cloth cap with a long visor, the executive staff of the bank leaped to attention, and became excessively affable — a social and professional gesture that never elicited a shadow of response.

He had a good riding horse and a pack of

Blue Tick hounds, and two high-stake poker evenings a week. He got his turkey and quail and deer every year. At sixty-six he was in perfect health, and drank one full tumbler of prime bourbon whisky every night of his life. His granddaddy, a drover out of Georgia, had homesteaded a big chunk of land and bought more, ranch land and Gulf land and Key land and bay frontage. His daddy, with very little fuss or notoriety, had acquired a lot more. It had been simpler for them to get it, hang onto it and make a profit off it. Purdy had to use the services of a sharp firm of attorneys and accountants. He had control of about twelve corporations, but he wasn't confused. He could read a financial statement with the same ease — and almost the same degree of pleasure — with which most men would read a dirty limerick. He drove a six-year-old car, listened to a twelve-year-old radio, underpaid his help, was generous with his friends, knew almost to the penny what he was worth at all times, and hated to see a month go by without adding to it. He was in citrus and celery, cattle and securities, motels and shipping, dredges and draglines, shopping centers and auto agencies. But the basis of all of it was land. He loved land with almost the same degree of intensity as he loved money.

He knew more about other men than they were ever able to learn about him. He knew the flaws and strengths and habits and vulnerabilities of every long-term resident in three counties who had a net worth of over twenty-five thousand dollars. Those men could be divided into three categories. There were those who had never had any dealings with Purdy. To them he was a mysterious, powerful, slippery old coot. Then there were those who had gone in with him on something and tried to get fancy and had got thoroughly stung. To them he was a vicious, crooked, merciless old bastard. Others had gone in with him and let him call the turn, and taken their profit. To that last group, Purdy was the salt of the earth.

The four men sat in comfortable old wicker chairs on the wide front porch of the ranch house. Purdy Elmarr was the eldest. Rob Raines was the youngest, twenty-seven, a solidly-built young man with a small mustache who had the manner of earnest reliability of the ambitious young lawyer. (A manner which, he had begun to suspect, was not helping him at all in his program of re-seduction of Debbie Ann.) On this day, in this place, he was so full of deference as to hover dangerously close to obsequiousness. He had the wind-and-weather look of the ailing enthusiast. After much thought he had worn a necktie, which he now knew was a mistake, but it was too late to take it off. It was his first invitation to the ranch. He sensed that his career was balanced on the sultry edge of this idle afternoon — and here it would be determined whether, in the far golden years, he would become Judge Raines, a figure of dignity, solemn with wealth — or ole Robby Raines, that lawyer fella they say had a real good chance and muffed it that time, back when old Purd Elmarr was still alive, making deals. Rob Raines wondered whether he had poured too much or too little bourbon into his glass. As the idle talk went on, with nobody coming to the point, he was getting more instead of less nervous.

It seemed as though J. C. Arlenton would drone on forever. He was Buddha fat, pink-bald, with little short thick hands and feet. He wore khaki pants and a white shirt and carpet slippers, and he had driven out in a Cadillac that was as dirty as any car Raines had ever seen. Rob knew he had been in the state legislature one time, a long time ago, and since then had shoved a couple of governors into office. He had a lot of grove land over in Orange County, and a good-sized building-supply business, and he was known to be in a few things with Elmarr. One of them was the regular poker session.

J. C. Arlenton sat hugging his glass with his little thick hands and said in a tone of complaint to the fourth man present, Corey Haas, "Now Corey, damn it, you know better'n to set right there telling me Wink Haskell ever had one dollar put into Sea-Bar Development. Wink, he never went into nothing without control and that was the reason how he lost out here and there, and Sea-Bar was one he lost out on, so don't you let him suck you in hinting on like how he had him a fine thing there, because Wink, he's like to do that way to you, proving how smart he is. When Sea-Bar sold that whole tract to Mackel, ole Wink didn't get one dime on account he wasn't in it, so don't let him hint you different."

"Have it your way, J. C.," Corey Haas said indifferently. "You've been down on Wink ever since he crossed you on that zoning thing and ever'body knows it."

Corey Haas was, in this matter, Rob Raines' ticket to join the discussion. Corey had thrown Rob a little bit of legal work lately. Of the four, Corey was the only one who wasn't a native Floridian, but he had come down from West Virginia so long ago there wasn't any perceptible difference in speech or manner. He'd lost a land-boom fortune so big that he'd spent the rest of his life trying to catch up to where he once had been. There were some who'd said he'd made it all back. He liked to get in on land syndicates. And he was in with Troy Jamison on Horseshoe Pass Estates.

"You stop chawin' each other a minute, we can get business out of the way and get back to drinking," Purdy Elmarr said quietly.

"Sure, Purd," J. C. said quickly.

Purdy Elmarr looked over at Corey Haas with a little glint of animosity in his faded old eyes and said, "Don't properly remember just how you come to go in with Jamison, Corey."

Corey looked uncomfortable. Rob, watching the exchange, suspected that Purdy knew exactly why Corey had gone in with Troy Jamison.

"I told you," Corey said. "It's on account of Mary being Charlie Kail's daughter before she married Bernard Dow, and her remembering how Charlie and me and Dow were in on a few things together, and when it looked like more than Troy could swing, they come to see me and it looked all right. And my end sure isn't enough to pinch anybody. I got forty-five thousand into it. It was like for old times' sake, Purd."

"Man has a right to throw his own money away, I guess," Purdy Elmarr said.

"I told him forty times he was going about it wrong," Corey said hotly, "but he's got control and he's stubborn, and there was no point bringing it to a head on account of she'd vote it the way he asked her to. So I've been just waiting."

"What were you figuring on doing?"

"Just waiting, Purd."

Purdy Elmarr smiled off into space. "I know that tract well, boys. I guess we all do. Little over eight hundred acres, with two thousand feet on the bay right opposite Horseshoe Pass. Joe Wethered had it and he passed on and June Alice Wethered had it and passed it onto young Joe and I remember it because he damn near lost it for taxes one time and I was hoping on picking it up. You remember old Joe used to have a fish shack there?"

"Remember it well," J. C. said.

"I got no quarrel with the figure Jamison paid for it. Eleven hundred an acre. Figuring conditions and location, I think it was bought fair and sold fair. I made me some rough figuring the other day. You take eight hundred thousand for that land, and with the clearing, grading, canals, hay fill, seawalling and all, you got to put in another seven — eight hundred thousand, maybe more. Then say a half million on streets, entrance, sewers and so on. But I figure you get two thousand prime lots that'll average out at eight thousand a lot, meaning sixteen million, or a gross of thirteen five, which sort of brings my interest to a head, boys. Now just how do you think he's gone wrong, Corey?"

"The big mistake, of course, was trying to engineer the whole thing at once. He shoulda took one little section and finished it off complete and nice, and sold it off to pay for the next piece, but he had to go right ahead and do it big, bulldozers, dredges, draglines all over the damn place, so every one of 'em had to be pulled off the job near two weeks back."

"That's the trouble with the little fellas," Purdy said. "They try to get big too fast. You take him. He was a little bitty house builder, only down here a few years, not big enough for anybody to pay any serious attention to, and making a little money here and there, so he up and marries Mary Dow and she's got just enough money so he gets to thinking big, and he loses it for her. But he got to be big for a little while. How much has he got into it, cash money, his and hers, Corey?"

"I'd say about . . . oh, three hundred thousand."

"They got more to put in?"

"By selling stuff. The boat, jewelry, mortgage the house, maybe they could find another hundred quick. But the way I see it, his nerves have got jumpy and he don't want to ask her to put every last thing in."

"How much would it take to save it?"

"Well, the land payments are spread pretty good, and I think maybe it could be done for three hundred thousand, no less."

"I expect they've come to you for more."

"I just couldn't spare more. My cash position isn't so good right now, Purd."

Purdy Elmarr grinned like an amiable old coyote. "I can tell just what you were fixin' to do, Corey Haas. You was going to set right there and let things get just as bad as they could get, where it would look like Jamison was going to lose the whole damn thing, and all of a sudden you were going to be able to put in cash to save it, but you'd want control, and he was going to be so grateful after being so scared you were going to do just fine, and once you had control you were going to run it your way, and slap one section together cheap and fast and soon as it begun to prove out you were going to unload your stock interest you stole from him, and make a big capital gain and get the hell out. And I bet you had that in mind right from the start, but you didn't know I was going to get interested in it."

"Hell, I didn't even know you were going to find out about it."

The three of them laughed. Raines felt confused. There were undercurrents he didn't understand.

"Now here's maybe what will happen. You set us up a little corporation so we'll be ready, boy. Ought to have a name. You're good on names, J. C."

"Uh . . . how 'bout Twin Keys Corporation? Riley and Ravenna are about the same length, and this land is chunk between 'em."

"Boy," Purdy said to Raines, "you check that name out with Tallahassee and set it up fifty and one-half percent to me, thirty-nine to Corey, ten to J. C. and a half percent to you instead of legal fees and all. Set it up minimum, boy. Corey, you look like you bit down on something soured you. Got anything to say?"

"Not a word, Purdy."

"Good. Now here's the way it'll work, Corey. Listen close. You set the timing. When things are as bad off as they're going to get, you tell Jamison you're peddling your stock to this Twin Keys Corporation for forty-five thousand, and getting out of this Horseshoe Pass Estates Corporation. Tell 'em it's me behind Twin Keys. And you hear I'll buy theirs too. That'll get 'em in the clear without much loss to speak of. Wouldn't want to hurt Charlie Kail's girl too bad. So Twin Keys borrows and buys up all the stock, then sets on it a while, and we get good estimates on just what it would cost to complete it, and what we can figure on getting back off sale of the lots, and then we sell the whole thing to my Ravenna Development Corporation and take us a good fat capital gain on the holdings of Twin Key stock, hear?"

J. C. stirred and grunted and said, "Ought to work out, Purd. Ought to work out good."

"Excepting for one thing," Purdy said gently. "We got to be sure Jamison don't get no he'p anyplace to bail himself out. Corey, you tole me this lawyer boy could find out what I was a-wondering about."

"He found out," Corey said. "Go ahead, Rob."

Raines cleared his throat. "Well . . . I was with Debbie Ann last night at a party at Jamison's and later at a beach party. I don't know exactly how much her father left her because I didn't ask her directly, but from what I was able to check other places, she got somewhere around three hundred thousand then. She doesn't have to touch it now because she gets enough alimony from that Dacey Hunter to live pretty good. I found a chance to ask her whether she'd invested anything in Horseshoe Pass Estates and she laughed at me. She said Troy Jamison had had a long talk with her about it three weeks ago, showing her the engineering plans and talking about potential and all. She said she'd told him that when she came into the money she'd had it taken out of the trust and put in an investment portfolio that was heavier in common stocks than the trust list had been, and it had been doing so good she certainly didn't want to disturb it for any land deal. She told him her father wanted her to be comfortable her whole life long, and that was just what she planned to be. She told him she couldn't help it if her mother was a damn fool about money. That didn't mean she had to be too."

"They don't get along so good? The girl and Jamison?"

"Not good and not bad either," Rob said.

Purdy spat over the railing into the yard. "Boy, what did you find out about that funny-name foreigner staying there? He got any cash money?"

"His name is Rodenska, Mike Rodenska. He's a newspaperman. His wife died a little while ago. He's got some money."

"Has he got enough?"

"I think he's probably got enough, if he wants to go in with Jamison. I don't know if Jamison has talked to him or not."

There was a long and thoughtful silence. "That's a risk I guess we got to take," Purdy said. "I've just about dried up every other place Jamison could go for cash money. Course, might be we could hedge it a little. Boy, you keep on seeing that Debbie Ann, and see if you can make you a chancet to hint to that funny-name fella the land deal is sour."

Rob said thoughtfully, "Of course it wouldn't be sour if Troy could get hold of . . ."

"Boy," Purdy said harshly. "One half percent of Twin Keys could be fifty thousand cash money."

"Oh, I didn't mean anything by what I just said, Mr. Elmarr. Not a thing. I was just working up to something else I think should be considered. I was wondering what there is to prevent Jamison getting in touch with, or being contacted by, one of the big land syndicates, say from the East Coast. They could see the potential in a minute. And he could still get out with a nice profit."

J. C. chuckled. "Run into that before, Raines. Tell him about that time they come in and tried to grab a deal Wink was interested in, Corey."

Corey laughed softly. "You can't make a deal that big quick and quiet. Wink found out long before it was going to be closed. So he started scrambling around. First thing you know the tract comes up for a zoning change and the Ravenna County Board of Commissioners tabled it for further study. Next thing somebody brings an injunction against the bay fill that was going on. Then it turns out maybe somebody got a little sloppy approving the title on the tract. With one thing and another, the Miami boys pulled out, and soon as Wink got it, all those little problems sort of got themselves ironed right out."

"I get the picture," Rob said, swallowing. "By the way. Jack Connorly has been after Jamison to run for Commissioner in November."

"Honest to God?" Prudy said with blank astonishment. He rocked his chair down onto four legs, slapped his knees, and began to gasp with laughter. When he caught his breath he said, "That Connorly is pure horse's ass, I swear. Gawd *damn!* Well, if he wants to make a big political figger out of Jamison, he better hustle his ass down the road, 'cause come November, Jamison is going to be back down to his proper size, building little bitty carports." All amusement disappeared with an almost startling abruptness. "Anybody got anything to add?"

"Just one little old thing I was saving, Prud," J. C. said, fat little fingers laced across his stomach. "I got this in such a roundabout way, it isn't worth trying to explain it. But it's a good guess Jamison has got him another woman. Don't know who she is, but she's staying at Shelder's Cottages on Ravenna Key, there on the bay side, just below Whitey's Fish Camp. Don't know if it will have any bearing on what we were talking about, but they say Jamison and Mary Kail ain't getting on so smooth lately, and the reason might be right there at Shelder's. You get any hint they're scrappin', Rob?"

"Nothing specific. I think he's drinking a little more than he was, from what Debbie Ann said. I thought it might be because he's worried about his project. Pre-development sales are way off."

"Nothing surprising about that," Corey Haas said. "He can't make any time sales and give title, on account he has to have cash money to get the mortgage release. And there's

98

a strong rumor with the real estate boys the development may never get finished. Jamison has cut down to one salesman, and they set in that office over there without much happening. Just be-backs."

"Just what?" J. C. asked.

"People use up an hour staring at a lot, scuffing their feet, then say we'll be back. But they never do come back."

"That about does it for now," Purdy Elmarr said. "You too dog-lazy to han' me that bottle, J. C.? Thanks. Here you go, boy. . . . "

A little over an hour later, his mouth slightly numbed by bourbon, Rob Raines plunged his little MGA west over bad roads toward the Tamiami Trail. Liquor made the world exceptionally vivid and slightly unreal. Thoughts, doubts, ambitions, boiled in his mind. Did I make the right impression? I know how they're using me, but are they also planning to use me in some other way I don't know about? This is the edge of the big time. One toe in the door. Handle it just right. No mistakes. Then there'll be fifty thousand, maybe thirty to keep after taxes and all, and they'll let me in on another one. Elmarr will still use Dillon and Burkhardt for most of his business, but they're getting pretty old. They took Stan Killian in with them, but Stan is a tanglefoot. They're all getting along. But they'll last long enough for me to get in solid.

He thought about Jamison. A sitting duck. He had that big advertising agency background, and he'd done well enough as a small builder, but he didn't have a chance against Elmarr, Haas and J. C. Arlenton. Jamison had no briefing on those kind of men. They'd tear him apart like a chicken and suck the bones.

He came out onto the Trail at the Stickney Point traffic light, and as he waited for his chance to turn south, all exhilaration faded and, without warning, he felt bleak, depressed.

Is this what I wanted? Is this where I was headed? He turned south, into a long line of traffic on the Trail, boxed behind a car from Ohio. The hell with it. I'll make mine. It's all legal. That's what the training is good for. So you know where the line is, and you can stay on the right side of it. That's what they use you for, to find out just how far they can go. And the closer to that line you can work, and still guarantee safety, the more valuable you are to those boys.

Forget all that idealism crap. It's just a blindfold they put on you, so you won't realize you're living in a jungle. Whatever happened to Jamison was his own fault. He was like a stupid caveman who'd gotten lucky and felled a big piece of meat, and instead of hacking off all he could carry and taking it back to his cave, he was walking round and round it, stone ax in his hand. It was going to spoil before he could eat the whole thing, so now a bunch of them were watching him from the bushes, waiting for the right minute to spring. They weren't even going to leave him with nothing — which they could. They were going to give him a little chunk to take home.

His widowed mother, Dolores Raines, called Dee by her garden club friends, sat fatly on her heels in the backyard, wearing her big straw hat, bulging green slacks, khaki shirt and gardening gloves, troweling a flower bed. She grunted erect as he approached, turned, beamed at him, and kissed the corner of his mouth.

"How did it go, sweetie? Are you going to be Purdy Elmarr's new smart young lawyer? I'm so proud of you, sweetie."

"I guess it went all right. It's just a little thing. I'm setting up a little corporation. Purdy and J. C. Arlenton and Corey Haas. We're going to pick up some land, maybe."

"We, sweetie? Are you really *in* with them?"

"Just barely, Mom. One half of one percent."

She hugged him and made a little squeal of ecstasy. "But it's a start, sweetie! Even if you only make seven dollars, you're in with some of the most powerful men in this part of the state."

"I might make a little more than seven dollars, Mom."

"You've had a lot to drink! I can tell by your eyes."

"Purdy Elmarr's liquor, Mom."

They grinned at each other with private understanding. "Now don't you get into any of those big poker games they have out there."

"He's not about to ask me. Yet."

"Later on, sweetie, let's go out to dinner to celebrate. Just you and me. A fat old lady and her wonderful, brilliant son."

"I'm sorry. I better change and go down and see Debbie Ann."

Dee's mouth grew smaller. "I know she had a silly crush on you years ago even though she was *years* younger than you — hardly past childhood and you were almost a man, but I really don't see what the great attraction is. She's a divorced woman, Robert. I haven't told you this before but I was actually *shocked* when I first saw her after she came back to live with Mary. She actually has a *slutty* look. I'm sure there are just dozens of really *lovely* girls around who would be delighted if you'd pay as much attention to them as you do to that . . ."

"Jealous?" he asked innocently.

"Oh, *you!*" She looked coy. "Maybe I am. A little." She frowned. "Sweetie, I just don't want my handsome intelligent son to get involved with a loose woman. I can remember how I used to worry about the two of you, years ago, wondering if she was . . . encouraging you in any way. She had that look, even then. I was *so* relieved when you broke up with her. And now, to have it start all over again . . . Really, sweetie, I *am* a woman of the world. I'm not an old prude. And I can see how she could be attractive to men . . . well, in a sort of *primitive* way . . . or you could say an *animal* way . . . and it wouldn't particularly *please* me if that's all you're interested in, but it wouldn't worry me the way it does thinking you might get *serious* about her."

"When I'm ready to get married, it won't be to her, Mom."

She looked intently at him, sighed and smiled. "Just don't let her trap you, sweetie. I guess it would be hard to trap a lawyer, wouldn't it. Run along then. I guess men just *have* to be like that. You can settle down after you're married, the way your father did. He certainly was no angel before he met me."

He went in the house and showered. He thought about Debbie Ann. He knew he had made a bad decision last night when he had ignored her objections, thinking that if he could arouse her, she'd let him into her room. But it had made her furious. He had been as angry as she was. What the hell difference could it make to her? She was divorced, wasn't she? And it had actually been so damn easy that first and only time, long ago. There had been girls before her, a very few, and a lot of girls and women since her, but it had never been like that. In his tipsy haste and clumsiness he had hurt her badly, and by rights that should have ended any chance of her response, but she had come out of the paralysis of the unexpected pain within moments, erupting into a greedy gasping frenzy that had at first shocked him, and then almost immediately depleted him. He remembered how she had cried afterward, and how she had looked, sitting on the blanket, her face contorted, tears flowing, sniffling, her small body red in the glow of a sun that sat cloudless on the rim of the Gulf, as she wriggled back into the damp swim suit. He remembered how she had kept shuddering there in the hot sun at each touch of his hands, keeping her eyes squeezed tight shut as though that somehow kept him from seeing her.

They had sailed back in dusk that turned into night, and she had refused to help with the boat, or look at him or speak to him. And after that, no matter how carefully he plotted, he couldn't make her do it again. He couldn't even get her alone.

When he heard she had come back for a divorce, even though eight years had gone by, the wanting came back, strong as ever. Last night had been the best opportunity yet.

As he dressed he told himself that he would have to hide his anger. Be very nice to her. Apologize extensively. Blame his insistence on alcohol. Because — and the thought chilled a little area in the back of his mind — if she refused to have anything to do with him, Purdy Elmarr would find out about it somehow. And he would be of no use to them. Any lawyer could set up a simple corporation. They weren't paying him fifty thousand dollars for that. He knew what they thought. They thought they were paying him fifty thousand dollars to continue sleeping with Debbie Ann. It was a small hedge compared to a sixteen million gross. It was espionage money. He wished he could start earning it in the way they thought he was earning it. So change the approach. Maybe humility would work. All in all, it was something the law texts had not mentioned.

And suddenly he realized he had a lot more at stake than he had counted on. He stood in shocked silence, thinking. If the deal went through, no harm would be done. It would be a private matter. But what if it didn't work? It would make a juicy story for Corey and J. C. to tell around Ravenna, Venice, Sarasota and Bradenton.

He could hear J. C. holding forth to a bunch of local businessmen at lunch, chuckling. "Purd, Corey and me figured we had that Jamison land practically in our pocket, boys. Hell, we even cut that Raines squirt in on a piece of it, on account of he'd cut himself in on a lot a pieces of somethin' else raht under Troy Jamison and Mary Kail's nose, so he was in a spot to steer it all our way a little, you know, but it just didn't work out. But I bet it was the nicest kind o' law work that boy ever had. Or ever will."

Rob Raines felt his face grow hot. A thing like that, a story that would accumulate artistic exaggeration as it passed from person to person, and lent itself so readily to coarse and obvious puns, could cook you for good. Ten years from now they'd still be telling it.

"See that fella cross the street? Rob Raines. I'll tell you how he got screwed one time."

Rob suddenly knew that those three men knew the additional risk he was taking. "God *damn* them!" he whispered. And he knew that the deal had to go through. He had to make it go through. Because, if it didn't, what had looked like the beginning of importance could turn out to be the end of any possibility of importance. It would not be the same in a city. But here, up and down this chain of Gulf-side resort towns and cities, the business and legal community was like one small town. Everyone knew your triumphs and mistakes, your golf handicap, your political opinions, your amorous adventures, the size of your father's and your grandfather's estate, and whether your mother had married up or down to produce you.

Had he previously established a public identity, had he made any particular start in establishing the legend of himself in the community, potential damage would not be as great. But he had been most careful. He had balanced the possibly critical opinions of the MGA and the sailing squadron and the addiction to rather expensive sports jackets, by subscribing to the opinions of the more conservative wing of the Democratic party, by avoiding divorce cases, drunk-driving cases and collision litigation, by serving on the hospital drive and the Community Chest, by entertaining and being entertained by the more responsible segments of Ravenna society. As an attractive young bachelor he had been able to be carefully selective. He had begun to acquire a small amount of estate work, and he had turned down one political opportunity that had seemed to him to require more work than kudos.

But should Twin Keys fall through, the results of the four careful years of practice would be bitched. He would be known as that young lawyer who was so eager to get cozy with the Elmarr group he had been willing to further his ambitions in bed. It would make of him a figure of fun. The community would not be indignant. Or cruel. They would be amused. It wouldn't be the end of him. But it would set a limit. He could go only so far.

And so it was a sobered, apprehensive and completely determined young man who drove south to Riley Key through the gaudy lights of sunset, his brown hands sweaty on the wheel of the agile little car.

four

At the Key Club at the southern end of Riley
Key, Sunday night was known, in the club
bulletins, as Family Night. The Club was
housed in an old rambling roomy frame structure that had originally been a hunting and
fishing lodge built by a Cleveland industrial-
ist. He had owned six hundred feet of land
from Gulf to bay, and had built the lodge on
the bay side, close to a natural lagoon that cut
into the Key from the bay side. When the
Cleveland man had died in 1923 a group of
his friends who had often been guests at the
lodge, remembering the freedom of their an-
nual visits, and the good times they had enjoyed, had banded together and purchased
the lodge from the estate and, after establishing ground rules and installing a Bahamian
couple to operate it, had incorporated it as the
ultra-private Key Club.

In 1932, after most of the members had
died physically or financially, the Club would

have folded had not one of the original members, who had retired to Florida at precisely the right time, been determined to save it as a club. He opened the membership list to suitable applicants in Ravenna, fourteen miles to the north, and in the much smaller town of Gulfway, five miles to the south. At that time there were also a few wealthy retireds, a very few, who had settled on Riley Key and were potential members.

The Club did not thrive, but it did continue to exist. It had been so solidly constructed of black cypress and hard pine that there were few maintenance problems.

By 1959, though the original structure was largely unchanged, the Key Club was fashionable, expensive, exclusive and beautifully operated. There were rental cabañas on the Gulf side for landlocked members and the guests of waterfront members lacking guest facilities. The entire structure was air-conditioned. Kitchen facilities were entirely modern. Lighting effects were dramatic and professional. The lagoon had been widened and deepened, the channel dredged and marked. There were dockage facilities for a considerable number of sizable watercraft.

Though it took a staff of sixteen to operate the Club and facilities, and monthly bills were prepared on the most modern of accounting equipment, and the initiation fee made the new member think thrice, the membership still insisted upon calling the Club homey and quaint, pointing out as evidences of quaintness the dark-beamed cathedral ceilings, the dusty throngs of stuffed fish mounted high on the walls, the enormous stone fireplace.

The shrewd and well-paid young manager of the Club, a graduate of the Cornell Hotel School, was called Gus by the membership, and, during his few years of tenure, had managed to establish a public personality which led the uninformed to guess that he had been born among the mangroves and had been yanked off a shrimp boat and charged with the confusing chore of running the Club. Gus was particularly adept in selecting and hiring bartenders and waitresses who were sufficiently casual with the members to be known and loved as characters, but never overstepped that invisible line of protocol and gave offense. Gus and the help never gossiped about a member to a member, never permitted an emotional relationship with a member to become established, ranged confidently back and forth within that narrow area between obsequiousness and rudeness — and knocked down every dime they could.

On the occasion of Mike Rodenska's first visit to the Key Club, the gathering was large and informal. April was more than half over. Most of the short-season winter visitors had left. House-guests were in short supply. Everybody told everybody else how wonderful it was to have the season over so you could relax and have fun with your friends. The night air was balmy. Tinted spotlights on palm boles dimmed the circus of stars overhead. Cruisers were arriving, and there were private cocktail parties on the cruisers and in some of the beach cabañas. The main bar was three deep. There was a constant roar of conversation, and rumble of the gentle surf, and the car doors chunking in the parking lot, and squealing of sunbaked children and incomprehensible cawings of teenagers, and clatter of crockery from the early diners, and swift swoopings of waitresses, and drinks held high and handed back. Polite hootings of dowager laughter, and hearty splashings in the lighted pool — and here and there the careful walk and wooden grimace of the alcoholic. It was Family Night.

If, during the day, you'd had a few knocks and a swim and some sun and a nap, you were ready. You cavorted under the dusty glass eyes of the fish who had lost battles long ago.

Mike, dizzied by the surge and noise in the bar, where the air-conditioning labored vainly against animal heat, made his way slowly to a side door and went out onto a broad porch. He looked in through a window. Shorts, halters, dinner dresses, cocktail dresses, swim suits. Gleams and glints of teeth, eyes and jewels. Skin of scarlet, pink, brown, taffy — in a shifting, laughing turmoil of shoulders and throats and thighs.

Voices came to him, blurred by the closed window: " . . . never had such a wonderful . . . went to Miami to . . . haven't seen you, darling, since . . . on the third flight to Havana . . . when she's looking sick . . . talk about new engines . . . for the silly girl he met in . . . menopause she doesn't . . . cracked up the car over in . . . that motel where Ruthie caught . . . good marks last year but . . . cold war doesn't mean we . . . remember that tarpon you . . . finished the marriage when she . . . sold it for two hundred a foot . . . in the hospital again with . . . backhand is weak . . . with strep throat only fourteen years old Tuesday . . . with a third martini is all . . . you should stop telling me what I should . . . give a stock dividend . . . before Betty's party . . . "

"Here he is!" a voice said, close and gay, and he turned his back on the window and saw, in the light from the window, Debbie Ann with a particularly handsome brunette with bangs and furry black brows and a look of insolence, and a broad compulsive mouth. "Watching the snake pit, Mike?"

"Nobody gave me a score card. I can't tell the players."

Both girls were in tailored slacks and seagoing blouses. They were the same height, both carrying drinks, both a little tight, but under control.

"Shirley, this is Mike Rodenska, our houseguest. Mike, Shirley McGuire. Mike and I . . . I was about to say we're roommates, but that doesn't sound right. Wingmates. We're both in the guest wing. We share a bath. That makes us intimate, doesn't it?"

"You leave it like a swamp. It's like living in a sorority house. Perfume, steam, hair in the sink. Soap."

"So I'm clean, but I'm not neat. I told you, Shirley. This may be an honest man."

"Nice to know there is such a thing," the McGuire girl said. She was almost a baritone. The contrast with Debbie Ann's little-girl voice was startling.

Rob Raines suddenly appeared out of the darkness. "I've been looking all over for you, Debbie Ann. Good evening, Mr. Rodenska."

"Hello, lover," Debbie Ann said acidly. "Shirley, I'm not particularly interested in having you meet Rob Raines, but I guess it can't be helped. Shirley McGuire. Now why don't you go swimming or something, Robert? Go tweak girls."

Raines looked nobly pained. "Please, Debbie Ann. I'd like to talk to you a minute."

Debbie Ann turned to Shirley. "I'll have to humor him, dearie. Take Mike to the Devans' cabaña. I'll join you there."

Mike left the porch with Shirley McGuire. As they walked toward the Gulf he said, "What's this cabaña deal?"

"Sort of a cocktail party. I'm staying with the Tennysons. She's my aunt. So I got drug to the Devans' party. You know the Devans or the Tennysons?"

"I'm new here."

"So am I, Mike. Let's not go back there. It's a herd of antiques. They keep talking about people I don't know."

"Suits me."

"Let's just walk on the beach." She stopped and emptied her glass. His was empty. She took his from him and put the two glasses on a bench, and they walked down the slant of the beach, angling away from the cabañas, toward the water.

"Hold it a minute," she said, and put one hand on his shoulder to brace herself, and took off her shoes. She slapped the sand off them and said, "Got a big pocket? Good. Here. Thanks."

"You known Debbie Ann long?"

"Ten days, I guess. Since I got down. I'm a project of hers. Sometimes it's fine. Other times, frankly, she gets on my nerves."

They were walking slowly at the edge of the gentle surf. "A project?"

"I guess we do have a hell of a lot in common, Mike. We both had a horrible marriage. We trade grim anecdotes. I'm two years older than she is, and mine lasted five years. She didn't have any kids. I've got a little boy three. Living with my mother in Richmond. The big difference is she got her divorce. I'm just beginning the route. So I'm a project."

"A new member of the club?"

"Something like that, I guess. I think you'd have to be a woman to understand."

"Is it a . . . kind of loneliness?"

She stopped so abruptly he walked two paces beyond her, turned back and looked at her, starlight meager on her face. "What's the matter?"

"I was warned about you."

"I'm harmless, Shirley."

"Are you? Debbie Ann said you're too damn easy to talk to."

"People have to talk."

"How many ever listen to you though? Got any cigarettes?"

"Cigars."

"Then smoke one, and give me a drag. I've been smoking too damn much since I got down here." She walked a little way from the water and sat down, digging her bare heels into the moist sand. He lit a cigar, sat heavily beside her, offered it to her.

She dragged deeply, coughed, inhaled again and handed it back. "Debbie Ann understands part of it. Loneliness isn't exact, Mike. It's something else. I tried to make it work. I honestly tried, long after my friends had started advising me to give up. Can you believe that?"

"Sure."

"So finally you make up your mind and leave the bastard, and set the wheels in motion. You're supposed, I guess, to feel free as birds. I came down here. I didn't know how rough it would be. It's very rough, Mike. You try to be yourself all your life. All of a sudden you're type-cast. You know? Young woman getting unhitched. Ready for adventure, or something. Nobody really *sees* you. As a person. They see a kind of symbol. And it gets you to wondering who you really are. It makes you feel lost and reckless. It's scarey, because you have the feeling you might do some really stupid thing."

"A case of no controls," Mike said.

"What do you mean?"

"When you lived with your parents there were rules. When you were in school there were rules. After school, before you got married, there were things you could and couldn't do. Pressure of society. Acceptable behavior of the junior miss. Now all of a sudden, no rules. There's even the reverse. A sort of pressure to make you let go of personal standards."

"That's exactly it! It's like . . . nothing to lean on. Nothing to really feel guilty about. Men make the automatic pass. I was part of a duet for five years and now I'm playing a single. And I just — don't know what to do with myself. Debbie Ann felt the same thing in a different way, so it helps to have somebody about your own age who understands the picture. But I can't be as go-to-hell as she is. I guess she's part of the pressure. You're pretty smart. I'm boring you."

"I'll let you know when you start to."

"A deal. I think I can look at myself pretty objectively. I'm not terribly bright, but I think I'm a warm person. And, let's face it, I've got a sort of sexpot look. Men are always getting the wrong impression. Women not so often. I can't walk without a wiggle, and I look like I'm pouting, which is supposed to be provocative, they tell me, and I've got this whisky-tenor voice and coloring the cosmetic people call exotic. But it's a big fake. Inside I'm a pretty prim gal, Mike. That's not to say my responses aren't whole-hearted. They're — thorough. But there has to be love. Anything without love would make me feel squeamish. But there's this . . . pressure. No rules. And maybe I'm the sort of person who needs rules and depends on them. It's a six-month deal now, a Florida divorce, and six months seems a very long time, and I don't want to turn into somebody I don't want to be, just because I feel forlorn and alone."

"If you're aware of the problem, you probably won't."

"I have the feeling I should stay clear of Debbie Ann."

"So?"

"Well, it might be a pretty good trick. She roped me into a beach picnic last night. I was too gutless to say no. And too bored. So I went and got too drunk, and so my day has been full of little remorses, and thank God no big remorses because my escort got even drunker. But you see?"

"I do indeed."

After long and curiously comfortable minutes of silence she said, "Debbie Ann briefed me. About you."

"Did she?"

"Yes. I was just thinking about it. Now I feel ashamed of spilling my problems. You must think they're pretty trivial."

"I don't, Shirley."

"There's something else you ought to know. You better keep your door locked, Mike. I wouldn't say that if I thought you would — welcome the attention."

"Oh, come now!" he said irritably. "For God's sake, Shirley. I've gone through a hell of a lot of years without having to drive off women with a club. I'm bald, fat and forty and — "

"And you were all sewed up so completely you wouldn't have even been aware of a pass. But now you're . . . available, Mike. And I think it's very sweet that you don't have any idea how attractive you are to women. Most men your age are totally convinced they're irresistible."

"The movies are after me every minute."

"A woman is always aware of strength and

120

gentleness and honesty, Mike. I guess it's a kind of . . . emotional reliability. That's why people talk to you. We're desperate young women, Mike."

They walked back up to the Club. They found Mary Jamison and she bought them a drink, signed the chit. Troy had reserved a table for six, for the four of them and a pleasant couple named Murner. They looked for Troy and could not find him. Mary decided they should eat. It was a fine meal. Throughout the dinner Mary looked strained, and Troy's chair was conspicuously empty. Debbie Ann filled the silences with empty chatter. She carried on a mock flirtation with Mike. Rob Raines joined the table after dinner. Mike noticed that Raines and Debbie Ann seemed to have arrived at a peaceable understanding. After dinner they went to the bar. Debbie Ann disappeared. The Murners said goodnight. Mary became involved in a conversation with the Laybournes. Rob Raines talked idly with Mike for a while and then said, "Let's take these out on the porch. I'd like to ask you something, Mike."

"Sure."

They went out onto the big unscreened porch and sat on the railing. The pool was closed, the pool lights out.

"Mike, I wanted to talk to you about something that may be none of my business. But I know you're a good friend of Troy's. And I think you're fond of Mary."

"Yes."

"Mary is a fine woman. Very loyal."

"What are you getting at?"

"I don't think Troy would tell you. I guess it would be a matter of pride with him. And a matter of loyalty for Mary not to tell you their troubles. But Troy is in trouble, Mike. Bad financial trouble."

"With Horseshoe Pass Estates?"

"Yes. He went into it too fast, without adequate capitalization. He wouldn't listen to his friends down here, people who know the local picture. He did pretty well as a small builder. But this is just too big for him. If he keeps going on the way he has, he may lose the whole thing, and Mary's money along with it."

"Have you told him this?"

"I've tried to, Mike. But he's a stubborn man."

"What do you think I can do?"

"I don't really know. I thought you should know about it, though. Troy has been trying desperately to line up additional financing. He's even tried to get hold of Debbie Ann's money. But she's scared of that project. Rightly.

Troy has the idea a few more hundred thousand dollars will get it over the hump."

"That much!"

"It will take much more than that, Mike. He could throw two or three hundred thousand more in the pot right now and all it would do would be delay the inevitable. And whoever goes in with him will take a fat loss. But I don't think he's going to find anybody."

"What can he do?"

"I don't know. It's possible that if he was willing to give the whole thing up, he might come out of it with a loss, a substantial one but not a crippling one. I've thought that, as a good friend of his, you might find a chance to talk sense to him. Has he talked to you about investing in it?"

"No."

"He might, Mike. And he'll talk about the tremendous potential. If and when he does, you might say that you'd like to look into it. You get in touch with me and I'll introduce you to a man named Corey Haas. He's put money into it, mostly because he was a close friend of Mary's father. The loss won't hurt Corey. But he can give you the true picture of how deep Troy has gone. Then that will give you something to go back to Troy with — questions to ask that he can't answer. And if you wake him up, you may be doing him and Mary a great favor. I'd hate to see them lose everything."

"Troy showed me around the area over there, Rob. I know they had to stop the development work because they ran out of working capital, but I can't see why it would take such an enormous amount to. . . ."

"Mike, when you start with eight hundred acres of bay frontage swamp, and you have to fill it up to grade, dig canals, dredge, sea-wall, put in roads, curbs, street lighting, sewage, drainage, landscaping, you run into a staggering expense."

"Couldn't he complete one small section at a time?"

"It's too late for that. I thought you should know the picture, Mike. It's a mess, frankly. He's licked and he doesn't want to admit it to himself. I suppose there's an emotional angle."

"How do you mean?"

"Nearly all of it is Mary's money. He could have plunged into this thing to make so much more that he wouldn't have any . . . feeling of dependence. And that could be why he can't look at it rationally. And why he's . . . perhaps drinking a little heavier than he should."

Mike looked at Robert Raines, at this sincere, competent, cordial, helpful, courteous young man — blocky, brush-cut and photogenically weathered — who lounged in the rectangle of light that came from the nearby window, one Dak-clad haunch on the cypress railing, raw silk jacket sitting neatly on husky shoulders.

"Come down for a rest, Mike boy," Mike said wearily. "Just slop around in the sun."

"I beg your pardon?"

"You are talking to me of course because I am gentle and honest and strong, and very attractive to young women. They are dazzled by the gleam of my very high forehead. It goes way back. And my athletic structure — just like Alfred Hitchcock's. I'm a father image."

"What?" Raines said blankly.

"I'm touched the way people up and tell me things. All my life people up and tell me things. Along comes some flack to my desk on the paper and tells me very confidential that Miss Bumpy Grind is staying at the West Hudson Hotel with a cheetah. With a gold collar. So I am very impressed, of course, and I am about to send over a throng of legmen, like covering an execution, when all of a sudden it begins to look to me like maybe he is talking to me because he has an angle."

"I don't understand."

"Robert, one chugs along through life and maybe picks up one or two survival ideas here and there. I've got one. The bastards come at you from all directions, and there's no wall to put your back against. There is a footnote to this one, at the bottom of the page, in six-point Caslon, saying everybody keeps his powder dry."

"Mr. Rodenska, you sound as if you think I was trying to work . . . some kind of an angle. I've told you all this . . . I've been frank with you because — "

"I'm easy to talk to?"

"Because Troy is in a jam and — "

"You'd hate to see me lose my money because I'm such a nice guy. Naïve, but nice. Thanks, Rob. Thanks a lot."

"Are you a little tight, Mike?"

"I'm just down here for a rest."

Rob stood up. He looked uncertain. "Well . . . I better see if I can find Debbie Ann."

"You're a lawyer. Lawyers have to maneuver people. I'll give you a message. When anybody looks directly at me, right into my eyes, which isn't normal, and doesn't do any fidgeting, which again isn't normal, and drops their voice level about a half octave and gets real grammatical, I just lay back and wait for them to bring out the three walnut shells and the rubber pea."

"Mr. Rodenska, you don't . . . "

"You go find Debbie Ann, and when you get a chance, you play poker. Play every night. Better stick to small stakes at first. They ought to teach it in every law school. You had a deuce down and an ace up, and you were convincing me you had aces back to back. Go find your girl."

Raines hesitated, and then left quickly. He looked back once. His leaving had the flavor of flight. Mike spat the tip of a cigar over the railing and lighted it. He wondered how many cigars he had gone through during this long day. He felt vaguely guilty, and out of that guilt came the great seventh wave again, rolling his heart among the stones. There was no one to chide him about the cigars. No one to give a damn how many he smoked. Nobody to keep count and lecture him.

When Mary appeared below him and looked up at the porch and said, "Is that you, Mike?" he had to wait two long seconds before he could trust his voice and answer her.

She came up the steps and said, her voice too casual, "I just found out Troy was on Tim Gosnell's boat for a long time. Tim says he was a little more sober when he left, so maybe he got home somehow. We might as well leave, if you're ready. There's always the chance he's taking a nap in a dark corner somewhere, but I'm through looking. If so, he'll wake up at daylight and walk home up the beach. It's nearly five miles, but it won't hurt him any."

"I'm ready. How about your daughter?"

"She just left with Rob. There's some sort of party down in Gulfway."

They walked to the parking lot. She gave him the keys, a spare set she carried. He drove the Chrysler north, through the area near the public beach where the cars sat dark in starlight outside the silent motels, and where a few neoned beer joints were close to their midnight closing, and north past a place where on the beach he saw the silhouettes of people around the red coals of a driftwood fire, and north past the big dark beach houses.

When he drove into the triple carport, parking between Mary's station wagon and Debbie Ann's little white Porsche Speedster, Mary said, "Will you come in for a nightcap?"

"I guess I better just . . ."

"Please, Mike. Just for a minute or two."

Her voice was still casual, but the appeal was clear. He went into the kitchen with her. She made the drinks and they carried them out onto the patio. Stars were reflected, motionless in the black surface of the small swimming pool. He sat in one of the big redwood chairs and she sat ten feet away on a hassock.

"Did you like the Club, Mike?"

"It's a gay place."

"Bernard and I used to belong. But living up on Ravenna Key, we didn't get down very often. It's much handier, living here. We get a lot of use out of it."

"The food is fine."

"How about the people, Mike? How about the people?" She laughed. "You told me you are a qualified people-watcher."

"I can't say much without sounding pretentious. I got this out of it. They seem anxious. I don't know why. It's as if they had the correct scoop that tomorrow a hurricane washes the Club out to sea. Or prohibition is coming back. Or sex is going to be outlawed. I don't know. They seem to try too hard. They press. And it isn't that a lot of them are retired, maybe a little too young. Most of them work. It's the same all over the country, I guess. But it seems concentrated here, somehow. Like they have to do everything there is to do right now. It gave me the jumps. It's contagious. I emptied two drinks faster than I like to drink, and I had to say whoa boy."

"I feel that too, Mike. It's . . . undignified."

"That's a word I was hunting for."

"But there were lots of nice ones there."

"Nice ones everywhere. I met one nice one. Shirley McGuire. She flattered me, laid it on with a trowel, butter from head to foot. I respond fine to flattery."

"Oh, she's Martha Tennyson's niece. A new friend of Debbie Ann's. I've met her, but I don't really know her. She's getting a divorce, you know."

"She told me."

"She's an . . . interesting looking girl."

"She talked to me, and that Rob Raines talked to me."

"What did Rob talk about?"

Mike crossed his fingers in the darkness. "Sailboats."

"He's very high on sailing. Debbie Ann crewed for him in Yacht Club races when she was practically a child. She has a silver cup they won. He seems very interested now, but I can't feel he's right for Debbie Ann. There's a sort of . . . heaviness about him. He doesn't seem to have the light touch."

There was a silence. He heard the ice rattle in the bottom of her glass as she finished the weak drink she had made herself.

"Mike?"

"Yes, Mary."

"About what you said this morning. I wanted you to come in because I thought I wanted to talk. But I don't. Not yet."

"Any time."

"I have to do some more thinking. And even then, I don't want to . . . drop my troubles in your lap. When I do talk, I won't be asking you to do anything. It will be just . . . to get my own emotions straightened out. And even that isn't fair to you. To have you come down here and then — "

"Knock it off, Mary. I'm your friend. I'm Troy's friend. I'll listen because I want to. Okay?"

"Okay, Mike."

He said goodnight to her and went out the kitchen door toward the private guest-wing entrance. The night was very still. The richness of jasmine hung in the air, almost too strong. He felt no desire for sleep, so he changed to swim trunks and slippers, took a towel and went over to the beach. After he was in he realized it made him uneasy to swim at night. The water seemed to have an oily texture. He could imagine monsters sleekly stalking this blundering thrashing chunk of live bait. When he stood up to walk out with courageous dignity, something brushed against his leg, and almost instantaneously he was fifteen feet from the water's edge, breathing hard.

Face of a hero, he said to himself. Race of a hero. They need you in the Olympics, Rodenska. New event. Fifty-yard dash in three feet of water. Symbolic, anyway. You get scared of the things you can't see. Comedy routine. Minnow nibbles fat man. Fat man roars out of water and then, with enormous nonchalance, peers up and down deserted beach to see if anybody was looking. Like Troy in Melbourne that time, when a lorry tire let go and made that prolonged and significant whistling, and when he came so damn close to dropping flat on the sidewalk, and then pretended he had stumbled.

Mike walked back and showered and went to bed, but his brain was a gaudy tin top, spinning and whining, his eyes glued wide open, his hearing acute. He guessed it was an hour later when he heard the car drift in with due consideration for those asleep. He walked over to the window, the terrazzo pleasantly cool against his bare feet. They sat there in the MGA, the parking lights on, talking in low tones. They got out of the car, met on her side of the car and kissed. Her back was toward him. He saw Rob's hands slide slowly down from the small of her back to cup her haunches and pull her tightly against him. She acquiesced for a few seconds, then wriggled free, made a mock gesture of slapping him, giggled in a high tinkling way, and spun toward the door.

"Tomorrow?" he called.

"Phone and find out," she said.

Mike went back to bed. He heard her stirring about in her room, with a quick tick-tack of heels which ended when she took her shoes off. He heard nothing for a long time, and then the soft closing of the other door to the bath they shared. A little while later the whispery roaring of the shower began.

He lay in darkness, moving closer to sleep, hearing her hum tunelessly above the shower sound, building pink and soapy and explicit visions of her, remembering what the McGuire girl had told him, and pretending in that drifting area of half-sleep that when she had showered she would come sweetly, moistly, silently into his room and . . .

Sleep was suddenly rolled back by his sudden contemptuous realization that he had imagined himself right into a state of acute physiological readiness for her — the shallow breathing and the sweatiness and the ponderous gallop of his heart and the knotted loins.

He rolled and thumped his pillow and said

to himself, Maybe you should go back into high school. Maybe start a nice collection of dirty pictures. An adolescent old man. It's a fleshy trap. The mind is entirely satisfied with continence. But it's the old ape body which strains with unreasoned desire. It knows how much time has passed. So it rests here, hairy, heavy, with all the scars and marks and saggings of forty years, all the blemishes and erosions of its ape maturity, waiting with a massive arrogance for the glands to force the mind into some sort of pretty rationalization which will clear the way so that it can again exercise its plunging primordial function, its mute declaration concerning the continuance of the race. It's an ape thing, squatting on its hairy haunches behind a screen of brush, slack-jawed, picking lice off its belly, watching the young females of the tribe, and making plaintive rumblings in its chest.

You know all the rationalizations it's trying to force on you. Health. Quiet the nerves. Natural function. And that most devious rationalization of all, entitled; What Harm Would It Do? No objective harm, of course. She's no hesitant virgin. She'd be incapable of attaching any emotional significance to it.

It's the subjective harm, Michael. To be desperately old-fashioned, the loss of honor.

It would be just a switch on the salesman and the farmer's daughter. You were asked down to relax and mend. The services of the daughter of the household were not included in the facilities available. And, because you have years to live, and nobody cares deeply how you live them, and sons to raise, let's beware of the sophistry that nobody gives a damn what you do. Because you *do* give a damn. When there's nothing left but your own image of yourself, it somehow becomes a more grievous sin to smear it.

Okay. You're noble. Go to sleep.

The shower stopped. He heard, at the limit of audibility, the tiny rusty sound of prolonged tooth-brushing. The other door to the bath closed quietly. And in the great emptiness of the tropic night he found sleep.

five

At eleven o'clock Mike had been on the beach over an hour. One week ago, at about the same time, he had been looking down from the high aircraft at the tiny chalk-scrawls of surf along the Atlantic beaches. And this Monday was another blandly superb day. A transistor radio, six inches from his head, canceled out any possibility of consecutive thought. He had a Havana station. It pleased him not to be able to understand the words of the singing commercials.

The sun glared red through his eyelids. Sweat ran down his ribs and the sides of his throat. When he become too uncomfortable, he could go into the water again. And when he became famished, he would go back to the house and eat. The present moments were reduced to the ultimate of simplicity.

But, a few minutes after eleven, Troy joined him on the beach. He brought a small ice chest containing cans of beer. He wore faded blue swim trunks and dark glasses. He settled himself beside Mike and said, "Got to replace the fluid you're losing, chief."

Mike sat up and said, "I'll recommend this hotel to all my friends."

Troy opened two cans, handed one to Mike. The beer was icy cold. Mike watched Troy. The glasses obscured his eyes. His hands trembled. He was tanned, but it wasn't a healthy color. There seemed to be a tinge of yellow-green in it. Though there was still a hint of heavy-boned power about his body, the muscles were ropy and slack, the belly soft.

"I thought you'd be over in your sales office," Mike said.

"I phoned Marvin early and went back to sleep. He can handle it. Things are slow right now. If he has to take anybody around, he can lock up and leave a sign on the door. I've been going slowly nuts in that place lately. Hell with it. I guess I was the belle of the ball last night."

"I didn't see you wearing a lamp shade for a hat. You just quietly folded your tent."

"Gosnell makes a wicked martini. My seams came unglued. Mary is full of pregnant silences this morning."

"How'd you get home?"

"It's a dreary story, old buddy. I crawled aboard Bart Speeler's Chris and went to sleep in the cockpit and the morning sun woke me up. I started wobbling up the beach and one of the Tomley kids picked me up in his beach buggy. Did you stay long?"

"We left a little before midnight."

"Enjoy the party?"

"I think so."

"Ah, we're a gay mad lot here on the Key." Troy finished his beer, scooped a hole in the sand and buried the empty can. He patted the sand down over it, smoothly, carefully, making a small and tidy grave. "Mike."

"Right here, sir."

"Yesterday, I was damn rude. I apologize."

"I needled you."

"Because I needed it."

Mike knew that in those few moments the old relationship had been reestablished. No more withdrawal. No more defenses. It made Mike feel glad, and in another way it made him feel weary, because the regained closeness implied an obligation he was reluctant to accept.

"I needed it a long time ago too, Mike."

"You were in bad shape then. Not like now."

"Maybe I'm headed for the same place again."

"That sounds jolly."

"Honest to God, Mike. I don't know. I can't even be honest with myself." He kept smoothing the beer-can grave. "Asking you down here. I said it was . . . for you. Good old Mike. My turn to help. Christ! But all the time I was thinking — somebody to steady me. And I didn't want to think I needed that. That's why I was so damn nasty yesterday."

"So it was a call for help?"

"I don't like to think so. How goddamn weak can I get?"

"How bad off is your project?"

Troy drew a fingernail cross on the beer-can grave. "It's like this. We rented twenty boards. Fifty dollars a month apiece. Three-year contract. The sign company got the locations and put them up. A thousand-a-month advertising expense. They're good boards. They show a picture of the place the way it should eventually look. Hell, I pointed one out to you. So we're behind in the rent. In the contract, when you get behind, the whole amount becomes due and payable. So Signs of Ravenna has turned it over to their attorney. They want twenty-six thousand bucks I haven't got. If I don't come up with it soon, they'll lease the boards to somebody else and I'll still owe the money — the corporation will. We've had to stop the newspaper ads. We can't give clear titles unless the customer pays cash so we can turn it over for release of mortgage, so I can't cut pre-development prices down far enough to move the lots to replace working capital."

"Bank loan?"

"They won't loan on land, only on our signatures. And only with personal balance sheets. And we've put everything into the kitty."

"Everything?"

"But the house, the boat, the cars and a little cash."

"How did you get into such a jam?"

"Too optimistic. Thought I could have all the engineering done at the same time. It's cheaper that way."

"Couldn't you develop one small part of it at a time?"

"With what, Mike? With what?"

"How much would it take to get into the clear?"

"Two hundred and seventy-five thousand. That would handle the costs of finishing the Westport Road section, three hundred lots, and the merchandising. The take from that, after mortgage payments, would cover the next section."

Watching him carefully, Mike said, "Rob Raines told me last night you were going to lose your shirt, and if anybody went in with you they'd lose their shirt too. He said if you asked me for money, he'd set up a date with Corey somebody and they'd educate me."

Troy's head had snapped up, his hand motionless over the beer-can grave. "So Raines is in it, too!"

"In what?"

"Haas would like to steal the whole setup. I'm not asking you to put your money in, Mike. I'm not asking you for a thing." His face changed, mouth going slack. "I don't think I give a damn. I don't think I give a hoot in hell what happens."

"Like New York?"

"Just like New York. I can always make three fast laps, but I fold on the clubhouse turn."

"Self-pity."

"Self-analysis, Mike." He turned his head away. He dug his fingers into the sand, then squeezed until his knuckles went white. In a dull voice he said, "It's like New York in another sense, Mike."

"How?"

"Jerranna Rowley is in town."

Mike felt as if he had been belted under the

141

heart. "What did you say?"

"You heard me. I don't know where she was. Out west someplace. There was an article about me in a building contractors' magazine. Just a column. Small builder with new ideas. One of those things." His voice was listless. "Just one of those things. She didn't even see it until the article was a year old. She saw it about four months back, in a damn dentist's office. So she got here in February. She's in a place on Ravenna Key. Shelder's Cottages. She phoned me at the office. I . . . I went to see her."

"You damn fool! Have you been seeing her often?"

"I guess you could call it that. There's a man with her. She calls him Birdy. Says he's her cousin. Who can tell? I guess the shakedown is more his idea than hers."

"Shakedown?"

"Nothing expensive. She's into me for — I don't know — six or seven hundred bucks." He took the dark glasses off and pinched the bridge of his nose. "I don't know, Mike. It's about that time things started to go sour. When she got here. I was supposed to see her last night. That's why I got drunk and didn't. Defensive maneuver. It's easier to get high than think about it."

"Troy! Goddamn it, Troy!"

"I know. I didn't want you to know about it. Pride, I guess. Right back in the same trap. Liquor, Jerranna and things going to hell."

"How about Mary?"

"Why, I suppose she'll get the same splendid deal Bunny got. Only it's going to be a little rougher on her pocketbook."

"Why wait for Halloween? You can soap dirty words on windows anytime. Be my guest."

"Ready for a beer?"

"Thank you kindly. For God's sake, Troy!"

Muscle bulged the corner of Troy's jaw. "You think I'm enjoying it? You think I get a charge out of wondering if I'm losing my mind? And don't think I don't wonder. Often. Sometimes I think it's as if . . . " His voice broke. He waited a few moments. "As if I wasn't put together right. A sloppy assembly job. Some bolts and washers left out. I . . . don't want to be what I am."

"Easy, boy."

"Isn't beer for crying into?"

"Can you stay away from her?"

"I don't know. I'm trying. I've tried before. I have the feeling this is my last try before I give up. That's the sort of thing I should have married. I should have stayed away from ladies."

"You told me a long time ago that if you ever saw her again, you might kill her."

Troy shuddered in the hot sunlight. "I came close, Mike. I came damn close. She knew how close I was. I had her by the throat. She looked at me. She couldn't talk. I could tell by her eyes she didn't give a damn. She wasn't scared. If she'd been scared, or fought, that would have done it. I was that close, believe me. I slung her away so hard she bounced off the wall and landed on her hands and knees and looked up at me with her hair falling down across her face and howled with laughter."

"Does Mary suspect anything?"

"I don't know. We don't have much to say to each other. I was careful at first. Now I'm not so careful. It's like I want to be caught, I guess."

"I could go see the Rowley woman."

"What the hell good would that do? What good did it do the last time?"

"Maybe she's changed."

"She's changed. But not in any way that'll help. Even if I want help."

"Don't you?"

"You must get awful damn sick of me, Mike."

"I should be inspirational. You know. Be a

man! Shoulders back! Eyes front!"

"I'm a man, Mike. In a limited sense."

"There's one thing about you. You get a compulsion to make a mess. Then you want to roll in it. Goddamn it, you enjoy it!"

Troy stood up. His glasses were back on. Mike could not read his face. He said flatly, "I'm enjoying every minute of it, every delicious wonderful minute of my life. I just couldn't bear to have it end." He walked away, his stride wooden.

When all of Ravenna Key was zoned in 1951, due to the dogged efforts of the Ravenna Key Association, every attempt was made to protect the future growth of the Key as a residential area. Based on estimates of future population, certain commercial areas were established which included most of the commercial enterprise on the Key so as to limit as much as possible the number of non-conforming businesses.

However, one small business area, midway down the Key, on the bay side, suffered what the owners termed a cruel blow. They insisted that they were being deprived of their rights, that all zoning was socialism. Their particular area was zoned residential. That made the four little businesses non-conforming. Under the law a non-conforming business can continue to exist, but it cannot be enlarged. And, should it burn down, it cannot be rebuilt. It is obviously very difficult to sell such a business. And such a discrimination discourages even normal maintenance.

The four business enterprises, shoulder to shoulder, reading them from north to south, were Whitey's Fish Camp, Shelder's Cottages, Wilbur's Sundries and Lunch, and Red's B-29 Bar. Whitey's Fish Camp consisted of a rickety shed where he sold bait, tackle, miscellaneous marine hardware and the random jug of 'shine. He had twenty ungainly scows, painted blue and white, an unpredictable number of five-horse outboards in running condition to be rented with the boats, a gas pump, a big compartmented concrete bait well for live shrimp and mutton minnows, a bewildering display of hand-painted signs, chronic arthritis, a vast moody sullen wife, four kids, an elderly pickup truck, and two ancient house trailers set on blocks near the shed. Whitey and his Rose Alice lived in one, and the kids in the other, and their septic-tank system filtered inevitably into the bay, where the blue and white boats were moored to sagging docks and tilted pilings.

Ma Shelder owned and rented out twenty

box-like cottages, arranged in two rows of ten, with just enough space between the cottages in each row so that a car could be parked between them. They were a faded scabrous yellow, with peeling orange trim and green tarpaper roofing, and little screened porches in front. In keeping with the times, Ma called them efficiencies. This was, perhaps, apt, because it would take a high order of efficiency to live comfortably in one of them. There was a wide creaking dock that extended out into the bay so the tenants could sun themselves. Ma lived in a spare cottage, one larger than the others, and nearer the road. The total landscaping consisted of getting a man in to cut things down when the area got too overgrown. Ma, in her day, had danced on three continents and in forty of the forty-eight states. She had raised four children, all dead. At seventy she weighed two hundred pounds, despised mankind, spent most of her waking hours sneering at television, had over twenty-eight thousand dollars in her savings account and was implacably determined to live until she was ninety.

Wilbur's Sundries and Lunch was a cinderblock structure that looked as if it had started out to be a two-car garage. Wilbur's slattern wife ran the lunch counter, listlessly scraping the grill between hamburg orders. Wilbur paced endlessly through the stink of grease, straightening magazines, dusting patent medicines, counting the packs of cigarettes, sighing heavily. Whenever a customer was spendthrift enough to leave a dime on the counter for the bedraggled blonde, Wilbur, despite his high-stomached bulk, would swoop from a far corner of the store like a questing hawk before the screen door had time to bang shut. On those few occasions when she reached the coin first, he would twist her wrist until she dropped it into his hand, and then, snuffling, she would run out the back door.

Red's B-29 Bar was a frame structure next door to Wilbur's. Red had only a beer-and-wine license. He opened at seven to dispense cold packs of beer to Whitey's rental customers, and remained open until midnight every night. He had draught beer, potato chips, salt fish, pickled eggs, aspirin, punch boards, a juke box, a bowling machine, a pinball machine, pay phones, a peanut machine, television, contraceptives, tout sheets, some crude pornography and endlessly boring accounts of his flyboy days when he was a C.F.C. gunner.

In spite of the overall grubbiness of the four little businesses, their sun-weathered look of defeat and decay, the community provided a reasonably pleasant refuge for low-income retireds. In fact, one elderly couple had been in one of the Shelder Cottages for over seven years. The man had his own boat and motor and kept it at Whitey's for a tiny dockage fee. Unless the weather was impossible, he fished all day every day. She stayed at the Cottages and filled her days with gossip and needlepoint. They ate some of the fish he caught and sold the rest. In the evening they would stroll to Red's B-29 Bar and have a couple of draught beers, play two or three games on the bowling machine and walk back. Once a week they would drive their old Plymouth into town for a cautious shopping trip, picking up the bargains she had found in the local paper.

There was a certain pleasantness about it. Sun, and the blue bay waters, and idle talk — a fish flapping on the floorboards of the boat — a wind chattering in the palmettos — blue herons stalking the mud flats — the endless brilliance of the nighttime mockingbird, exhausting all the variations of his theme, while a dove talked of sorrow amid a whippoorwill's insistencies. Night wind creaked the hingings of the old metal signs, and the widow in Seven cried out in her dream. Rain puddled the dust and hushed the fronds and hurried across the roofs. The high sun swung by, and the years

149

swung by, and spiders as big as tea cups spun webs the size of doors. Every year the traffic was heavier on the Key Road, boats more numerous in the bay, fish smaller and fewer.

At three o'clock on Monday afternoon, Mike Rodenska, in the station wagon borrowed from Mary, parked near Ma Shelder's Cottages. He got out and stood in the white glare of sun on bleached bay shell, then walked around and looked down the double row of cottages. The little porches were empty. Bugs droned the litany of siesta.

A spare old man in sagging shorts, his chest brown as raw coffee, came walking around one of the cottages.

"Pardon me, sir."

"Eh?" He stopped and looked irritably at Mike.

"I'm looking for a woman named Rowley."

"Don't mean a thing to me."

"She's with a man called Birdy."

"Oh, them. Sure." He scratched the bleached fuzz on his chest. He turned and looked. "The car's there. Number Five. So they're in there, or they're up to Red's Bar. You the law?"

"No."

"Hoping you were."

"Why?"

150

"Friend of theirs?"

"No."

The old man glanced toward number Five again, and lowered his voice. There was a New Hampshire flavor in his speech. "D'be no use pretending this is the Parker House. Ma doesn't give a darn who she rents to long as she's full up. That pair, they don't even have the common decency to pretend to be married. T'aint like I'm a prude, young fella. I've been around the world nine times and seen things that'd make your blood turn to water, and for thirty-forty years I was wild as they come. Far as I care, they could do it right out here in the open, waving flags, and to me it wouldn't matter no more'n if they were Airedale dogs. But there's *some* folks here get upset easy, and those two, they don't even care enough to pretend they're legal. And him renting her out, pimpin' for her, that doesn't set too well. When I said that about the law I was thinking of two things, young fella. Either somebody complained loud enough and long enough so the law is looking into it, or I thought maybe the law was catching up. They got that look of people always on the run for one thing or another, and if you're not the law and not a friend, I'm just thinking maybe you've come here as a customer, and if you did I've talked too damn much, but I can't feel sorry."

"Not that either, friend."

"I can tell looking at you, you ain't going to tell me what business you got with those two no matter how I try to find out. So I'm wasting time, mine and yours . . . They not there, you try Red's."

Mike walked slowly to number Five, through the heat and silence of the afternoon. A five-year-old Mercury was parked beside the cottage. It had been altered to sit low on the rear wheels, snout in the air. The windshield was cracked, the body beginning to rust out. It had, at one time, been given a coat of green house paint. It had a look of long and dusty distances, of a hundred thousand miles of going nowhere in particular very fast.

He banged on the screen door of the small porch. The inner door was open. He could see into the cottage where an angle of sun struck a frayed grass rug, a soiled wadded pink towel, a Coke bottle on its side near the towel. He banged again. The place had the flavor of emptiness. He walked over and looked at the car. Torn upholstery. A plastic doll in a grass skirt hanging from the sun visor. Oklahoma plates. Bald tires. Comic books piled in the back seat.

He had a sudden odd feeling about the car. A presentiment of disaster. It seemed to him that he had seen the same car many times. He had covered accidents. He had seen this car before, warped and twisted into ruin, flame-seared and clotted with blood after the bodies were taken out. The wrecker would be looking for a solid place to plant the big hook. And the dangling doll would be there, and the peeling stickers from far places, and the welter of trash in the back seat and on the floor. These were the vagabond cars, the twenty-four-hour cars, dropping like bombs through the many dawns, heading inevitably toward that rendezvous with a pole, a tree, a truck, an abutment.

He walked back out to his car, saw that Red's was so close there was no point in driving. He walked past the sundries store, where a bulky man with a pinched face was putting the evening newspapers in a rack, the Ravenna *Journal-Record*, the Sarasota *News*. BERLIN CONFERENCE STALLED . . . FIVE DIE IN ARCADIA SMASH . . . TORNADOS LASH KANSAS . . . VENICE BYPASS OPPOSED . . . YACHT AGROUND AT BIG PASS. . .

He pushed the door of the bar open and walked into a dark and noisy place. After the outside glare it took long seconds for his eyes to adjust. There was a clattering whine of an air-conditioner, the drone of compressors in the coolers, the rattling and thudding of the bowling game, the hysterical braying of a television host giving away a twelve-dollar food mixer to a woman with a face like a shy pudding while thousands cheered.

The great tumult, after the silence outside, gave him the impression that he had stepped into a large, busy, jostling celebration. But as his eyes adjusted and his ears sorted and identified the sounds, he realized that there were only four other people in the place. There was a scrawny man with a rusty brush-cut and white eroded face behind the bar, leaning on his elbows, talking above the television din to a brutish-looking young man in a white T shirt and khaki shorts who sat on a bar stool, bare brown powerful legs locked intricately around the legs of the chair. They both turned to look idly at Mike. The bartender's eyes were a sun-bleached-denim blue. The young man had an inch of forehead under a towering pompadour of glossy, wavy blond hair, small deep-set simian eyes, a tender little rosebud mouth, and a jaw that bulged with bone and gristle. On his left biceps, across the cantaloupe bulge of his flexed arm was the complicated tattoo of a faded pink rose in full bloom.

Jerranna Rowley was at the bowling machine, competing with a wide-bellied young man in gas-station khaki. Mike moved onto the stool nearest the door, ordered a draught beer, left the change from his dollar on the bartop. Red moved back to continue his idle conversation with the wavy blond. Mike half-turned to watch Jerranna. He saw her bend, and aim, and concentrate and roll a strike and give a snort of triumph.

When she turned and looked toward the television, awaiting her turn, he saw her face clearly. What was she now? Twenty-five? So little change. The same round face and oddly small head, and welter of mussed tan hair, and the pale gray eyes that bulged a little, the fatty contours of the mouth framing the large, ridged, yellow-white teeth, the long neck and the narrow shoulders. She wore knee-length tight red pants, a jersey T shirt of narrow red and white horizontal stripes, with the red of the shirt the wrong red to wear with the red of the pants. She wore dusty black ballet slippers, and her bare ankles looked soiled.

He noted the changes, one minor, one major. The minor change was a puffiness around her eyes. The major change was in her figure. She had that same scrawniness, the loose, indolent, shambling, somehow arrogant way of handling herself. Her breasts, small, high, sharp, immature, widely separated, obviously unconfined under the jersey shirt, were unchanged. The change had occurred from lean waist to knee, and was accentuated by the red pants. There, in thighs and buttocks and lower belly she had become heavy, rounded, bulging, meaty — a gross and almost obscene flowering. It was a startling contrast to the rest of her, as though she were the victim of a casual assembly of the major portions of two different women.

The game ended. She won. She thrust out a narrow palm and he heard her crow, "Pay me, boy!" The voice was rawer, huskier, more ribald in its overtones and nuances. The man paid her. She turned, grinning, and walked toward the bar, and he noticed something he had not observed before, that she was slightly knock-kneed. Halfway to the bar she turned and looked at Mike. And stopped abruptly, lost the grin. She looked puzzled. She nodded to herself and found a grin of slightly different shape, more mocking, and came directly toward him.

He got up from the stool. "Always manners," she said. "I remember that. I know it's Mike, but the rest of it is gone."

"Rodenska," he said, and briefly clasped

the skinny chill of her outthrust hand, noticing the fading saffron hues of a great bruise that reached from the edge of her sleeve to her elbow.

"I thought about you a lot. You were so cute that time. Honest to God, you were so cute, Mike."

"I was a doll."

The beefy man had gotten off his stool. He came over to them, thumbs in his belt, his face dangerous in its utter stillness.

"What makes?" he asked, his voice high and thin, unsuitable for him.

"An old friend, Birdy. Birdy, this is Mike."

"Hiya," Birdy said. Muscles bunched the arm as he put his hand out. Mike braced himself for a childish display of strength that might be highly painful. But the hand in his was warm, dry, soft, so utterly boneless and flaccid it was like grasping a glove filled with fine loose sand.

"Where'd you know him?" Birdy asked.

"It was when I was in New York the first time, a long time ago. Five years maybe. He was buddy with Jamison. Like I told you he told me an old friend was coming down but that was all he said and I didn't know it was Mike. This was the guy I told you, honey, tried to bust me and Troy up but he didn't have the picture."

"How about that!" Birdy said.

"It's like they say, a small world," Jerranna said. They both stood and smiled at him. Though the mouths and faces were in no way alike, there was a chilling similarity in the smiles. They looked at him with a kind of joyous malevolence, an innocent evil, like two small savage boys — one holding the cat and the other holding the kerosene.

"You just happened to drop in here?" Birdy said wonderingly.

"Not exactly."

Birdy studied him. "Oh." He turned to Jerranna. "Find out the pitch," he said, and went slowly back to his stool, swinging his shoulders as he walked, lifting a slow hand to pat the fat glossy sheaf of hair over his ear.

"Two brews here, Red," Jerranna called and got onto the stool beside Mike's.

She turned on the stool, forked her hair back with spread fingers, and beamed at Mike. "It's good to see you, cutie." She touched a fingertip to her lips, reached out and touched the dampened tip of the finger to the top of his head. "You lost something up here, Mike. A fella told me once a perfect way to save your hair. Save it in a cigar box. How about that? In a cigar box."

"You've changed a little."

She slapped the hip pocket of the red pants. "Just call me Satch. Honest to God, nothing I do does any good. All kind of exercises. You'd die laughing watching me. You wanna hear a hell of a measurement? From top to bottom I'm twenty-six, twenty-two, thirty-seven. Isn't that a hell of a thing? Birdy says I got me a low center of gravity. He says I'm one-third Miss America. Birdy's got a real sense of humor."

She gulped the beer with automatic greed, her long thin throat working. The years had coarsened her. He had detected a certain sensitivity, a capacity for imagination, in the girl in New York. But the years and the roads, the bars and the cars and the beds and the bottles — they all have flinty edges, and they are the cruel upholstery in the dark tunnel down which the soul rolls and tumbles until no more abrasion is possible, until the ultimate hardness is achieved. So here she sat, having achieved the bland defensive heartiness of a ten-dollar whore.

But there was more than that. She had retained that unique sexual magnetism which had no basis in either face or figure. It was a dark current generated in some unthinkably primitive source, a constant pressure which

159

tugged the male mind into grubby yet shamefully enticing imaginings. In the back alley of the mind of every man there is a small, black, greasy pool of evil, an unawakened capacity for foulness, a place of guilt. She could walk through your house, past all your prides and glowing purposes, ignoring your display of awards for small victories, and take you out the back door and down the alley to the brink of the blackness you have learned to ignore, and point at it and smirk with an ancient wisdom and say, "See what we found?"

If all men are alcoholics, she is the bottle. If all men are compulsive gamblers, she is the gaming table. If all men are thieves, she is the open, unguarded safe. If all men are suicides, she is the knife, the rope, the bullet. In fair exchange for your soul she offers self-disgust and unavoidable repetition.

The tug of evil was, if anything, stronger than before.

"Who is Birdy?" he asked.

"Sort of a kissin' cousin. We teamed up a long time ago, Mike. Over a year. We been all over hell and gone. When there's a couple you get in less jams. And it's easier to make out. What's on your mind, Mike? You trying to be a blocking back for Jamison again?"

"I guess so."

"He says he got in real bad shape after I took off. Drunk himself out of his big job and into a crazy house."

"That's right."

"But he's doing okay again, isn't he?"

"Do you care?"

"Sure I care! He's not a bad guy. But like I told you before, anything he does to himself isn't *my* fault. If a guy goes overboard, he goes overboard."

"Sure, Jerranna. Sure. And you came down here by accident and phoned him by accident."

She frowned "Well . . . I didn't especially want to. But we weren't making out so good and I saw that thing about him and tore it out of the magazine and showed it to Birdy and told him about New York and all. You know, you get older, you think of angles. I wasn't high on coming here, but Birdy and me had never been in Florida together, and the other times I was here it was Miami and Jax only, and he kept at me until finally I said okay. And you know . . . hell . . . if you've had a guy on the ropes one time you want to find out if you still got that old black magic."

"You found out you've got it."

"Sure thing. I set it up with him and he came over to the cottage and I'd sent Birdy the hell away, and for about fifteen minutes I'd thought I'd had it. He spent fifteen minutes marching back and forth, calling me everything in the book, yelling at me, acting like he was working up to beating me up. Those old poops that live there must've got a real earful that night. Then he made a big jump at me. Scared hell out of me. And the next thing I know he's hanging onto me and bawling into my neck and telling me how much he missed me."

"What's this shakedown angle?"

She stared at him. "Would you kindly explain that, please?"

"Shakedown. How do you explain it? Money. He's given you money. There must be a reason. To keep you from going to his wife?"

She gave him a look of complete disgust, followed by a short explosive laugh. "Good Christ! Shakedown! I tell him we're running broke so we got to go over to the east coast and get jobs, so he gives me a hundred or one-fifty and we stay."

"It's a living."

"Mike, don't get it in your head we'd stay in this stinking place the rest of my stinking life. One day maybe soon it'll be me or Birdy getting up and looking around and saying, 'Let's roll it.' And in twenty minutes we'll be packed and gone, and it may be noon or midnight when we take off. That's the way we are. That's the way we want to be. It's the only way to ball it, cutie, the only way to keep the moss off the rock."

"So it's just like it was last time, Jerranna?"

She bit the corner off her thumbnail. "Just about. Hey, you know what you can buy now? Safety belts for bar stools. Isn't that a jazz?"

"Hilarious."

"You want to try to beat me a game?"

"No thanks."

"Where was Troy last night? I hung around because he said he'd show but he didn't."

"He fell over a martini."

"It figures. He just can't handle it good. He ought to let it alone."

"Think of the reasons he has to drink."

"Look at how I'm bleeding, Mike. You're still cute. Say, you know you got a real good tan? Birdy tans good, but I just get all over freckles. Buy me another brew. Hey, Red!" She turned on the stool to face him more squarely. "You know, you walked out on me one time. You going to do it again? I know what you're thinking. I always can tell when somebody is thinking the way you are."

"You told me that the last time. Do you have to get approval from Cuz?"

163

"No. It's like this, Mike. I do what I want. He does what he wants. And he doesn't care because it isn't his main kick anyway. He's a real seldom man."

"With or without approval . . . no thanks."

"Still scared of your wife, I bet."

"That's it. That's my trouble. I'm chicken."

"Too bad, Mike. Real too bad."

"Suppose I could dig up a thousand dollars. That would take you two a long way."

"Why would you do that? You Jamison's brother?"

"Would you take it and go?"

"What if we were about to go anyway?"

"Then I made a thousand-dollar mistake."

"You wouldn't have it on you."

"Not exactly."

She studied him, chin on her fist. "We should trade in that bucket. It's got a high-speed shimmy. Drives Birdy nuts. I'm interested, Mike. But he gets funny sometimes about the money thing. If he gets the idea anybody is trying to buy him, he flips. So let me put it to him easy. He's got a lot of pride. You know. And I can let you know. You got a phone?"

"I better stop by."

"This is Monday. Come by Thursday with the money. It should be in tens and twenties,

Mike, on account of it's hard for us to change bigger money. They always want to know where we got it. Somehow I've never given much of a damn about money. Funny, isn't it? There's a skinny old poop in one of the cottages came creeping up offered me fifty dollars. He's maybe a hundred and nine — age and weight both. Saved it up out of his Social Security, I betcha. Maybe one day I got to go that route, but I'm not ready yet. Anyhow, it woulda killed him. You going someplace? Aren't you even going to finish the brew? I can if you can't. See you Thursday, boy scout."

The door swung shut behind him. The sun, low over the Gulf, glared into his eyes. A red truck went by, stirring up a small whirlwind that pasted a piece of newspaper against his leg. The air smelled like hot asphalt and dead fish. He took a deep breath and said a filthy word and walked slowly to the station wagon.

He drove into Ravenna, wired his bank for money, and got back to the Jamison house at dusk. Debbie Ann and Shirley McGuire were walking slowly from the beach toward the house, laden with gear, gleaming with sun oil.

He met them after he had parked the car and gotten out.

"I'm a hundred and nine," he said. "I've

165

saved a fortune out of my Social Security. The three of us could go to Ceylon, swim at Mount Lavinia, have tall frosty ones at the Galle Face, dine at the Silver Faun, wander through the botanical gardens at Kandy, and be back here in a week. All set?"

"My goodness!" Debbie Ann said. "Could you survive it?"

"It will probably kill me. That's what I'm counting on. Incidentally you both look sweet, fresh, pretty and decent. It's a sort of contrast I won't explain at the moment."

"Have you been out in the sun all day without a hat?" Shirley asked.

"Oh, this is just senility in action. It's a kick I'm on."

"Go sit by the pool, Ancient One," Debbie Ann said, "and pretty soon we'll be slave maidens and bring you something tall, cool and delicious."

He had noticed the other cars were gone. "Where is everybody?"

"Troy is probably working. Mother Mary borrowed my little bug to go to some kind of committee meeting. Durelda went home early with a toothache. We're on our own, buddy."

But Mary returned before the girls had finished changing. They all had a drink by the pool as dusk turned to night. Shirley agreed to stay for dinner if she could help. She phoned her aunt and explained. Her call to her aunt emphasized in everyone's mind that Troy hadn't arrived and hadn't phoned, but no one spoke of it. They delayed dinner and finally ate, and after the women had cleaned up, they played bridge.

Shirley was Mike's partner. It was almost immediately obvious that Mary and Debbie Ann were the superior players, and could have won handily if Mary had been able to keep her attention on the game. She alternated between brilliant play and gross error.

The talk was aimless, a bright and meaningless thread woven through the dark fabric of tensions. There was the click and whisper of the cards, the bright cones of light, the idiot faces of kings and queens, the perfume of the women and the gleam of their hair — their light voices and the small formalities of their smiles.

The rites and codes of the game had, in time, a strangely hypnotic effect on him, leading him into a fantasy that at first amused and then disturbed him. He slumped, heavy-lidded, and looked at the quick oval glintings of their fingernails and thought, 'This is a deceptive plastic, almost natural. Their eyes are made of finest tinted glass rolling realistically in a special lubricant. Debbie Ann's brow took a long time to make, inserting the delicate copper-gold wire into the delicate plastic, warmed by the mesh of the invisible heating system.'

And he thought that he was utterly alone in the world, easing his emptiness with these clever toys, able to pretend, for a little while, that they were real. But in time he would tire of the game and get up and go to each of them in turn and expose the little control panel set into the small of each tender back, and press the proper silvery stud. As he did so, each face in turn would go utterly blank and dead and they would get up in a wooden way and walk off one at a time to a closet where they belonged and line up, glassy and motionless in the darkness. Should he want one of them to cook for him or sing for him or swim with him, he had only to make his selection, press the proper stud, clearly marked, and the programmed behavior pattern, a card with a printed circuit, would drop into place. This is what we have had to do since all the women left. And if there is need for love, there is a stud for that, a choice to make, programmed after the patterns of the great courtesans, nimble, tender, delicately avid, quite realistic, utterly without significance.

Live comfortably with a Demi-Girl. Our model has a half life of a thousand years. Buy the assembled model or the kit. Delivered with five hundred program cards. Catalogue of ten thousand other cards immediately available. The General Electronics Demi-Girl is powered by a wafer of thorium, completely shielded for your protection. At your command she will Dance, Quarrel, Play Chess, Shovel Snow, Discuss the Esthetic Theories of Bergson, Recite Dylan Thomas, String Beads, Play Darts, Play Golf at the Selected Degree of Skill, Cut Your Hair, Mow Your Lawn, Prepare Beef Stroganov, Play the Accordion.

Wear-Pruf, set for 98.6°, free of blemishes and imperfections, guaranteed lifelike, basic wardrobe included in purchase price, tireless, never ill, faithful. Specify height, weight, coloring, and simulated age. Immediate delivery. Visit our showrooms. Time payments can be arranged.

I am alone, he cried, crouching and howling back in the desolated ballroom of his mind, his anguish echoing amid the bedraggled crêpe paper and soggy balloons of the party that was forever ended. So damned awful alone. No kiss for the bruise. No apron to hide in. . . .

"I've had enough," Mary said. "How about you people?"

"Golly, it's nearly midnight," Shirley said. "I didn't realize."

"Nightcap before I drive you home?" Debbie Ann asked.

"No thanks, honey."

After they left, Mary went to the edge of the living room and stood looking out at the patio. There was a rigidity in her stance. She stood with her head slightly tilted, as though she were listening to something very faint and far away.

His empathy for the little signs of agony made him feel ham-handed, dull, awkward. "Mary?"

She turned slowly, rubbed the back of her hand against dampness under her eyes, smiled in a crooked way and said, "Stupid, I guess."

"Is it?"

"It's . . . wondering what I'm doing wrong. Not knowing the right way to handle it."

"Believe me, you're not doing anything wrong."

"I've tried so many things some of them must be wrong. Scenes. He walks out. Indifference. He doesn't seem to care. Where did he go, Mike? Oh, I don't mean now, tonight. He went somewhere, inside hinself. I love him. I can't find him. It's so damn difficult trying to be an adult. When he . . . shames me."

"It's a kind of sickness, maybe."

"He's never told me very much about . . . what happened to him in New York before he came down here. It was pretty bad, wasn't it?"

"Pretty bad."

"Mike . . . if I knew all about it . . . if you could tell me, if it wouldn't be a kind of disloyalty for you to tell me . . . it might help me understand. We used to have such . . . fun."

He sat down with her, sat close beside her on the couch, and told her. When they heard Debbie Ann drive back in he stopped, but she went to her room without coming in. At one point she took his hand and clung to it tightly, and he did not believe she was consciously aware of doing so. He tried to make it as factual as the ten thousand news stories he had written.

"This," she said blankly, her eyes very round, "is the very same woman?"

"But you shouldn't get the idea this is . . . you know, a fatal fascination. I don't know how to explain what I feel. It's like a symbol of something. Of a flaw. Somehow he hates himself. She's a club he beats himself with. I

171

know him, Mary. He's a good man. That's the hell of it. From the time the war ended until that mess in New York it was like he was pulling something inside himself tauter and tauter, straining at something, and then it snapped, and, like a compulsion, he destroyed everything that meant anything to him. Bunny is a fine woman. You're a fine woman too, Mary. You fell in love with the goodness in the guy. It's a sickness. And I think there's a pattern. He'll try to destroy everything this time, too."

"I won't let him, Mike. I won't let him do that to himself. Why should he — depise himself?"

"I don't know. He had a little psychiatric treatment last time. Not much. The doctor said he didn't respond well to the treatment, wouldn't cooperate. He had the idea it all went back to a thing during the war. He got that out of him with sodium pentothal."

"What happened?"

"First you got to understand this was a decent kid from a decent home, bright and sensitive and essentially kind. We had to turn a lot of those kids into killers, fast. It didn't leave any mark on the louts. It never does. But it can be a hell of a thing to do to an imaginative kid. He volunteered himself into the

Corps on December eighth when the lines were long. They did their best to brutalize him in boot camp. He's got ability. He can do a hell of a lot of things well. They pushed him up fast. We were learning how to fight a war, and making mistakes that would sicken you. As a sergeant, a platoon leader, after forty days of nightmare, he got sent a stupid, pointless patrol in command of ten men. Later on, when he'd gotten smarter, he would have gone far enough to be out of sight, dug in, and come back at dawn and faked a report. He made the patrol. It didn't accomplish anything. He was ambushed and lost six men and managed to get clear with the other four. They were cut off. They had to make a big circle. They crawled. A snake got one in the throat and he died in ten seconds. They got separated from another one somehow in the darkness. He was never seen again. Three left. Once a big Jap patrol walked by, close enough to touch. They didn't know where the hell they were. Later a sniper got one of them through the head, and the other in the belly. He dragged the wounded one away. A two-hundred-pound man. He finally got back to the lines, fourteen hours overdue, carrying the wounded man on his back. But by then the wounded man had been dead, they estimated, for three or four hours. Once we got drunk in Melbourne. He told me about it, telling it as if it was a long funny story, grinning. He laughed when he was through and then he started to cry. I never heard a man cry like that. I hope never to hear it again. He felt it was his fault, losing them like that. The ambush, the snake, getting lost . . . all his fault. Ten guys he knew well. Ten guys who believed he could take them out and bring them back. It's a good bet nobody could have. Maybe something snapped right there. Maybe that's when they should have taken him out. But they left him in and he made them a good officer and later a good company commander. Before that patrol, maybe it had all been sort of brave and glorious adventure to him. After that it was just dirty, bloody work. And he learned his trade."

"My God," she said softly. "Oh, my God."

"I don't know, Mary, but I think that's as close to the reason as anybody is ever going to get."

"And that woman is just . . . I'd like to see her."

"I think it would be better if you didn't. I think it would just make it harder to understand, seeing her."

"Could we get him to a doctor?"

"I could try. I could try to do that."

"You think she'll leave?"

"I'm sure she will. But I don't know when. Maybe Thursday when I give her the money."

"I'll pay you back for that."

"No point in that. It's hard to get used to the idea a thousand bucks isn't important money. But it isn't. And . . . you might get cleaned out, Mary. I guess you know that."

"I know it. Yes."

"It scare you?"

"A little, I guess. Yes, it does. But . . . what is happening to Troy is more important. I don't . . . need all this. I didn't earn it. We could live on what he was making before, as a builder. Debbie Ann has her own money. It would just be the two of us."

"I want to poke around a little. I want to look into that land deal. There's something funny about it."

"Poor Mike. You came down for a rest. We're all leaning on you. It isn't fair. Tell me what you think I should do. How should I . . . react?"

"You won't like this, Mary."

"I think you should get the hell out for a while."

"Go away when he . . ."

"You're one of the things he wants to de-

175

stroy. Like I said, sort of a symbol of self-destruction. Going away takes some of the pressure off him, the need to hurt you and keep hurting you."

"I — I guess I understand."

"You ought to pack and leave in the morning. Tell him you want to go away and think things over. Don't be emotional about it. Pick a spot and tell me, so I can be in touch with you. It got rough after she took off the last time. It might get just as rough again. I'll do what I can. The land deal, the doctor, the woman."

"Mike. Mike, I'm so . . . "

"Where will you go?"

"I . . . don't think I want to visit anybody . . . and I don't want anything fancy. I think I'll drive over and stay in the Clewiston Inn. No. That would be too far. I wouldn't feel right about it."

"Why don't you just drive up to Sarasota and check into a motel and give me a ring when you're settled?"

"All right. I'll have Debbie Ann drive me up so you'll have a car here. She can tell you where I am. I can come back by cab if there's an emergency, and she can come get me if there isn't. I . . . don't know why I should feel better. All I'm doing is leaning on you."

Her eyes were wet. He kissed her good-night, an impulse which surprised him but which she took gratefully and naturally, clinging to him for a short shuddering moment.

After he was in bed he spoke to himself harshly. The big mister fixit. Self-appointed. What do they matter to you? What does anybody matter to you? Just the boys. What thanks did you get last time? Did they strike off a medal?

He wanted, dolefully, desperately, to be back in the house in West Hudson. When you were in one room, it was as if she was in the next room. The little sounds of housekeeping. That wild little yelp of exasperation when she broke something or burned something — a sound that was almost, but not quite, a dirty word. The quick fragrance. The things around her that she touched and loved.

So lie in this strange bed and go over all the times you were cross and cruel, the times you made her cry, and all the gestures of affection you never made, the presents you never brought to her, the days that had gone by without an avowal of love.

But there had been that one thing denied to so many others, the chance to say goodby. "It's like I'm running out on you," she had said. "No time to pack. No time to sort things. No chance to clean the closets. You'll have to love our grandchildren enough for both of us." He had promised her he would be duly doting.

He lay in the three o'clock darkness. A car went down the Key. A night heron flapped by, hooting with maniacal derision. Tears, heavy as oil, ran out of his eyes. His hands were fists. His throat felt rusty. He heard an airliner.

six

He slept late on Tuesday. When he got up, the Chrysler was back and the Porsche was gone. Durelda gave him breakfast on the patio. She said her tooth was better. She said the mister was sleeping and the missus had gone away for a little trip.

After breakfast he drove into Ravenna and found a stationery store and bought a package of coarse yellow paper and some soft pencils. It was the special armor of his trade. Operating on the smallest hints and clues, he had often, in the past, dug out stories that had nudged people in high places out of their upholstered niches in city and county government. It was no special trick. It required merely sturdy legs, a consuming diligence, and the knowledge that to most people the sweetest possible sound is their own voice. They can never hear it often enough. And everybody likes to give the impression that they are very well informed. To Mike Rodenska the miracle was not that chicanery was revealed but that it was so often successfully concealed.

He went first to the small sales office just inside the pretentious entrance to Horseshoe Pass Estates and talked to Marvin Hessler, the salesman-employee Troy had introduced him to when he had shown Mike the property. Marvin was wary at first, but after Mike had managed to give the impression that his investigative efforts might serve to put the project back on its feet, and thus protect a job Hessler had begun to be dubious of, he got complete cooperation. He scrawled key words as memory aids on the coarse paper, folded twice, bulging the pocket.

He looked at land which had been cleared and land which hadn't. He saw half-dug canals with banks that were collapsing because the sea-walling hadn't been done. He saw where the dredging had stopped, and where they had run out of fill. He looked at the plot map, read the restrictions and specifications which had been filed with and approved by the Ravenna County Board of Commissioners. He studied the engineering reports, the list of lots already sold, the clips of the advertising campaign, a copy of the original land purchase agreement.

The initial contact always gives you a lead to a few others. It is a geometric progression. He went to the office of the elderly, somewhat ineffectual-acting lawyer who had set up the corporation. By then Mike had become a Mr. Rodney, a staff writer for a large picture magazine which was contemplating doing a story on a typical Florida land-development project — not one of the monster ones, and not one of the little grubby ones — one about the size of Horseshoe Pass Estates. He got some information from the lawyer. He had lunch, picked up his cash from Western Union, added a couple of hundred in traveler's checks and opened a bank account at the Ravenna National Bank, where he talked for over an hour with an amiable, elderly, low-pressure vice president about the opportunities for investment in Florida land. After he left the bank he became Mr. Rodney again, and talked to three real estate agents until he found one that suited his purposes, a brown, wiry, savage little woman in her fifties who had been born in Ravenna, who envied and despised the people who, through her efforts, had made large pieces of money in real estate, who was a confirmed and vicious gossip, and who seemed to know every local landowner and every parcel of land in the county, and every slick trick that

181

had ever been pulled on the unsuspecting. Her name was Lottie Spranger.

After talking a half hour in her office they went across the street to a curiously tearoomy sort of bar and drank Cokes in a booth.

"A story like that wouldn't hurt this area a bit," she said, "and I'm all for it, but you're making a terrible mistake picking that Jamison mess out there opposite the pass. Sure, it's a pretty piece of land, but it's dead."

"You keep saying that, Miss Spranger, but I don't quite see how it's dead. Their sales office is open."

"I'm not one to gossip, but I'll tell you just what happened there. For your own good. Jamison is a fool, came down from the north, built some little houses, nothing special, then married Mary Kail who was married before to Bernard Dow, and he died and left her a stack of money. Jamison got his hands on that money and got big ideas and went in too deep. I'd say it's a good buy for anybody right now, buying good lots in there at the price he's got 'em down to, but people can't see that. They haven't got patience. Pretty soon Jamison is going to be dead broke, and then he's going to have to unload his equity for whatever he can get for it, and the wolves are just setting waiting to jump. After Jamison is out, whoever gets it will finish the development and clean up. There's millions in that kind of deal. That's choice land. There isn't much of that left on this coast. It'll be a high-class development. I'll tell you this. Jamison fought pretty good there. He's tried to sell treasury stock, bring people in with him, tried to borrow, tried to move those lots. Nothing has worked."

"Who are these wolves you mention?"

"There's big ones and little ones. This deal is big enough to interest the big ones. Purdy Elmarr. Wink Haskell. J. C. Arlenton. They sit way back quiet, but they run Ravenna County, Mr. Rodney. They make out like they're just old cracker boys, but they're made of money, and all that money started with land, and they still buy swap and sell land. And when any of 'em hanker to own a piece of land, there isn't anybody going to come in from the outside and grab it away."

"So you think somebody is after the Jamison land?"

"I do."

"Why do you think so?"

"Because he had too much bad luck for it to all be accidental. Dredge broke down. The work crew dug a whole canal in the wrong place and had to fill it up. They put fill too high around tree trunks and lost a lot of good trees. All this adds up to money, and he didn't start with enough at first. Then there've been rumors about how he couldn't give you a good deed to a lot there, and how it never would be finished. I tell you, when you're in the selling business, rumors like that can hurt bad. Somebody wants it. I don't know who."

"I was talking about this project of mine to a young lawyer named Raines. He said the whole thing would fall through, that Jamison couldn't save it. Was that an example of these rumors?"

Her shrewd eyes narrowed. "Hmmm. Rob Raines. Dee Raines' boy. Now what in the world reason would he have to bad-mouth Jamison? He's seeing Mary's daughter, I hear. Nice looking boy, but he's got an awful cold-looking pair of eyes on him. You know, if he could work his way in with . . . Say, he has been doing some law work for Corey Haas. Jamison took Corey in with him on account of Corey being so close to Mary's father and Bernard Dow a long time ago. And taking Corey in with you is just about like carrying a snake in your pocket. He's a slippery one, that Corey. I must be getting old and stupid, I didn't add that up before. Sure. Corey would love to ease Jamison out of there, and I'll bet he hasn't put in a dime over and above what it cost him when they set up the corporation. Corey isn't real dishonest, but he's so close to it you can't hardly tell the difference. Corey goes into things with old Purdy Elmarr sometimes, and this is just the sort of thing to catch Purdy's eye. Yes sir. It would be Purdy working with Corey, and Rob Raines sticking close to that Debbie Ann to keep in close touch with what's going on. Nice law work *that* is!" She gave an evil snicker.

"I guess I better pick a different development."

"Oh, this one will move fast enough soon as old Purdy gets his hooks into it. I'm sort of glad it's Purdy instead of Wink. Or Corey Haas all alone. Purdy pushes hard, but he isn't merciless. He'll set it up so Jamison and Mary Kail won't lose everything."

"I'm grateful to you, Miss Spranger."

"All I've done is talk. It didn't cost me a thing."

The day was gone. He went back to Riley Key. The Chrysler was gone. Debbie Ann was prone on a poolside mattress, her sun top unlatched, her sun shorts rolled and tucked to expose the maximum area. As she was entirely in shadow, it was obvious she had fallen asleep. The scuff of his shoe on the patio stone awakened her. She lifted her head, then sat up, holding the bra top against her, craning her arms back and latching it. Her face was puffy with sleep, her light hair tangled.

She yawned widely and said, "Wow! I folded. Where've you been all day? I got back at two. I'm going out to dinner with Rob so I sent Durelda home. No point in her staying around. You wouldn't mind eating out, would you? Just go down to the Key Club and sign Mommy's name."

"I'm thirsty," he said. "Bring you a beer?"

"Sounds good." He opened two cans, brought her one, and folded himself into a bronze and plastic chaise longue. "I've been a tourist today. Was Troy gone when you got back?"

"Durelda said he went out about noon."

"Did you get Mary settled?"

"Yes. A very nice place up on Longboat Key. Corny name. Lazy Harbor. The phone number is in my purse. What's going on, Mike?"

"What did she tell you?"

"She said she had to get away for a little while to think things over. I asked her if she was going to think about divorce. She said no. She was pretty quiet on the way up."

"So I guess she told you as much as she

wants you to know."

"My God, you'd think I was eleven years old. I'm an elderly divorced type, remember?"

"It's probably a good idea to get away, get some perspective."

"While Troy works himself up to being a genuine alcoholic, keeps some tramp on the string, and loses the family fortune. It wasn't a big fortune, but it was comforting while it lasted."

He studied her. "Is there anything you really give a damn about, Debbie Ann? Anything that really concerns you seriously and deeply?"

"No, thank God! I don't want to be involved in anything but kicks."

"Any plans at all?"

"Nothing that isn't frivolous. What got you on this sober dedication routine anyhow?"

"Are you concerned about Mary's happiness?"

"I'd like her to have it. She had it and now she hasn't. Nothing I can do is going to turn it back on, like a switch."

"True."

"Speaking of frivolous, why don't we make Rob take us both out? He'd hate every minute of it. We could be very flirtatious and he wouldn't dare yelp. For some reason he's being terrible good. A real little gentleman. I suppose he's figured out a new approach, but I don't know what it is yet. Won't you come along?"

"No thanks. I've got a little work to do."

"Work?"

"Sorting some notes."

"Writing a book?"

"I might."

"Oh, I forgot! Two letters came for you. Durelda put them in your room.

He got up quickly. "Excuse me," he said. "Probably the boys.

One was from the boys, two letters traveling with one airmail stamp. Mickey told him Tommy had been very homesick, but he was getting over it. They seemed to like the school well enough. One of the boys had taken to calling Mickey Round-End-Ski and the fight had been broken up. They were taken to the headmaster who turned them over to the athletic instructor, who had put gloves on them and let them work it out. Now they were good friends. The work was hard. They were way behind the others, but they were getting special help so they could catch up.

The other letter was from a friend on the paper. After he read it, he reread the boys' letters. Poor lonely devils. He heard Debbie Ann in the bathroom, heard the shower running.

A few minutes after the shower stopped, his bathroom door opened. She stood in the doorway, artfully draped in a big chocolate and white towel, her smile wide and utterly innocent. "Was it from your boys? Are they all right?"

"They're fine, thanks."

"That's nice."

"I'd ask you in," he said, "but they got a tough house detective in this joint."

She made a face at him. "Poo! It's just friendship, Mike."

"You can't trust me. I'm queer for towels."

"I could take it off."

"That's enough kidding around, Debbie Anm," he said gruffly. "There's no sense in it and no future. So back up and shut the door."

She widened her eyes. "My goodness! The man can't take a joke." She backed into the bathroom and shut the door, firmly.

"Have to beat them off with clubs," he grumbled. "Little old irresistible me." But he decided his second reaction was right. It would do no good to try to joke with her on her level. She would just become bolder. And then, in a parody of enticement, in a burlesque of seduction, she would manage to

189

wind up in his arms, and then it wouldn't be parody or burlesque any longer, and she would have had her opportunity to not only satisfy her curiosity and make her soiled and ordinary little conquest, but also to save her own pride by faking great consternation and saying, afterward, in a stricken way, "But I didn't mean this to happen, darling! I was only joking! Really I was. And suddenly everything got . . . out of control."

Or, if she was a little more vicious, and it was quite possible she was, she would go only far enough to be certain that he committed himself, that he made the unmistakable pass, and then scramble away from him and be very upset about the whole thing. They had the right words long ago. Trollop. Baggage. Wench. He wondered if Dacey Whatsis knew how lucky he was to get rid of her. And he hoped Mary would never see her daughter clearly. Mary deserved a hell of a lot more than she was getting.

He stretched out for a while, then changed and went over to the mainland and ate and went to a drive-in movie. Two westerns. The good guy finally nailed the bad guys. He rode back to his room, tall in the saddle, lean, noble and deadly, rolling a cigarette with one hand and shooting hawks out of the sky with the other. He was always a hell of a wing shot.

Troy wasn't home yet when Mike got in, but was home and sleeping when he left in the morning. He had sorted out the important pieces of information. He talked to two more men who contributed a little, more in the line of confirmation than anything new. He drove to where yellow bulldozers and draglines were working and talked to the man who had bossed the Horseshoe Pass Estates job. He questioned him closely about the bad luck he had had on the job, and when he became convinced the man was lying, and not interested enough to lie very well, he felt he was ready to tackle Corey Haas. Corey Haas managed his varied business interests from a small office in a shabby old building on West Main in downtown Ravenna.

He was a gaunt stooped man in his late fifties, with bad teeth, a threadbare suit, thinning hair dyed a violent purple-black, an artificial affability in his manner, the grey rubbery face of a retired comedian, and a firm over-prolonged handshake.

"Rodenska? Aren't you the fella visiting Troy and Mary? Sit down. What can I do you for on this beautiful day?"

"I guess I wanted a little free advice, Mr. Haas. I got talking to Rob Raines the other night about my putting some money into Horseshoe Pass Estates. I know you own stock in it."

"Eighteen percent," Haas said with a wistful smile. "They're right pretty stock certificates."

"Rob didn't think it was a good idea, but I guess he didn't want to say anything about his girl's stepfather, so he told me you're an honest man and you'd tell me the things he didn't want to."

Haas shook his head. "Now, I could paint a big wonderful picture for you and I could make it sound good, and maybe we could take your money away from you, Mr. Rodenska. But it wouldn't be right, and it wouldn't be fair. Frankly, I got stung. I figure I've lost my money. Oh, I may come out with some if we can ever unload the whole corporation, but I just thank God I didn't have more to put into it, or I might have, and that would be gone too. I only got in on account of knowing Mary's daddy so well, and knowing her first husband — lot older man than Troy, and I hate to say it, but a lot smarter man too. It's pitiful that girl has to lose her money that way. I can go into details that probably wouldn't mean too much to you, Mr. Rodinski."

"Rodenska."

"I'm sorry. Man likes to hear his name said right. Were you thinking of any sizable amount?"

"Three hundred thousand, maybe."

He pursed his lips and shook his narrow head. "Wouldn't help. It's too late for that. Throwing good money after bad. Rob did right sending you to me. It would be a turrible mistake. I can go into details about what them problems are, but like I said . . . "

Mike pulled a sheaf of notes out of his pocket. "Care if I go into details?"

"What? What's that?"

"Want to hear what I think of it?"

"I don't see how you'd have much of an idea about — "

"Let's try it and see." Mike began to talk, carefully, explicitly. At first Haas looked dazed. And then all expression went out of his face. His eyes were watchful. From time to time he reached up and touched his throat with his fingertips and swallowed.

Mike put his papers back into his pocket. "Those are the figures. Those are the problems. Three hundred thousand would more than bail it out. You know that. I know that. Troy knows that. I'm going to loan the corporation three hundred thousand, and take Troy's and Mary's stock as security. I didn't come here for advice. I came here to tell you something, Haas. I'm going to hire a detective. And if there's any more bad luck out there, and he can prove who caused it, like your bribing that construction clown to goof off, you're going to have a conspiracy suit on your hands. I'm sorry I can't get your eighteen percent back from you. You stand to make a lot of money out of it. And it's too good a thing for you to ever let go of. That's all I have to say to you."

"Just a minute," Haas said quietly. "Sit down, Mr. Rodenska. I thought you were just a newspaperman."

"That's all."

"You would have made a hell of a good businessman. You still might."

"A glorious ambition."

"Eh?"

"I just collected facts and suspicions, Haas. I did some legwork. That's all."

"That's all," Haas said bitterly. He seemed to be trying to make up his mind about something. He waited long minutes.

"All right. It won't hurt me none to admit something else has been cooking, and when it all blew up and the dust settled, Jamison would be out but not hurt too awful bad, and I'd have me a bigger piece of it. It's worth waiting for the size money that thing'll make. So I'll tell you this. Detective or no detective, I can work against you and give you a hell of a lot of problems one way or another. Or I can work with you, and things will smooth out just fine."

"What's on your mind?"

"I'll split the risk with you. One-fifty apiece, hear? We'll juggle the stock around. You're in for a third, I'm in for a third, and the Jamisons are in for a third. You and me, we'll run it right."

"No thanks."

"Why not?"

"Mister Corey Haas, I wouldn't go in with you on a ten-cent pail of water if we were both on fire."

"That's a rough way to talk to a man, Mr. Rodenska."

"I can make it rougher."

Haas smiled. "You're new here. Jamison was new. Don't have any idea what makes the wheels go around here. You just bought yourself a mess of trouble. Go into it if you want, newspaperman. The more I think about it, the more I don't think three hundred will quite do it."

"We can try," Mike said, and left.

He placed a call to Purdy Elmarr from a drugstore booth. An hour later he was seated on Purdy's front porch, with a bourbon in his hand. The old man gave an impression of ageless strength that did not match the frailness of his voice over the phone. There was no cordiality in him. He looked out toward the highway, his face still.

"My basic deduction, the reason I came to see you, may be entirely wrong, Mr. Elmarr. So I can save both of us time by starting with a question. Are you interested in any way in Horseshoe Pass Estates?"

There was a long silence. The old man spat over the railing. "Keep talking."

"As I told you, I'm a newspaperman. Ex-newspaperman, at least for a while. I've done a lot of interviewing. I listen to what people say and how they say it. And I remember. I want to give you as near a verbatim conversation as I had today with Corey Haas as I can manage. There's no point in telling you why I came to go to him. But I did. Here is what was said."

Except for the infrequent lift of the glass to the lips for a measured sip, the old man was motionless as a lizard. Mike wondered if he was really hearing any of it, or if he was far off in one of the misty reveries of senility.

"That's all. I said, 'We can try.' I left and phoned you within the next five minutes."

Purdy Elmarr stood up and went to the table and fixed himself a fresh drink, slowly, carefully. He went back to the chair, sat down and said, "He'p yourself any time you feel like."

"Thanks."

"One thing. That Raines boy bring up my name?"

"No. It was just a guess."

"Never liked newspaper people. Spent my life keeping my name out of the papers. Every time you open a paper, there's the same damn fools grinning out at you. So I never got to know one. Why'd you bring this to me?"

"It seemed like a good idea. And somebody told me you aren't . . . merciless."

"Have been. Can be again if I have to. One third to him, one third to you, and one third to Mary Kail and her husband. Pretty. But you didn't like that. I know you're telling me exactly how it was, because you got the figures right, and that's just how Corey would say things. What are you after?"

"I like Mary. I don't like Raines and I don't like Haas."

"I don't have to like the people make money for me. So you're just going around doing good?"

"Call it that."

"You could come out with a nice profit. They'll want to cut you in. Mary will anyhow. Nice girl. Haven't seen her in years. Is that the only money you got?"

"Yes sir."

"Funny you want to risk it all in something you don't know anything about."

"It isn't very important to me. When it could have been, I didn't have it. And got along fine."

"I got stacks of money, son. If there was twenty of me and we all went hog wild, we couldn't spend down to the end of it. Don't use it for anything special. Just like piling it up."

"I can see how that could be."

"I like you. You aren't the least damn bit scared of money. Most people come here act a little trembly, like I'd bite hell out of them."

"There are things I'm scared of. Money isn't one of them."

"He wanted one third of it. It's the second time he's acted cute on the same project. Corey is getting awful hungry, seems."

"I guess so."

"I'm going to break a rule. I don't generally tell people my plans. Then if they don't work out good, I don't have to explain anything. I'll tell you a couple things. You keep them to yourself. I wouldn't tell you if I thought you couldn't. First off, put your money into that thing. I've give up wanting it. Second, you won't have no trouble of any kind. I'll talk to Corey. If there's trouble anyway, come to me and I'll tell you how to fix it."

"Thank you, Mr. Elmarr."

"Now here's the last thing. You can think about this some. I'll talk sweet and pretty to Corey Haas. I think I'll last another five years. He should too, if he doesn't kill hisself. I'd say about five years from now, sooner if I can do it, Corey Haas is going to be walking the streets with his skinny old tail sticking out through his raggedy pants a-wondering just what in hell happened to him. He tried to cross me a second time, and I shouldn't have let him get away with it the first time."

Prudy Elmarr turned as he spoke and looked squarely at Mike. The faded old eyes were like bits of a wintry sky, and he wore a slow barracuda smile. In a very few moments Haas had been tried, sentenced and executed.

"I guess you know why I don't keep on saying thank you."

"Do I?"

"Some of this is because you're probably a decent enough man, Mr. Elmarr. But you feel like it's smart to play it safe, too. Because I'll be quiet. Otherwise I might be crazy enough and lucky enough to get the whole thing in print."

"You know, we got us a little poker group meets out here."

"I'm not that crazy or that lucky, Mr. Elmarr."

The old man thumped his thigh and gave a wild high cackle of laughter. "Damn if I don't like you some, son. Never thought I'd see the day. Northun fella. Newspaper fella. Foreign name on you. Just tell me one thing. What got you started digging on this land deal? What got you to wondering?"

"Rob Raines acted too anxious about keeping me from putting any money in it."

"Ummm. See how that could be. Just another kid lawyer. Gawd damn! New crop every year. But a man can't find him a good one any more. Seems like every year they're hungrier. Want to get rich right now, and don't give a damn how they do it, long as it's a little bit legal. They don't seem to have anything on the inside of 'em any more, any old-time rules of what a man can do and can't do. They wear everything on the outside. Raines looked possible, but damn if I felt right about a man willing to mess around with a girl for

200

more than that one good old-fashioned reason. Guess I'm losing my judgment about folks. Want to take a look at some nice pups I've got?"

"Thanks, but I'd better be getting back."

The old man cackled again and said, "People just don't do that to Purdy Elmarr. I say come look at the pups, they say sure thing. I say go gnaw down that oak, and they say how far up from the ground, Purd? Anything to get close and cozy to where the money is. Maybe one time you could bring Mary out, just to say hello. Not her husband. Just her."

"Why not her husband?"

"He's got another woman, and I don't want a cheatin' man settin' foot on my prop'ty." He spat over the railing. "And he can't handle his liquor. And he was pig stupid about how to develop that land. You put your money in it, boy, you handle it yourself."

"You keep in touch with things, don't you?"

And once again he saw the barracuda smile as Purdy Elmarr said, innocently, "Why, people just seem to keep coming out here telling me things."

Elmarr walked out to his borrowed station wagon with him. "Glad you come out," he said. "I mean that. I told you what I would do, and that makes it a deal, so on account of it's a deal, I'll shake your hand. It's the only time I ever shake a man's hand. Shaking it for hello and goodby is just damn silly. It gets to mean nothing. Here."

He shook the spare leathery hand, and they exchanged conspiratorial smiles, and he drove away from there.

All you could do — all you can ever do, Mike thought — is make the best guess you can about a man, and play it that way. The rough road brought out the rattles and creaks in the station wagon. The low sun glared into his eyes when, almost an hour later, he turned toward the bridge to Riley Key. It was five-thirty when he reached the house.

Durelda came to the carport just as he got out of the car and said rapidly, her eyes round and white in her dark face, "Miz Debbie Ann says I was to tell you case you come home 'fore my husban' comes to pick me up — the sheriff called twicet and final got 'hole Miz Debbie Ann telling her the mister got hisself messed up on drunk driving, and it was two hundred dollars cash money to get him out, so Miz Debbie Ann borrowed it here and there and took off maybe a hour ago to go down bail him free."

"Thanks, Durelda. Was there an accident?

Anybody hurt?"

"Nobody said nothing about anybody hurt, but he went and messed up our car some ways."

He went into the house and phoned the Ravenna County Sheriff's office and got hold of a deputy who told him Troy Jamison had been released about twenty minutes ago.

"He was definitely drunk?"

"I wouldn't know, mister. He missed a curve on Ravenna Key and he put that Chrysler smack through one of his own sign-boards, and he couldn't walk. This was two o'clock in the afternoon, mister, and he threw up in the patrol car, and when they brought him in here he was yelling that Marine Corps song but you couldn't hardly understand a word of it, so what do you think?"

"Oh. Where's the car?"

"I don't know, but that girl, that step-daughter I guess it is, arranged something about it."

"And he wasn't hurt?"

"Man! Tomorrow he's going to feel like somebody's spooning his brains out with their thumbnail."

Mike thanked him and hung up.

The white Porsche, with the top up, snorted into the drive five minutes later. Debbie Ann got out quickly, her face rigid with disgust. "It's somebody else's turn now," she said. "Anybody's." She turned and walked swiftly toward her room.

"Hold it!" Mike said sharply. She turned and waited for him. He took his time catching up with her. "Want to clue me in on it?"

She seemed to relax a little. "They called up because he . . ."

"I know most of it. I talked to somebody in the sheriff's office. I just want to get a few details. He was still here when I left this morning. When did he get so . . ."

They were keeping their voices down. "I don't think he slept last night. He had a bottle in the bedroom. I didn't see him leave here, about eleven. Durelda did. She said he left woobly. Isn't that a dandy word? Woobly."

"How about the car?"

"It's been towed into Carson's in Ravenna. I didn't see it."

"How about a lawyer?"

"I phoned Rob. He wasn't exactly eager, but he said he'd take care of it. I explained what happened, told him the names of the arresting deputies. The county police patrol the Keys. He said it didn't sound like he could fight it. About all he could do would be to ask Troy to plead guilty and then he'd see if he could get permission for him to drive his car during daylight hours for business purposes only, and whether that would be granted right now or three months from now would depend on the judge. He won't have a regular license for a year."

They both turned and looked toward Debbie Ann's car.

"Things seem to go to hell in all kinds of ways around here," Debbie Ann said.

"But you don't give much of a damn in any case."

"Thanks. I must try to keep remembering that."

"Does he need a doctor?"

"He needs a bath," she said, and, turning, opened the entry door to the guest wing and went inside.

Mike walked out to the car and opened the door on Troy's side. He sat slack in the bucket seat of the Porsche, staring ahead, slack fists resting on his thighs, mouth agape, coppery stubble on his jowls, his white shirt ripped and soiled, a purple bruise on his left cheekbone.

"Come on, boy. Get out."

Troy didn't stir until Mike shook him and repeated the order. He made slow work of getting out of the small car. Once out he fell back against the car. Mike caught him by the arm and then, supporting a good portion of his weight, led him slowly, blinking, dazed, barefoot, soiled, to the house. He took him through to the master bedroom, eased him into a small straight chair and got him out of his clothes. They were beyond repair. He performed the distasteful task of going through the pockets before he bundled them up to take out to the trash baskets by the garage later.

He left Troy there for a moment while he went into the big tiled bathroom and got the shower going at the right temperature. When he went back to the bedroom Troy was sitting, his head almost between his knees. Mike got his wrists and pulled him up and wrestled him gently into the bathroom. He could detect vague attempts at cooperation. He got Troy into the shower but when he handed him the soap, it slipped out of his hand. Mike sighed, stripped down to his shorts, found a bath brush, and scrubbed Troy as if he were a sleepy, spiritless horse. He pulled him out of the shower, perched him on a bath stool, toweled him dry, found clean pajamas and got him into them.

He leaned close to him and said, "Sleeping pills! Have you got sleeping pills? Where's the sleeping pills!" He slapped Troy lightly.

"Sleeping pills!"

The eyes tracked a little and he made an aimless gesture toward the medicine cabinet. "Blue," he mumbled. "Blue'n white. Lil bo'll."

Mike found the little bottle. Blue and white capsules. The dosage was one. And no more than two. In Troy's condition, one should do it, one should take him beyond that state where, after three hours of semi-sleep, alcohol induced, he would wake up with nerves like icy screaming wires.

He fed him one, poking it into his mouth, sluicing it down with water. When he pulled him off the stool he nearly lost him, nearly went down with him at the unexpected lurch. He turned one of the beds down, got Troy into it. He put his own clothes back on, took his first good look at the room. It was in shades of blue with a deep blue rug, and had wide doors that swung open onto its own tiny private patio where there was a table and two chairs. Atop Mary's dressing table was a big colored photograph in a plain silver frame. He picked it up and turned it toward the light of the dying day. It had been taken on a boat, the two of them sitting side by side on the transom, Troy and Mary, brown, grinning, holding hands. The ensign was snapping on its staff — a fat white wake boiled through blue water — there was wind in Mary's dark hair — in the background, far away, was a tall sailboat, and close at hand a gull was caught in one teetering instant. Good composition. A vivid little piece of happiness, frozen in place by Kodak.

And again, with no warning, the towering wave smashed at him, slamming him down into savage undertows. Not enough pictures of her. All the chances gone. Camera dusty on a shelf on the days she laughed. And he was far away from love, tending a drunk.

"Mike," Troy said in a blurred way.

He put the picture back and went to the bed. He was certain Troy, up until then, had had no idea who was helping him. So this was a return of lucidity on the edge of sleep.

"What is it, boy?" He sat on his heels by the side of the bed, his face a foot from Troy's blurred face.

"Mary took off. Gone two days." The words were slow, the efforts of pronunciation clear.

"I know."

"That isn't why . . . this."

"What reason then, Troy? Why this?"

Troy closed his eyes for so long Mike thought he had gone off, but then he opened them again. "It's . . . a thing in my head. It's

208

there, Mike. It's been there . . . long, long time."

"What kind of a thing?"

"Right . . . in the middle, Mike. Round. Black thing. All . . . knotty like . . . black rubber ball of dead snakes. So there isn't room . . . room in there for me. Didn't want to tell anybody."

"A long, long time?"

"Went . . . away by itself. Came back." Suddenly he lifted his head from the pillow and reached out and caught Mike by the shoulder with fingers that dug so strongly Mike wheezed with pain. In a voice suddenly clear and strong he said, "I had it licked today, Mike. I made it go away. I felt so damn good. I knew all the things I had to do. I sang, Mike. I was drunk outside, but 'way down inside I was sober like I've never been, seeing everything about me like I was on a hill looking down. And I *knew*, Mike. Everything was going to be right for me. I'd licked everything by myself." His hand fell from Mike's shoulder. His head dropped back to the pillow, voice blurred again. "Then they were pulling me out of the car. Didn't know where the hell I was. It's . . . back again. It . . . takes up too damn much room."

"Here is what we are going to do, Troy,"

Mike said. He spoke slowly, distinctly, precisely. "We're going to find a doctor for you. He will make that thing go away and stay away."

Troy closed his eyes. "Sure," he murmured.

"You can't handle a thing like that yourself. You should have told Mary, me, somebody."

Troy sighed.

"When you know something's wrong, you can get it fixed."

Troy had begun to breathe heavily, slowly. Mike looked at him for a few moments. He got to his feet. The cramped muscles of his legs creaked, and his knees popped.

He picked up the bundle of ruined clothing, closed the bedroom door quietly behind him, and, after he had disposed of the clothing, took the number Debbie Ann had given him out of his wallet and phoned the Lazy Harbor Motel on Longboat Key. There were evidently phones in the rooms.

Mary answered. "Oh, Mike, I was hoping you'd call yesterday, and if you hadn't phoned I was going to wait until seven and then phone you."

"Is this a private line here?"

"Yes. What's happened?"

"Something bad and something good. The bad isn't too serious, Mary. Just messy." He told her about the arrest, the car, told her Troy was in bed asleep.

"I shouldn't have gone away like this. It was a bad idea."

"No, it wasn't. Maybe it brought it all to a head. I've got news on the land thing, and I guess it's good news, but it isn't the good news I meant." He told her about Troy's confession of the black object in his head.

"I'll come back right away."

"Now wait a minute. He talked to me. He promised he'd see a doctor. I'll get one lined up. I'll refresh hell out of his memory if he pretends to draw a blank. I'm no shrinker, but I don't think this is physical. You know, a tumor, anything like that. I think it's a kind of anxiety. I think he scared hell out of himself today, and I think that's good. I think we're getting someplace. But I'm afraid if you come roaring back, he's going to back off into a defensive position again, and maybe we won't be able to get him to cooperate. Do you see what I mean?"

"Yes, but . . ."

"I'll be talking to him tomorrow. And then I'll be in touch with you, Mary, and I swear if I think you can help me get him to do something constructive about this, I'll yell for you. I promise."

"All — all right, Mike."

"Cheer up, honey. I think we're moving in the right direction."

"That sounds like an order. All right. I'll cheer up."

"I talked to an old duck today who wants to see you sometime. Purdy Elmarr."

"Purdy! My goodness, how did you happen to meet him?"

"It's a long story. I'll tell you the whole thing later on. I'm an expert on Florida land development all of a sudden."

"Mike, would you do one thing for me?"

"Of course."

"If . . . it should happen that you don't think it would be wise for me to come back, after you talk to Troy tomorrow, could you come up and tell me what's been happening? Phones are no good. Not for a thing like this."

"It might be Friday instead of tomorrow."

"That would be all right. But phone me tomorrow anyway."

"Sure."

After he hung up he looked at Troy again. He was reasonably certain Troy wouldn't stir for at least fourteen hours. With luck he'd sleep through the more desperate symptoms of hangover.

As he walked back into the living room,

Debbie Ann came in, eyebrows high in inquiry.

"I got him hosed off and sacked out," Mike said.

"Good."

"I just talked to your mother."

"That's what I wanted to ask you about, if you or I should phone her. Is she upset?"

"Sure, she's upset."

"Is she coming back?"

"Not right away. I told her you did a fine job of taking care of things."

"Up to a point."

He shrugged. "You couldn't have helped me with what I had to do."

"I've had more experience than you might guess, Mike. Dacey tied on some beauts. It's quite an experience, swabbing off lipstick and wondering whose it is. I just got fed up with him, with Troy, on the way back."

"Why? What happened?"

"I think he thought I was somebody else. I couldn't understand him very well, but he certainly called me all the names in the book. He started with slut and went on from there. Of course, deep in that alcohol fog, he may have known exactly who he was talking to."

"Have you given him cause?"

"That's a funny damn question."

"I just wondered whether he ever got that towel routine you worked on me."

Anger went out of her. "Why, I'm just a simple little affectionate girl-type girl," she lisped, "and I just can't understand why the menfolks keep getting wrong ideas about me, I swear I cain't."

"That ends the discussion, of course, which is just what you wanted to do. You've got more defenses than a radar system."

"So let's not tire ourselves out emotionally, Mike. There are more practical things to consider. Food. Drink."

"You look all gussied up for a date."

"I had one, but I just canceled out. I couldn't stand the thought of all that polite, humble attentiveness from Rob again. He keeps looking at me like a spaniel begging me to throw a stick so he can show how wonderfully he can bring it back. I had one meager idea. I looked in the deep freeze. There's a steak in there the size of a coffee table, and a charcoal grill over at the cabaña, so let's get into beach togs and phone Shirley and I'll pick her up while you do something important about some drinks and the charcoal."

Rob Raines had been within minutes of leaving to drive out to the Key and pick Debbie Ann up when she had called him and had broken the date with such a bored, irritable, arrogant manner that it cut deeply.

"But I thought we could just . . . "

"I don't want to do *anything*. I just don't feel like *seeing* you. Isn't that clear enough?"

She had hung up on him. After a few seconds he put the phone back on the cradle.

His mother called to him from the kitchen. "Who was that, sweetie?"

"Uh . . . Debbie Ann."

She came into the hallway, licking chocolate from her thumb. "She just can't leave you alone, can she. You're going out there anyway, but she just has to call up and . . . "

"She broke the date, Mom. She . . . doesn't feel well."

"Ha! If I know *that* one, she's got somebody else all lined up all of a sudden, and she knows she can lead you around by the nose any old time, and she . . . "

"Cut it out, will you?"

"You don't have to yell at me, sweetie."

"But you keep on bad-mouthing her every chance you get. I get sick of it."

"The only reason I even *asked* about the phone call at all, Robert, was on account of I thought it might be Purdy Elmarr calling you, or Mr. Arlenton or Mr. Haas. You know, sweetie. Your new business associates. I'm so proud of how well you're doing, honey."

He shrugged and went to his room. And a half hour later Purdy Elmarr, much to Rob's astonishment, did call him.

"Raines? Elmarr talkin'. Wondered how you're comin'."

"Oh, I'm coming along fine, just fine," Rob said heartily. "I'm getting the Twin Keys Corporation all set up just the way you said you wanted it, and . . . "

"Any fool knows how to set up a little corporation, boy. You think I'd bother phoning you to ask about that?"

"Well . . . I guess not, Mr. Elmarr."

"Then you know what I am asking about. I want to know about that funny-name foreigner."

"Mr. Rodenska? Well, sir, I talked to him, like you suggested. I think I got it across pretty strongly that he'd be making a mistake going into Jamison's project with him."

"You tole him it was real sour, eh?"

"I got that across all right."

"And he believed you?"

"Yes sir. I'm . . . pretty sure he did."

There was a long silence during which Rob got more and more uncomfortable. "Then maybe you can tell me this, boy. Maybe you can tell me how come that Rodinsky fella is going all over town asking a lot of questions about Horseshoe Pass Estates."

"I . . . I didn't know that, Mr. Elmarr."

"You're supposed to know stuff like that. Has Rodinsky talked to Jamison about loanin' him money?"

"I don't really know."

"Then you better start hustlin' your tail to and fro and be a-findin' out some of these things you don't know, boy. Or we can get right impatient with you, hear?"

Purdy Elmarr heard the nervous protestations as he slowly placed the phone back on the hook.

seven

Though Mike had entered into the beach arrangement with many reservations, it turned out to be almost astonishingly pleasant. By the time Debbie Ann got back with Shirley, there was still a pink line of sunset low over the Gulf. Just as drinks had been fixed, a couple, neighbors named Briggs and Mildred Thatcher, came walking north along the beach, heading home.

They accepted a drink, confessed a lack of plans, inspected the steak, and agreed to help with it, provided they could contribute one large bowl of salad. It was already made and on the ice, so Briggs went home and drove back with it.

As it was obvious Shirley and the Thatchers would see the news item on Troy in the morning paper, Debbie Ann told Shirley and the Thatchers of Troy's mishap, telling it in a joking way. She covered her mother's absence by saying she was visiting friends. All in all,

Mike thought she handled it very well.

And he soon found he enjoyed talking to Briggs Thatcher. He was about forty-five. They had two girls in college in the north. Briggs had been almost at the peak of a highly successful career as an industrial designer when he had had a coronary that had nearly killed him. Now, after one year of being an invalid, and a second year of being cautious, he was getting back into his profession slowly and carefully. He worked at his home on the Key, on small projects for the firm he had once owned. He had an agile, unorthodox intelligence, and his wife, Mildred, was a mimic of almost professional calibre.

After the steak, perfectly done, had been consumed to the last scrap, they sat around in the big deck chairs on the cabaña porch and talked with that special intimacy sometimes achieved with strangers. The dark water was phosphorescent, and the stars looked bright and low.

Mike had gathered that the Thatchers kept themselves from participating in some of the attitudes of the residents of the north end of the Key. He was cued by Mildred's imitation of Marg Laybourne, high comedy which could have been vicious, but wasn't. So at one point he said to Briggs, "I guess all this, this social community, is sort of a unit. But I'm not up on the tribal customs."

Briggs said, in his dry way, "It takes a little while to get the picture, Mike. These people call themselves Floridians. We're guilty of that sometimes. But it would be like our embassy people in Mexico calling themselves Mexicans. We've got our tight little structure here. Same as on Ravenna, Siesta, Manasota, Casey, St. Armands, Longboat — all these exclusive sandpits along the west coast. Own houses, pay taxes, vote — but it doesn't make us a part of Florida. It's like a bunch of cruise ships. Come the hot months, the cruise will be over, and eighty percent of us will flee north. When we're here, we don't accept the environment. We alter it. Air-conditioning. Screening. Bulldozing out the natural stuff and replacing it with tropical exotics for the next freeze to kill. We've got our clubs and maids and gossip and pretty boats and yard men and confused offspring. The Kodachrome life. But it isn't Florida. Not their Florida."

He made a wide, nearly invisible gesture toward the mainland and continued, saying, "Oh, there's some fine people living snug in this icing on the cake. Productive human beings. But too many of them are rootless. So they fill their days with a special emptiness made up of garden clubs, cocktail parties, social vendettas, adventures in pseudo-culture, hypochondria, semi-alcoholism, random fornications, sports cars, and when it gets so dull that even they become aware of it, they take all their frantic aimlessness to Jamaica or Cuba or Nassau. And brag about their hangovers when they get back. But I'm the big serious wheel. I sit around designing a new soap dish. Significant."

"We're all just a mess," Debbie Ann said.

"Not as messed up, honey," Briggs said, "as the sixteen-to-twenty group, the children of these people. Charge accounts, Club memberships, no obligation to go get an education. They knock themselves off on the highways with miraculous efficiency, and the drama of mourning is intense but short, because when you've ceased feeling very much of anything else except the sensations of self-gratification, it's tough to summon up legitimate grief. I will now knock this off, to the audible relief of all."

"But you can live here," Mike said. "Without going native."

"If you have some purpose beyond watching the golden years go by. And if, like Mildred and me, you can get a certain amount of amusement out of watching the monkey cage, and throwing the random peanut."

"It's all those wooden-headed colonels that get me down," Mildred said. "They think people are troops or something. There ought to be one day a month set aside for them, so they could stride about clanking their medals and yelling atten-shun."

"My anti-militarist wife," Briggs said. "One of them once ordered her to go get him a drink. Sure you can live here. The sand and the sea, et cetera. Enjoy it. Be my guest."

There was a long time of lazy talk. World problems were settled. And the impromptu party ended. The Thatchers drove on home, forgetting the empty salad bowl. Debbie Ann and Shirley did the minor scullery work required. Mike thanked them and said goodnight and went for a walk south down the beach.

He was standing, staring at tracks of swift phosphorescence a few feet from shore, wondering what was causing them, when Shirley McGuire said, "Boo, you all."

She was two feet from him. The soft sounds of the waves coming in had masked her approach.

"Turn your back while I get back into my skin. Like putting on long johns."

"I'm sorry."

"Where's Debbie Ann?"

"She wanted to drive me back to the Tennysons' but I said I'd rather walk — it isn't much over a mile — and I asked her if she wanted to walk with me, it's so beautiful, and she said no thanks. So when I was thinking it was all kind of spooky and deserted and there was a figure in the distance, and I was going to make a big circle around it, it turned out to be you. Want to walk with me?"

"Sure. And carry your shoes again, even."

"Not necessary. These are for beach walking."

After they had walked in silence for a while she said, "That was especially nice tonight, Mike."

"I thought so."

"It's something I've missed. It was like that around my home, that kind of talk. But not after I was married. I should have been smart enough to see that it was a bad sign that anything abstract made Bill uncomfortable."

"So you quit because the talk was bad?"

"Don't be nasty, Mike. The bad talk was a symptom. Bad drinking was another. And getting beaten up was another. You say you'll stick it out for the sake of the chee-ild, and then when said chee-ild sees you get hammered to your knees in front of his high chair, you start wondering how much good it's going to do him to grow up in that kind of an environment."

"I'm sorry. It's too easy to make a cheap remark."

"A marriage can be impossible, Mike. Mine was. That's all. I had it just about as rough as it can become, and this is just as much convalescence as it is divorce. I'm not trying to unload my troubles. I just . . . want you to know this isn't self-indulgence. Okay?"

"Okay."

"So we drop it. I've been thinking about you. And all this going on with Troy. You're like the man who came to dinner and found out he was expected to cook it and serve it and clean up afterwards."

"It makes me feel important. You know. Needed. One of life's empty little pleasures."

"Ah, you're a bitter man, Rodenska."

"No, I can't be bitter, baby. A little fat man is never bitter. He just pouts. You got to have the big lean type to be bitter."

"You are *not* a little fat man. You're just . . . dignified in a stocky sort of way, and you have nice shoulders and nice eyes."

He stopped in the starlight and beamed upon her. "Say, you come through nice."

"Okay. Tell me something nice about me."

They started walking again. "Okay. To-night when you said anything, it made sense. You talked just enough, and not too much. You laughed in the right places. That's what you need for a good group. People who all laugh in the right places."

"Mother said beware of men who compliment you on your mind."

"The rest of it? Hell! You look like Lamour should have looked when she used to do those South Seas things, only a little more on the savage side."

"Me got faded sarong, sailor man. Cook plantain. Share grass hut, maybe?"

"Baby, I just got off that ship out there and I didn't know there was nothing like this in the world. You know what I'm going to do? I'm just not going back to that ship, ever."

"Sailor man likes photogenic little coral atoll? Photogenic sarong. Sailor man likes . . . ah, God, let's drop it."

"What's the matter?"

"Every little while the bottom falls out of any mood I'm in. Games don't last long these days. Don't mind me. I should have gotten a place of my own. My aunt and uncle are just too damn solicitous. And indescribably disapproving. Poor little Shirley. Know what I want to do?"

"What?"

"It's pretty silly. Maybe it's self-conscious."

"Try it on me."

"I would dearly love to get revolting, sloppy, stinking drunk. With somebody standing by to take care — somebody I could trust not to let me do anything horrible or sick. I feel as if it would . . . release some kind of tension. And afterward I want to have a hangover so bad, I'll never want to to do it again. One of these days, when I'm ready, will you be the male nurse?"

"Where do you want this debauch?"

"Somewhere private. I don't want anybody to see me in that condition. I'm very prim and conventional. I'll think of a place."

"Let me know."

"Hey. Here we are! It turned out to be a real short walk, Mike. Thanks." She turned and put her hand out to him, standing up the beach from him where it was so sharply sloped her eyes were level with his. Her face was clear in the starlight. Her hand was small, warm and slightly, not unpleasantly, moist. Black bangs and heavy black brows shadowed eyes, and a triangular paleness of face, narrowing to the broad line of the mouth.

They said goodnight and he waited there until she turned under the night light over the side door, and waved at him, and let herself in. He turned and walked slowly back the way they had come, thinking about her. Where they had walked side by side in moist sand their prints were sharp and clear.

She doesn't look like what she is. So who does? I've marveled at them — statesmen who look like pickpockets, murderers who look like scout leaders, whores who look like seamstresses, bankers who look like football coaches.

Bless you, Shirley McGuire. After they have tumbled you over the reef, and torn all their raggedy holes in you, walk safe ashore. No rats in the roof of your grass house, baby. Fruit on every tree. No hurricanes. Stay dry when it rains. Have some love, not for earning it, but because you can give some — and that's the only way you ever get any back.

The Gulf sighed, like the steady breathing of some ancient hibernating thing. The night crabs marked his passage. When he got back to the house he stood for a moment on the beach and looked at a star.

That's the way they'll find out what we were, he thought. They'll go whistling up there and settle down and look back right along this path of light from me to the star. Train their instruments and take a look at light rays fifty thousand years old. What were those creatures back there, down there? One of them stands on a beach in the ancient past. On a wrinkly ball of mud and water. Looking up. Why did they do what they did? What were they thinking about? Were they aware, as we are aware, or was it just a refinement of instinct which almost simulated intelligence?

Go to bed, Rodenska, before you flip. Before you bug yourself with the ineffable grandeur of your night thoughts. Go wash your fangs and lie down.

On Thursday morning at nine when he walked into the main part of the house, Durelda said, "Moanin', Mista Mike. Worl' all covered up white and misty."

"Moanin' to you, Durelda," he said. He saw a quick glint of amusement in her eye. He wasn't intending to mock her, and she knew it too. But it didn't hurt anything to let her know he was aware of being Uncle-Tommed. It was a part of the essential defenses she had raised against her environment. It was a maintenance of established order, and thus comforting to all involved.

"Suppose I set you in the dinin' aye-ria on account everything's soaked wet on the patio this morning." The final word came out with a crispness of diction that matched and replied to his gentle dig at her.

"That'll be fine."

"Miz Debbie Ann isn't up and the mister isn't up and I got no idea what he'll want."

"I'd plan on just juice and coffee when he does get up."

"Your eggs same way today?"

"Same way every day, thanks."

"Sun'll burn this yeer fog away quick."

The morning paper was on the table. He found the item on Troy on the bottom of page three, headed BUILDER ARRESTED. It was short and reasonably fair, neither exaggerated nor underplayed. Estimated damages to the car were four hundred dollars, plus eight hundred dollars other property damage.

After he finished breakfast he went quietly to the bedroom and looked at Troy. He didn't look like anybody who was about to wake up. There was a sour musty smell in the room. He decided he would have time to run in and get the cash for Jerranna from the bank. After he got the thick packet of tens and twenties from the bank, he looked up Signs of Ravenna and went to the sign company and talked to a reasonable man about the boards for Horseshoe Pass Estates. Despite Mike's assurance that soon he would be in a position to make some fair settlement on the previous contract and set up a contract for a slightly smaller program, the man was reluctant to promise any cooperation. But after Mike, smiling confidently, said, "Mr. Purdy Elmarr is anxious to have this project run smoothly. Why don't you give him a ring?" — after that the man said he would phone the attorneys and tell them to delay action on the past due contract until Mike had a chance to make arrangements.

It was a little after eleven when he got back. Troy was in the shower. He came out to the patio at eleven-thirty, in a blue mesh sports shirt, spotless beige slacks, clean-shaven, in an obviously ghastly condition, physically, mentally, spiritually. How come, Mike thought, a hangover is comical, like a black eye, or somebody slipping on a banana peel and cracking their pelvis?

Troy lowered himself carefully into a redwood chair and said, "I drank so much water I've got the bloat."

Durelda came to the doorway and said, "Fix you up something, Mist' Jamison?"

"I'll try some black coffee, thanks." As soon as she left Troy said, "Take a good look at a fun-loving playboy."

"Got any questions?"

"I cracked up the car and spent some time

230

in the drunk tank. Debbie Ann got me out. You got me to bed. Is that the essentials?"

"Yes."

"Was anybody hurt?"

"No."

"Thank God for that. That God for there being no kid on a scooter or a bicycle. Another thing. Does Mary know?"

"Yes."

"She told me when she took off for me not to try to get in touch with her. She said you'd be in touch. Did it make you feel important, relaying my little disasters?"

"For God's sake, Troy."

"Is she coming back today?"

"No."

"I don't think I could take her on top of everything else. She's so goddamn noble and understanding and unselfish."

"She's all three of those, truly."

"And I'm a pig? It follows."

"You're sick."

"That's just about the most meaningless thing you could say."

"How about that thing right in the middle of your head, Troy? It takes up too much room. It's round and black and lumpy, like a ball of black rubber snakes. You thought it had gone away yesterday."

Troy stared at him, his eyes pinched almost shut, his face slack. Mike could sense his enormous surprise, his fear. But in a few moments he saw the forced smile he had expected. "Now who's sick, Mike? You giving it to yourself right in the vein?"

"You told me about the round black thing, last night."

"I don't know anything about that."

"I think you do."

"I was as drunk as a man can get, Mike. I was out on my feet. I probably babbled. Drunks talk nonsense. You're a fool to take stuff like that seriously."

"I did. You promised to see a doctor."

"That's a promise I don't remember. I don't keep promises I can't remember. What's wrong with you? I haven't got time for nonsense like that. I've got work to do."

"I looked into that too the last few days, Troy. I think I know a way you can make out all right."

Durelda brought the coffee and put it on the wide arm of the chair. As soon as she had gone, Troy said, "It was only a question of time until you got your nose into that too. Somewhere you got the idea you can run my life better than I can."

Mike looked at him for long heavy seconds.

232

He got up. "You can go to hell, Jamison. I'll be gone from here in twenty minutes."

He'd walked ten feet before Troy said in a different voice, "Wait a minute, Mike."

"You want a chance to see if you can make it worse? I don't need proof. You can. You're good at it."

"No. I want to say . . . I'm sorry. It was a hell of a thing to say. I didn't mean it. I'm . . . not myself. Sit down."

Mike sat down again, wary and still angry. "Only because of Mary, boy. Not you. Take your choice, boy. You're either sicker than you'll admit, or you're a worthless s.o.b. Take your choice."

"Great choice."

"I'm fresh out of alternatives. You weren't raving last night. There's something wrong with you. If you don't think so, see a doctor and prove there isn't. Or go to hell, believing you're sane."

"Now I'm nuts. Is that it?"

"Your actions aren't rational. They're self-destructive. They were like that once before."

"Now a few drinks is suicide."

"For some people. How about that doctor?"

Troy turned his face away. He waited long seconds. "Maybe there is . . . something going wrong. And maybe it scares me a little.

But I can work it out myself."

"You're doing so well at working it out yourself. Unbelievable!"

"Get off my back!"

"The doctor, boy. The doctor!"

"Listen. I'm in no shape to make a decision like that now. Today. For God's sake, give me a chance to unwind a little."

"How long will that take?"

"Let's talk about it tomorrow, Mike. Tomorrow. Nothing is going to be any good today. The only feeling I've got about today is to try to live through it. That will be the only project I can handle. By tomorrow afternoon I can talk about this thing and make sense."

"All right. We'll leave it that way."

"What's this about the development?"

"That will keep. Don't think about that. Think about yourself. For once in your life, try to look at yourself as a stranger might."

The attempted smile was a horrid grimace as Troy said, "It's a lot easier not looking too squarely at some of the things you do."

"For you, it's time."

"The thing is, I've never felt like a bad guy, really. I act like one. Then I want to get away from myself. But that's the one thing they won't let you do. That's the big trap."

"What are you going to do today?"

234

"Be a vegetable. Lie in the sun. Take a nap later. Even standing up makes me feel weak and sweaty."

"You'll stay around? You won't leave?"

"God, no!"

Mike spent the brief time before lunch writing to the boys. He had lunch alone. Debbie Ann had gone into town to have lunch with somebody. Troy didn't yet feel like eating.

After lunch he finished the letters and mailed them on his way to Ravenna Key. He got to Red's at two-thirty. Birdy and Jerranna weren't there. He asked Red about them. "Haven't been in yet today. Probably at the cottage."

He went to the cottage. Birdy sat on the floor of the small porch, bare to the waist, intently weaving some unidentifiable object out of long thin leather thongs. His thick fingers were nimble, his expression intent. Muscles pulsed in his chest and shoulders as he worked.

He looked up, the fingers still working. "Go on in, hey. She's sacked out. She said you'd be around." He had made no attempt to lower his voice.

"Did she tell you what I'd . . ."

"Mike?" she called, her voice faint and grainy with sleep.

"Go on in, hey," Birdy said.

He went inside. Venetian blinds cut the white light to thin slivers. Doors stood open inside. There was a small living-room, a small bedroom, a bath, a kitchen corner in the living-room. The place was a welter of clothing, magazines, empty bottles, unemptied ashtrays. She had been sleeping on the living-room couch. She sat up as he came in, combing her hair back with the spread fingers of both hands, yawning so widely he saw where back molars were missing. She wore crumpled white shorts and a red canvas sheath top.

"Christ!" she said. "Sleeping in the daytime gives me a mouth like a bird cage. Dump the stuff off that chair and sit, Mike."

He picked the pants and magazines off the chair, tossed them onto another chair and sat down, facing her.

"I brought the money."

"I told you, Birdy," she called. "He brought it."

"That's nice," Birdy said sourly. "That's real nice."

"So what's the deal?"

She yawned again, and shuddered. "Somebody walking on my grave. The deal? That's the trouble. A deal. It's another way to say I get pushed around. You know?"

"Not exactly. It's a thousand bucks. I'm not flipping you a four-bit piece to stop singing."

Birdy came in, blocking the light from the doorway for a moment, and then leaned against the door frame just inside the room. He patted his hair. "It's still a deal, buddy. You pay us and we say, 'thank you sir, oh thank you sir,' and take off."

"Maybe we're not getting through to each other," Mike said patiently. "Or maybe I'm stupid. I'm paying you to do something. Paying you damn well."

"And you don't care if we like it here or not. You don't care if we're ready to go yet," Birdy said in a complaining tone. "People are always pushing."

"Won't you go sooner or later?"

"Sure. Sometime."

"So go now and get paid for it."

"That means we're doing what you want, not what we want," Birdy said.

"That's why I'm paying you!" Mike yelled. "To do what I want instead of what you want."

"You see?" Birdy said. "Pressure. All the time pressure. And I don't like it. No matter where we go then, we got to get used to the idea the only reason we're there is you pushed us out of here."

"Doesn't the money mean a damn thing?"

"That's a nice piece of money," Birdy said.

"Don't you want it?"

"Sure, we want it."

"Then what the hell kind of an agreement *do* you want?"

"I talked it over with her," Birdy said. "I didn't think you'd come up with it. I said if you did, okay. You can give it to us. Like a present. Then after you give it to us, no strings, then we decide if we'll leave. Maybe we will and maybe we won't, but that way we're not being pushed around none."

"Do I look like a sap?"

"Buddy, I don't know what you look like. You figure she's poison for your pal. You want her out. Did you ever think of asking real nice, no money or anything, please take off?"

"Frankly, no. But if that's what you . . ."

"It's too late for that now, buddy. That's what you do first. And if it don't work the money comes next. You bitched yourself, buddy, thinking you could buy us. So you only got one choice left. Leave the grand and we'll think it over."

"I'll tell you one thing," Jerranna said. "Troy was getting kinda boring, but not yesterday, man. Yesterday he was real crazy. Yesterday was full of kicks. I saw in the paper

238

he didn't make it home."

"So now you'll stay even if I turn over the money."

"Did anybody say that?" Birdy demanded.

"That crazy Troy wanted to trade punches with Birdy. He smacked Birdy one good one, and Birdy hit him — pow — and I swear to God he slid eight feet on his back and got up laughing so hard he was crying. He was having a ball yesterday."

"I'm not getting into any kind of crazy arrangement about the money, the way you people want me to do it."

"Suit yourself, buddy," Birdy said.

Mike got up and said, "There's no reason why you can't take it away from me, I suppose."

"Then it would be the same thing," Birdy said.

"What do you mean?"

"We'd have to leave. We're people, like anybody else. I took it away from you, it would be the same deal again. If we were going anyway, we would. I would. You're heavy and you look solid, but I could snap your back across my knee."

"Good for you."

"He can pick up the front end of a new Caddy," Jerranna said.

"If I *don't* give you the money, will you stay longer?" Mike asked, feeling confused and desperate.

"The way I feel right now, buddy, when both of us get ready to leave at the same time, we'll take off, and I don't know when. You don't get with things very good. You don't come on very fast."

"I feel like I'm dreaming this damn conversation," Mike said. He stood up and pried the bills out of his pocket and looked at them stupidly. He sighed and opened the packet and slowly counted out five hundred and put the rest in his pocket, placed the five hundred on the table.

"What's that for?" Birdy demanded.

"It's a present," Mike said thinly. "For two lovely people. I like your eyes. I like your hairdos."

"And we go or stay. It's up to us," Birdy said.

"Yes. This is — a gesture of undying friendship."

Birdy grinned. "Man, now you're coming on better. You could even get with it, you keep straining."

"Stick a gold star on my forehead," he said and walked wearily out. When he was ten feet from the porch door Jerranna said something he couldn't quite catch. And then they both began laughing. Mike flushed. When he got to the station wagon, he could still hear the laughter, very faint and far away. He drowned it with an angry roar of the engine.

Conned, he thought. Conned out of five hundred bucks. I'm not with it. I just can't come on. I can't dig the tribal customs. What the hell kind of a code of honor is that? And how much did Troy leave with them yesterday — as a touching gesture? It's like you try to give a shark a cheese sandwich to stop gnawing your leg, and the shark says that as a moral, upstanding shark, he can take the sandwich only as a gesture of friendship. Give it to me, boy, and I'll decide later on.

He went back to the house. Debbie Ann was still out. Troy was napping. So he went out and swam and fell asleep on the beach and awakened in time to see the last bloody segment of the sun slide into the Gulf.

I can pick up the front end of a new kiddy car, he said. I could snap Shirley's wrist across my knee, after a course in calisthenics. And I can sure as hell give money away.

Some days the world seemed a lot less real. This was one of those days.

eight

On Friday morning he left the house at nine before Troy was up, and while Debbie Ann was having breakfast, and drove up to see Mary. Though the peak of the tourist season had passed, the Tamiami Trail was thick with cars from Ohio, Indiana, Iowa, Michigan. The cars were dusty from travel, the rear window ledges cluttered with Kleenex boxes, fruit, seashells, coconut masks, children's toys, yellow boxes of camera film.

As he neared Sarasota the tempo of the traffic slowed for the long, tawdry, dangerous strip of commercial slum — juice stands, beer joints, drive-ins, grubby motels, shabby sundries stores, tackle shops, shell factories, gas stations, trailer parks, basket shops — all announcing the precariousness of their existence with big cheap bright signs imploring the passer-by: STOP — BUY — EAT — SHOP — CUT RATES — SALE — BARGAIN — SPECIAL. Here and there were trim, tidy, attractive operations,

242

lost in the welter of potentially bankrupt anxiety, in the dusty flavor of a dying cut-rate carnival. Tires yelped and horns brayed indignation as people cut in and out of the lines of thirty-mile-an-hour traffic.

The road widened as he entered Sarasota. He found a marked turn through an exceedingly complicated interchange, swooped around a bay-front drive and on out over bright new bridges to St. Armand's Key where the leggy brown girls walked in their short shorts, and there were a great many convertibles. He found his way to Longboat Key and drove past some vast and florid hotel ventures along the Gulf front and, just when he was wondering if he had passed Lazy Harbor, he saw the high blue and white sign ahead, with a plywood sea gull balanced on one wingtip on top of it. He parked by a long low pink building, asked for Mrs. Jamison, and was told she was out by the pool. He found her in a deck chair in a white sheath swim suit that accented her tan, her long legs burnished with oil, big black sunglasses with coral frames, cigarettes close at hand, an O'Hara novel propped on her stomach.

"Pardon me, Miss, but haven't I seen you someplace before?"

"Oh, Mike!"

"I generally don't try to pick up young girls," he said, and moved a chair closer to hers and sat down.

"It must be this suit. I bought it Wednesday, and yesterday when I was walking over on the beach, I was whistled at, by a boy Debbie Ann's age. It made me feel horribly smug. This suit must do something special."

"You do something nifty to it, maybe."

"Stop it right now, or I'll become unbearable. What's happening, Mike? How is Troy? Don't you think I ought to come home?"

He told her about Troy, how he was reacting. It took a long time. She had a lot of questions. Then he told her about Jerranna and Birdy and how that had worked out.

"They sound like members of a different race," she said wonderingly.

"Martians, maybe. I don't know. It's a kind of evil, Mary. Psychopathic. I saw one like him once, a younger version. Killed his parents. They wouldn't let him have the car keys. He was indignant. Why the big fuss, he wanted to know. They wouldn't let me have the keys. I got sore. They didn't have any right not to gimme the keys, see? I had a date."

"And have you ever seen anything like her?"

"Never. A lot of them almost like her, but without that something added, whatever the hell it is."

Mary kept at him to describe Jerranna more completely. But words merely made her sound totaly unattractive, and made Mary feel baffled by the whole thing.

"I've had a chance to think about Troy," she said, "and about the things you told me about him. I've been wondering something. I want to know what you think."

"Go ahead."

"Could a man . . . a man like Troy . . . have such a fear of failure, which could come from a feeling of guilt, have such a great fear of failure that through some sort of reverse, compulsive thing, he forces himself to fail? In two businesses and two marriages, probably the four most important things in his life?"

"It's a thought. It could be right. The neurotic ambitious pitcher who can't help serving up that fat pitch, that home run pitch."

"Oh, Mike," she said in a lost voice, "I don't know what to think."

"Maybe it was just drunk talk. Just that." He felt a sudden unreasoning contempt for himself and for his involvement in this thing. It was unreal to be here, sweating in the sun, talking to a brown handsome woman beside a

245

tourist pool. "We all take the big swing with amateur psychiatry. What does it mean? What do we know? So Troy is another alcoholic, and we make a big thing out of it."

"It's a big thing to me, Mike."

"I shouldn't have said it that way. Hell. It's the alcoholic cycle, isn't it? Build everything up so far and then tear it all to hell down and start again. But how many starts does a guy get in one lifetime?"

"I better come home, Mike. Now."

"I don't know. I felt sure I was being smart. He's trying to smash everything he cares about. So if you're out of the way, I thought . . . now I don't know what I think. I feel as if I'd been meddling. Maybe an occupational disease. Come home — stay here — how important is it to you?"

She looked away from him. A little muscle moved at the corner of her jaw, and her throat looked taut. She pitched her voice so low he found himself leaning forward to hear her. "I want to say . . . it's terribly important. But that's a pose, isn't it? Noble Mary, forgiving and understanding. My own retouched photograph of myself. It . . . isn't as important as it was. It never will be, Mike. Never again. That foul woman. He went from me, to roll in filth. So I wasn't enough. Something inadequate." She looked directly at him, her eyes brilliant, and said abruptly, "A lot of this warm protective desire to understand the poor sick man is crap, Mike." She banged her fist on her naked thigh. "He hurt me! He made me ashamed! He hurt me! He hurt me!"

She bent forward from the waist, face in her hands, in a quiet agony. On the other side of the pool a sheep-faced woman stared, nudged her husband, spoke secretively to him, still staring, the explosions of rapid sibilants audible across the pool. He opened his eyes solemnly and the two of them stared at Mary. There had been a slight flavor of childishness in her outbursts, a little of petulance, but it was mostly a mature woman in that special area of pain reserved, in irony, for those who know how to give.

He wanted to reach out and touch her, but did not want to make the little scene more interesting to the couple opposite them. He sat in discomfort, thinking how easy it was to hurt the good ones, how impossible to hurt the bad ones. Vulnerability, he said to himself, seeking for that epigrammatic quality, is the curse of the thinking classes.

She lifted her face, fighting for, then achieving an illusion of composure, and said in a small weary voice, "I'm so damn tired of being so stinking decent about everything. It was easier to get away from him than you know, Mike. I . . . snapped at the chance, with a pretty show of reluctance. The least I can do right now is be honest with myself and with you."

"Mary, this honesty thing is tough. The pretending is so easy. There is maybe about four of me, and only one is real, so once in a while, like for character or something, I have to go down into a hole with those three other guys and lay around me with a club so I'm the only one left. But they win sometimes. How do you tell the player without a scorecard? I'll give you this. I admire you. I'll do it up in needlepoint. You can frame it. Like home sweet home."

"Don't you make me cry, darn you."

"Okay, let's try a change of pace. Now I'll tell you how I'm becoming a big land merchant. They call me Mike the Dealer. I've got the secret of this land-development kick. You've got to hate trees. A tree has to offend your sense of ugliness, so you bulldoze it the hell out of there, and asphalt the whole area. Then you put up eighty-six lousy little forty-thousand-dollar houses and you're in."

He told her about his adventures. He made her laugh. Laughter took the agony out of her eyes, made her visibly younger. It took so long to tell that he stopped while she went and changed to a yellow sunback dress, and then he drove her to a garden restaurant where, under a pink umbrella and with the pleasant distractions of a fashion show of beach wear and a small and tender filet, he finished it. She felt sorry for Corey Haas. She told Mike he was brilliant. He told her he had known that all along, but it was difficult to get anybody to perceive it. She told him that if he was actually, seriously considering risking his money, he needed his head examined. And that had a double meaning which put shadows back behind her eyes. He said he would risk it out of greed, maybe, having always wanted to see how a millionaire felt on the inside — smug or nervous.

So, after some silence, not particularly awkward, they got back to Topic A.

"I don't want to go back right now," she said with a certain defiance, "even if I felt he does need me, which I don't quite believe somehow. I need myself. I'm getting reacquainted with Mary."

"Then the thing to do is stay."

"But if I stay here, it leaves it all in your hands."

"So I'll try to cope. No obligation. Should I

sit on the beach in mourning? There is a thing you should know about. Buttons called it the Curse of Rodenska. I've got used to it. I can explain it this way, Mary. Suppose I was convicted of murder and sentenced to death. The day before they're going to finish me off, the warden comes to the cell. He sits down and looks at me sadly. I'm all braced for words of compassion. So he says, 'Look, Mike, I've got this problem I need your advice on.'"

Mary laughed. "Oh, Mike, honestly — "

"Everybody does it. Should you be different? If all I had to do was lie on your beach it would make me highly nervous."

And so, promising to keep her up to date, he took her back to Lazy Harbor and drove back on down to Riley Key. It was nearly four when he arrived. He looked across the beach before he turned into the drive and saw Troy stretched out, alone, in the sun.

He changed to swim trunks and walked down onto the beach and sat on his heels beside Troy.

"You could even be human," he said.

Troy rolled up onto one elbow. "It took until noon today. You've been to see Mary? Thought so. Spare me any play-by-play, old buddy."

"I wasn't going to present a report, old buddy."

"The words would be familiar. I'm tearing her heart out. I don't deserve such a fine woman. And so on."

"For a nearly hundred-percent bastard, Troy, you run in luck. You not only get the friendship of a sterling type like me, but you marry real good women."

"It's a knack. I'm a great guy. I'm a war hero."

"About Mary, set your mind at rest, war hero."

"How so?"

"One time a guy on our street bought a dog. The dog didn't adore him enough. So he got a stick and beat on it, but for some reason the situation got worse. He couldn't understand it."

"Pull up a cracker barrel and we'll spit on the chunk stove to hear it sizzle."

"I'm just homespun, Troy. True blue. She'll be back, I suppose. But it won't be the same deal you had."

"Something precious has been forever lost?"

Mike studied him. "You're a great guy, Troy. You're a prince. You need that shrinker."

"Anybody who doesn't agree with you is sick?"

"Let's say you're scared, Troy."

The word dented Troy's mask of bland amusement, ironic arrogance. The word twisted his mouth. Mike watched him regain control.

"Scared of what, old buddy?"

"What's happening to you. Because you don't know why it's happening. Or how it's going to end. You know it's going to end bad. You don't know how bad. Nobody knows how bad. So everybody's scared, Troy."

"I'm scared. I'm sick. I'm a mess. So I need a drink. That's indicated, isn't it?" Troy got up and walked toward the house. Mike stood up and watched him. Troy strolled. He ambled along, scuffing sand. But his back muscles were rigid. Very casual, Mike thought. Like a thief walking past a cop. What gutted him like a fish, Mike wondered. What hollowed out the empty man?

Mike swam. He stood, winded, in the clear water. A fish the size of his thigh, wearing a black and white striped suit, swam by with slow, purposeful dignity, heading north. You got lousy taste in clothes, Mike told him. A self-made fish. So you don't know how to dress. You buy mail order stuff from Playboy, and all your employees snicker behind your back. Find a good tailor, buster.

Mike waded out. He prodded his belly and

told himself all this swimming was making him hard and lean and dangerous. Rodenska, soldier of fortune. They all wondered who the tanned stranger was, with that look of far places in his eyes.

Wait until Buttons sees . . .

He turned and squinted through the water in his eyes at the fat red dying sun. Go on down, he said. Don't bother to come up again. Stay down. It isn't worth the trouble.

So he went back to his room, and when he shut himself into the shower stall, he sang his shower song. Not exactly a song, without much of a tune. Up half the scale — boom, boom, boom, boom — and back down — bum, bum, bum, bum. It resonated well.

The alcohol was working on Troy. Mike nursed his drinks and listened. Good old maudlin garrulousness, he thought. Paddlin' maudlin home. Every drunk has the conviction he is unique, and all drunks are alike. A few tears for Bunny. A few lies about the war. Tears for the daughter. Tears for Mary. Some jokes, badly told. Owlish laughter. The world is down on me. Nobody cares. The bad luck I've had. Jesus! Bathos instead of tragedy. Alcohol loosening the mouth, dulling the eyes, causing the expansive, uncertain gesture.

Paralysis of the cerebral cortex. No judgment in choice of words or thoughts. The fumbling tongue. Mike watched him. This had been the lean and deft young officer, good at love, good at killing — full of a quickness. Now the chronological age was forty, the apparent age fifty. A pulpy drunk, bragging now of many conquests, some of them obviously imaginary.

When does life end?

Shirley and Debbie Ann arrived at eight. They were both in shorts and sandals and sleeveless blouses — Shirley in dark green Bermudas with a white-and-green striped blouse and golden sandals — Debbie Ann in off-white shorts and a black blouse and red sandals. They had been to a large and informal cocktail party down the beach. They stood just inside a cone of light, both of a height, a dark one and a fair one, shapely, slightly flushed, close to laughter, twenty-five and twenty-three, the frosted cone of light picking up the highlights of perfect teeth and the fluids of their eyes and the fresh moistness of underlips, the slant of the light accenting the breasts hammocked in dacron, the both of them standing slightly hipshot with forward pelvic thrust and tilt.

I have been here before, Mike thought.

This is an advertisement in full color. The plates cost a fortune. They have just stepped out of their convertible Spumoni in front of this Jamaican villa. Real clean women. Sixty-bucks-an-hour model fee.

But there was something a little out of key in the advertisement. These two lacked the scrubbed, vacuous sterility of ad models. They had come half-laughing out of the night, out of the hot night, slightly feral, with a moist and sensual pungency about them, their tanned roundnesses bespeaking their elemental service to the race. Toast lightly and serve with gin. He stared blandly and approvingly at the projections of breasts and narrowness of waists, at curved ripe mouths and lilting eyes, and thought, which twin had the baby? No stranger could have told.

They both talked at once, the wee little voice of Debbie Ann alternating with Shirley's gamin croak. "A hell of a big dull party . . . but with gaudy goodies, a long table full. . . . And what is *he* celebrating? . . . Is this a party like . . . ? Invite us, sir. . . . I love smaller groups . . . Same poison, Shirl? . . . Let's put on some musica. . . . The lights are lovely. . . . Poor Troy's got the wobblies."

And so it became, in a somewhat limited sense, festive — with music and dancing girls.

And a little later, with Shirley in a suit borrowed from Debbie Ann, swimming girls, accompanied in the small pool by Troy, while Mike located suitable ingredients and constructed a monster sandwich. The swim sobered Troy somewhat, and the girls, though they continued the martini route, seemed to maintain control — at least as much control as they had arrived with. The girls changed back to their shorts and blouses. Quieter music was stacked on the changer, and the volume turned down.

When Mike looked at his watch he was surprised to find it was a little after eleven. He had been sitting for some time in a double chaise lounge affair with Shirley. They had circumspectly switched to beer. They were in a far corner of the patio, shadowed from the lights by the broad leaves of a clump of dwarf banana. He had enjoyed talking with Shirley. They had gotten off into obscure and esoteric areas of philosophy, such as why do the fattest women wear the shortest shorts, and how big can tail fins get, and could you market a cigarette that was eighty percent filter, with enough tobacco for three drags. Nothing personal, nothing weighty, nothing pretentious. No drunk talk. No flirtatious innuendos. Just a couple of people talking in the tropic night, finding it easy to make each other laugh.

So why should I feel guilty? Mike asked himself. So we are lounging here on this double deal, and those brown legs have a very sweet shape stretched out right there, ankles crossed. So she is somewhat slumped, and props her beer can on the delicate convexity of her little tummy. So with those black bangs and that pointed chin and all that mouth, she somehow keeps reminding me of a cat. (Her eyes tilt a little, no?) So she smells good and the jasmine smells loud around here. So she is thoroughly girl, and I am, as an unkind traffic cop would put it, slightly under the influence. Am I making passes? No. Am I thinking of making a pass? It is a subject for idle speculation. But there is no intent, judge. And who wouldn't? What redblooded American newspaper bum wouldn't be thinking somewhat along those lines? Don't feel guilty, Rodenska. Some days you tire me. Some days you are an old lady, indeed. Rodenska, dwell on this. The same year you found out what girls are for, she was missing her mouth with the pablum.

Troy and Debbie Ann were at the other end of the patio, beyond the pool, and they had been talking quietly and inaudibly together for a long time, and with a flavor of intensity that made Mike uneasy, though he could not guess why.

"One enchanting little deal at that big dull party, Mike," Shirley said aimlessly, and with a slight trace of bitterness. "A very brown man of about sixty, known hereabouts, they tell me, as a tireless tennis player. He had found out what we will delicately refer to as my status. But I didn't know his, which seems to be professional widower. Anyhow, he kept calling me, 'my dear.' Very uncle about the whole thing, you know. He said divorce is an emotional shock. His name is Van Cly or Van Clay. Something like that. He said the dangerous time is when the knot is finally cut, and he offered a suggestion of what to do with myself. And like a damn fool, because I really thought he was being quite nice, I had to ask him what he had in mind. So he said he had a nice little motor sailer, a jewel, not too much boat for one man to handle, and he knows the Bahamas like the back of his hand, and it would give me the perfect chance to relax. We could go around the Keys or through the canal and the lake, and spend a lazy month cruising the islands. He would show me places few people ever saw. 'It would be so *good* for you, my dear.' By that time, finally, I had the picture, so I got all hopped up about the idea and said it would be wonderful, and my mother and my little boy would enjoy it just as much as I'm sure I would. And all of a sudden he got very vague about the whole thing."

"You are a cruel girl. You spoiled all his fun. Just think, you could have been a rich man's plaything, and when he tired of you, he'd sell you to a native chief."

"And I'd end my years in a crib in Port Said, a pitiful, broken thing, chanting my dreary invitations to sailors of all nations. Golly, I really missed a good thing, didn't I? I wish I could remember that old clown's name. Troy will know. Troy? Troy."

She swung her legs off the chaise and stood up. "Hey! They're gone!"

Mike stood up too. "We better check the cars. That's the one thing neither of them are capable of doing right now."

But the wagon and the Porsche were both there. Mike took the keys out of the Porsche and pocketed them.

"Maybe they're just walking on the beach," Shirley said.

They went back to the patio. They looked at each other and looked away, uneasy. "Mike, we shouldn't have left them . . ."

"Are they teenagers?" he demanded irritably. "Are we chaperones?"

"But . . ."

"I know. I know. I know. Stay right here a minute."

He left her there and, with a little crawling of apprehension he checked the master bedroom, the other bedroom in the main house, and finally the guest wing. No locked doors. No melodramatic confrontations. He went back to Shirley, where she sat crosslegged on a poolside mattress.

"We seem to be alone at last," he said.

"Can we be sued for libel for what we were thinking? I guess they're just walking on the beach."

He sat in a nearby chair. "You know her. I can only guess. What . . . how much would she be capable of? She's his stepdaughter."

"I was worried. Is that an answer?"

"I guess so."

"Maybe it's what he's capable of."

"Right now he's trying to nasty up his life as completely as possible."

"Oh."

"Look. Do you like her?"

"I don't know, Mike. I don't trust her. She's amusing. And we have so much in common. Like her? You know, that's getting to be an old-timey sort of question, isn't it? Do people go around liking each other any more? Or just enduring. I like you, Mike. But with most people — I just keep my guard up, and lower it as much as I dare. I don't understand the things people do any more. I used to think I did. I don't any more. I can't put myself in their place, I guess. It's a world full of strangers. The world's a big cruise ship, and you don't want to get committed too far because the cruise ends. Why should you ask me if I like her?"

"I liked Troy a long time ago. I loved him. That's an old-timey word too, for a friendship between men. So once you love, in any way, you make a commitment. Give away a chunk of yourself. So he's calling the debt now. I don't like Debbie Ann. I think maybe she's a monster. I like Mary. And you."

"Thank you, Mike."

"Shirley, I got left behind somewhere. I'm put together of old-timey parts. I don't react modern. I'm still on this good-and-evil kick. Okay, it hit both of us, soon as we found they were gone, they went off to crawl in the sack. Right? So I say, on one level, worse things happen all the time, don't they? It's incestuous only on a legal basis, no? It's a forty-year-old man, a twenty-three-year-old woman, unrelated. So I ask myself, why the sweat?

Isn't copulation getting about as casual as shaking hands in certain circles? Who is going to tell on them anyhow? But all that fast talk I give myself doesn't work so good. Maybe they're walking on the beach. Maybe not. If they're doing what we thought they were doing, then I'm just full up to here with outraged indignation, righteous horror. A real bluenose. Because it is evil. Capital E. Rodenska is old-timey. That's my message to you."

"Evil," she said thoughtfully, "not because of the act itself, but who it can hurt. Mary, mostly. That's what evil is, hurting people."

"Would that be your only rule? That's pagan, isn't it? Shouldn't there be rules of behavior? If Mary never knows, Mary isn't hurt. That's the way practically anything could be justified. You have to have a rule book and a scorecard."

"They keep changing the rules and nobody keeps track of the score any more."

"I'm inner-directed. That's the new-timey word for old-timey. You're a child of your times, Shirley. So you're outer-directed more than I am. You go most by what people think of you, and I have to go almost all the way by what I think of me. So, contemplating a deal like what we thought, I get horror, and, honestly, what do you get?"

262

"Not horror. It would just be . . . offensive to me. It would make me feel crawly, because it's an offense against good taste. Like watching your bridge partner peek into somebody's hand. Maybe a little more than that because it's in an emotional area. Maybe more like being in a supermarket and watching some woman bashing her four-year-old around and shrieking at him in public. You wonder what it's doing to her and doing to the child, basically."

"I don't like to think what it could do to Troy. A man who despises himself can do a lot of filthy things, Shirley. Symbols, maybe. But what if he goes too far? What if he does something that really sickens him beyond his capacity to endure it? Then what does he do?"

She yawned. "The questions are getting too hard, Gramps. You are so old and wise. And the party is over. And I am pooped. So walk me home, huh?"

"I guess I can hobble along beside you, youngster. Wheezing."

They went out into the night. They saw the running lights of something big, far out in the Gulf. The slow and meager swell curled lazy, thumped the beach, hissed and sighed.

As they walked toward the road she said, "Tomorrow I am being taken out fishing. By uncle. We'll be after kingfish. I hate fishing. Have you been out on Troy's boat?"

"Not yet. I looked it over. It looks nice."

"I haven't been out on it either. Debbie Ann says it's dreamy. And very, very fast. I haven't even had a close look at it."

He remembered later how casually he said, "Let's go peer at it by moonlight. We can stand on the flying bridge and pretend we're cruising the Bahamas. I'll be showing you places nobody ever saw before."

"And how's *your* tennis?"

They cut diagonally across the raked sand of the wide yard toward the boat basin where the *Skimmer III* sat pallid and quiet, moored to the pilings of the dock, serene in starlight. They made little noise as they walked across the sand. As they neared the boat he heard a curious creaking, an oddly familiar yet momentarily unidentifiable sound, audible over the surf sound when they were six feet from the boat, as rhythmic as the sea sound, but considerably faster. He did not yet understand when Shirley grabbed his arm with surprising force, pulling him to a stop. She made a hissing sound. He looked down into her eyes, dark and wide in the moonlight, and then suddenly realized that the quickening sound came from the cabin aboard the *Skim-*

mer III , the surging and creaking of the nautical bunk, the strenuous, cyclic pulsations of a mating, that only rhythm in the world which is almost as old as the cadence of the seas.

And they turned away, quickly, like thieves who had been challenged in the night, and before they had reached that point a few feet away where the metronome of the flesh would be buried by the night sounds of the Gulf, full confirmation came in the thin, raw cry of a woman, so like the daytime sounds of the terns, full of pain and triumph and self-mocking.

They walked quickly to the beach and walked three hundred yards without a word to each other. Then Shirley paused and walked more slowly up the slope of the beach and sat down at a place where a storm had cut into the beach sand, leaving an abrupt two-foot miniature cliff, as comfortable as a hassock for sitting. He sat beside her. She dug cigarettes and lighter out of her straw purse, lit his cigarette and her own. She snapped the lighter, a sound like a pistol being cocked in the darkness.

"Pretty," she said, and her tone was not pretty.

"We don't know for sure that it was Debbie Ann and — "

"For God's sake, Mike! Why don't you go

make a formal identification? Take their fingerprints."

"All right. We both knew it when they took
off. Suspicion confirmed. Charming girl, isn't
she?"

"And he's a doll."

"I have a bad feeling, Shirley. I think bad
things are going to happen."

"Have happened, don't you mean?"

"I don't know what I mean. All I know is
Mary deserves a hell of a lot better from a husband and a daughter."

"Juicy gossip for Riley Key."

"Are you going to spread it?"

"How would you like a smack in the mouth,
Rodenska?"

"I wasn't accusing you. Settle down. I was
just wondering how it would get around."

"It isn't any great trick to tell about a man
and a woman when you see them together in
public. It always shows. People always guess.
They're either too utterly casual with each
other, or too tensed-up. Mary will sense it
right away. It stinks, Mike."

"It stinks."

She shoved the burning end of the cigarette
into the sand and stood up. "Now you have a
longer walk."

"How so?"

"I was sleepy enough to go right back. But that — tender little episode has made me restless. We're going to walk right on by the Tennysons'. Okay?"

"All the way to the Club, if you want."

"I'm not *that* restless."

"Is conversation in order?"

"I'll let you know when it is. Mike, I am being awfully irritable. I'm sorry. Give me a little while and I'll be all right again. Right now I feel a little sewery, as if the girl on the boat was me. Could be me. I think I'll stop being chummy with Debbie Ann. Not all of a sudden. I'll taper off."

"Sound idea."

And so they walked in silence, not as quickly as before, walking where the sand was hard-packed, past the Tennyson house and on down the long wide empty beach. The night was utterly still. Palms fronds were cut out of black metal, striped with silver along the edges from half a high-riding moon. The beach was gypsum, left over from an alpine movie of long ago, held in place by a wrought-iron Gulf that infrequently, casually, lifted and thudded against the sand.

Mike had begun to recover his composure as premonitions of disaster faded. She walked neatly and placidly beside him, their moon

267

shadows black against white sand.

She made a small sniffling noise. When she made it again he looked at her and saw that she was walking with her head bowed, her shoulders slightly hunched.

"Hey!" he said softly and stopped.

She faced him, lifted her head reluctantly, and he saw the tear tracks on her face, rivulets of mercury.

"Hey, girl," he said gently. Such gentleness was a mistake. It crumpled her face. It brought out of her a hollow yowl of grief and plunged her against his chest, clutching at him, sobbing and sniffling against his ear, shuddering within the circle of his heavy arms, so automatically and protectively placed around her. He heard the strangled gulpings, rasping breath, little cries of loneliness. The top of her shining black head came to the level of his eyebrows. The straw purse thudded onto the damp sand.

He made the automatic and traditional sounds of comfort. There, there. And, Now, now. And, It's all right. There, there. Take it easy, honey, patting her slim shoulders and back with a big earnest clumsy hand, supporting, against him, most of the weight of her.

A woman is soft and fragrant. A weeping, trusting woman is compellingly appealing.

The ape-thing had been crouched back there in the brush, somnolent, half-dozing, scratching its hairy chest and belly, and peering from time to time at the females of the tribe. Suddenly he selected a female, stood up on knotted bandy legs, thumped a stone fist against a bass chest, grunted and came waddling out of the brush into the clearing where the female stood, curious, half-poised for fight. . . .

Mike Rodenska could not pinpoint the precise moment of transition. He knew only that he had been standing trying to comfort a weeping young woman, and that he had been feeling fatherly and awkward as he waited for the storm to diminish. He had been glad, he knew, when it started to diminish. But somewhere along in there, things had changed. It was a new relationship. Perhaps their mouths had come together by accident. But there it was. Her mouth upon his in a raw, warm, soft, compulsive insistence, taking eagerly the weight of his mouth. His hands, moving not in comfort but in more intricate design, readying her. Her fingers stabbing into the meat of his back. Her hips beginning to pulse against him, her breasts hard against him, his right hand sliding down to cup her haunch as that great elemental force dizzied them, beseeching them to find a place, very near, to lie down and join themselves together.

The alarm bells were all going off in the back of his mind, and there was a little man back there, very busy, running around stuffing rags between the clappers and the bells, deadening the clamor. She ripped her mouth away and made a convulsive sound and thrust so hard against his chest she pushed herself back and away, off balance, almost falling, but recovering to stand six feet away, breathing deep and hard, black hair wild across her face.

"My God, God, God!" she said, panting.

"I didn't . . . I wasn't . . . I didn't mean to . . ."

"Oh, Mike."

"Look. Don't cry again. Just do that. Don't cry."

"I won't cry."

"This was just an accident that didn't happen. Okay? Nobody's fault."

"I'm an accident walking around looking for a place to happen. Looking for a person to happen to. Me and Debbie Ann. Oh, Christ!"

"Feel sorry for yourself. It sounds dandy. I didn't start it. You didn't start it. My God, would we want to? What the hell is this place tonight, a convention hotel, maybe? Listen,

Shirley. Look around. Moonlight, tropic night, beach, and a couple or three drinks. You can figure that a lot of people have got carried away under much worse conditions. So who are we? Invulnerable? You broke it up. I didn't. I knew I should, but I kept telling myself I'd get around to breaking it up in just a minute or two. Sure! Like maybe by dawn. You broke it up, so select a medal. But don't go bleating around about being sorry for yourself, or being just like Debbie Ann."

And suddenly, astonishingly, she was laughing. Genuine laughter. Not a trace of hysteria. He felt abused and indignant. Don't laugh at the little bald man, honey. It ain't polite. Then he sensed that she was laughing at both of them, and he saw how funny it was, how it was funny in a very special way, so he laughed too, and it felt good to laugh. As they walked back toward the Tennyson house the laughter kept coming back, and each time it was a little less than before, and by the time they got there it was all gone.

"What a crazy, crazy night, Mike!"

"I've spent quieter evenings."

"I'd like to fall in love with you, Mike. I think I could. I don't think it would be hard to do."

"Don't give it a thought. Please. I've got enough problems."

"All right. I won't fall in love with you. You know, I feel better than I have in months and months, right now. Tears and laughter. Therapy, I guess. From now on I'm going to be all right, Mike. From now on I'm not going to take myself so darn seriously."

"It's a sound program."

"And I've been thoroughly kissed. That's sort of a reassurance."

"As if you needed any."

"Thanks, Mike."

"Don't mention it."

"Goodnight, Mike. If there's anything I can possibly do about . . . the mess at the Jamison house, let me know."

"Sure. Good night, Shirley."

He walked back alone, quite slowly, only half-aware of the beauty of the night as he did some cautious probing within himself. I kissed a pretty woman. Nothing else happened. A lot else could easily have happened. Or maybe not so easily. Who can tell? But let's say it could have. What then? It would have put me right on Troy's ball team, playing left field. Because I can't feel casual about a thing like that.

All right. So I feel relieved I didn't get into

a mess. But I feel more than that. Strengthened, somehow. In a way I don't understand. Because we laughed at ourselves? Maybe. Because I accept concern and involvement in the lives of Troy and Debbie Ann and Mary? Maybe that's some of it. But here is what I know. Those big waves are going to continue to come at me when I'm not looking. And they'll hurt. But tonight, somehow, I got my feet planted a little better. The waves won't do quite as much damage. And I can feel a little sorry that they won't. So I cannot yet look squarely at the idea of being alone, but I can look sort of sideways at it.

When he got back he took a chair off the cabaña porch and placed it on the beach, facing the Gulf. He sat there a long time. He struck up a lazy conversation with Buttons. What do you think, kiddo? I think you're still letting people take advantage of you, Mike lamb. Leaning on you. The Curse of Rodenska. Okay, I am, but it's something to do, and they need somebody, and I haven't been able to do much of anything anyway. What about Shirley? What do you want me to say about her, Mike? She's young and pretty and reasonably bright and pretty mixed-up. Don't take her on as a problem. Take somebody on, some day, Mike, but not because you think they need you. Wait until you need them. Okay, but how about the way I all of a sudden found myself climbing all over her? I knew you were going to get around to that, Mike. What are you after, a clear conscience? Absolution? *I* am certainly willing to testify you've never been exactly backward in that department. But you won't get any built-in excuses or forgiveness out of me. Your degree of continence is your own problem, my boy. Now that my concern is . . . academic, you have only yourself to live with. But I can tell you you've never been cheap — if that helps you any. Thanks, girl, but that wasn't exactly what I was digging for. I know, Mike.

So he dozed there, and when he opened his eyes the world had changed. He felt a little chilly and stiff. The gray of dawn had come. He yawned, growled, fingered his chin stubble, and carted the chair back onto the porch. There was a line of red in the east. He felt totally relaxed and slightly surly, and a little bit reckless.

Reckless enough or, as he later admitted to himself, curious enough to creep up upon the *Skimmer*, board her with great stealth, and move forward along the side deck until he could look down into the cabin. There wasn't enough daylight yet so that he could see distinctly. He didn't particularly wish to see with total clarity. He looked down through the oblong of screening. They lay entangled in the bunk, a blanket across their hips. Troy snorted in his sleep. Mike could see enough of a pale scramble of limbs to know the two of them were there, but not to be able to tell which was which.

A tender scene, he thought. I will be the loving dicky bird and go gather dead leaves and cover them up.

He stepped ashore, scowling, and trudged to his room, went to bed, and fell into sleep like stepping into a mine shaft.

nine

At eleven o'clock on Sunday morning, as Mike was on his second cup of coffee and had just lighted the first cigar of the day, Debbie Ann came out onto the patio and joined him at the small table. She moved quickly and smiled a cordial greeting. She wore pale blue linen shorts and a white shirt with long sleeves, cut like a man's.

"Durelda tells me you've eaten enough for three. She's very pleased with you. All I can manage is hot tea, and a small experiment with dry toast."

"Hung?" he asked.

"Uh *huh!* Totally."

He looked at her with inward awe. She gave a superficial impression of daintiness, freshness and good health. She looked not quite seventeen. He looked at her dispassionately and marveled at the duplicity and resilience of woman. Her mouth had a bruised and pulpy look. There were dark shadows under her eyes. A scratch on her throat disappeared into the white shirt. And he had noticed that when she had seated herself, it had been with a trace of awkwardness, a barely perceptible wince of pain or stiffness.

The little filly had had a hard ride over the midnight steeplechase. Brown hands had lifted her over the moats and stone walls and brought her, winded and sprung, back to the stables.

He also detected a smugness about her, a little flavor of accomplishment, the end product of stolen satisfactions. Yet there was defiance commingled with the smugness, and perhaps some doubt. She was like a naughty child who would, through the blatant innocence of her poise, attempt to evade the deserved spanking.

Durelda served the tea and toast and went back to the kitchen.

"Saturday night comes around a little too often," Debbie Ann said. "Somebody should change something."

"We lost track of you people around eleven o'clock."

She raised her eyebrows. "Oh, did you? You two seemed so enthralled with each other I didn't think you'd notice if the roof blew off."

"She's a nice girl. Fun to talk to. But en-thralled isn't the word. Sorry. I'd like to be more exciting, but I can't manage it."

"Maybe you don't get enough encourage-ment."

"Where did you go?"

She had bitten into the toast. She took her time before answering. "Oh, we walked up and down the beach to sober Troy up, and me too, I might add. And then we did a little moonlight swimming. Nothing very exciting. Is Troy up yet?"

"I haven't seen him."

"He'll have a head again. Not as bad as last time, but a pretty substantial one."

"Who are you trying to kid, Debbie Ann? Me or yourself or Troy or your mother? Or everybody?"

She clattered the teacup down and stared at him. "Kid who about what? Make sense." Her eyes were wide and utterly innocent.

"Before I walked Shirley home we went over to take a close look at the boat in the moonlight."

"Oh," she said in a small voice. She turned dull red under her tan. "Oh! That's a little embarrassing, friend."

"Just that? Embarrassing?"

With narrowed eyes she said, "What would

you like me to do? Tear my hair out? Beat my head on the wall? Set fire to myself?"

"Those aren't bad ideas, but maybe you could feel a little ashamed. A little guilty."

She shrugged. "Not particularly. It's better if nobody knew. But you do know. And I'm assuming it was an accident. It's too bad, but it isn't exactly the end of the world."

"All right. It isn't the end of the world. I'll buy that. But it's a filthy relationship. Shameful."

Her smirk didn't quite come off. "Moral judgments so early in the morning? Come now, Mike. Loosen up. It was just one of those proximity things. That's all. Nobody's fault. It's been building for a long time. That ole black magic. And sooner or later it was going to happen, and it did. A little debauch, to clear the air. It isn't really meaningful, Mike."

"To Mary?"

"Her marriage is bitched up beyond all recognition, and you know that as well as I do. What did she lose by what we did? Nothing at all."

"I keep wondering what she'd think of you."

"Oh Mike, really. Can't you guess? If she ever finds out — and I don't see why she has to — I know just how she'd react. Even if I gave a detailed confession, she wouldn't listen. It would be her poor baby trying to conceal a case of drunken rape for the sake of the family honor, to avoid scandal. I'll say to you that it *was* a little sneaky, and mostly my fault — hell, entirely my fault — and probably it shouldn't have happened, but it did and it's over and it might happen again and might not, and who can tell? But you don't have to act as if I'm a criminal or something."

He frowned at her, studying her. "I guess I don't understand. You seem more mischievous than vicious. But you can perform a vicious act of seduction, a dangerous, damaging act, and have no more idea of the meaning of that act than a sand flea. You can even defend that act."

"And why not? It's a big busy world, Mike. Lots of things go on."

"I guess it's because you're empty," he said. "Empty in a way you don't comprehend. It's like being a psychopath. You have no basis for morality, do you?"

"That has the reek of church talk, doesn't it?"

"All right. You are Godless. A reincarnation of the same scented bitch that has appeared and reappeared in history. I thought they were evil women. Consciously evil. I didn't know they were just empty. It's kind of disappointing in a way. It takes the drama out of it. They weren't overthrowing kings and princes and kingdoms out of malice after all. They were just satisfying a little clitoral itch, and when things started falling down they probably looked around and said, 'Who, me?' "

She stared at him with a flat, surprising malevolence. "*Now*, I get it."

"You get what?"

"All this literate lecture routine. You didn't make out with McGuire, did you? So you get righteous about the whole thing. I'm real nasty. And if you'd made it, my friend, you wouldn't have one word to say, would you? I'm so sorry, dolling."

She laughed, and he sensed she was trying to make her laughter sound completely genuine, but her eyes were not right for laughter. There was a wariness in them. The laughter sounded more artificial after it had stopped.

"We can't communicate," he said. "Words don't mean the same things to us. It makes me scared about my two boys. I don't want them to get as far away from reality as you are, Debbie Ann."

"Reality! If anybody is living in a dream

world, it isn't me."

"You sure of that?"

"Positive."

He stood up and looked down at her. The sun was bright on the table and on her hair. She looked up at him politely, with an assured half-smile.

"Honey," he said. "Just you hope nothing happens to wake you up. Because if you ever wake up, you're going to have to look in a mirror. And you won't like it. That is my message."

He sensed that had he been within range, she would have raked his face with her nails. "It must be comforting to be so holy. What has anybody ever done for me? I'll do anything I damn please. I've got no obligations to anybody."

"You have to eat scraps and they beat you and beat you. Things are rough everywhere."

"I can't understand all this fuss over . . ."

He didn't hear the rest of it because he had walked away, feeling sickened. He went to the guest wing and washed his hands. He was annoyed at himself for even trying to talk to her. Something was happening to people. To the young ones. Maybe, he thought, we've taken something away from them and haven't given them anything to replace it. Maybe human nature does change every thousand years or so, and this is the time of change. I don't like it. They figured out what made the dinosaurs extinct. A batch of fast little mammals sprung up, and they lived off dinosaur eggs. They didn't give a damn for dinosaurs. They just loved those eggs. Wonder what happened to them when there weren't any more eggs.

He had alerted Durelda, but it was not until two o'clock that she came out onto the beach and told him Mr. Troy was up. Debbie Ann had gone boiling off somewhere in her car. Somehow the word had been spread that the Sunday routine at the Jamisons' was finished. There was pedestrian traffic up and down the beach, but nobody stopped at the house for the buffet brunch.

He gave Troy a few minutes and then went up to the house. Troy sat on the patio drinking black coffee. He was clean-shaven, dressed in fresh slacks and a crisp sports shirt. His eyes were bloodshot and he had the shakes so badly it was difficult for him to light a cigarette.

Mike sat at the table and said, "Another nice day."

"Certainly is."

"Lot of people on the beach."

283

"Are there?"

He made Mike feel uneasy. There was a curious remoteness about him. There was too long a delay before his automatic replies. His eyes had a curious staring look, a look almost of blindness. Mike suddenly realized where he had seen that same remoteness before. He had seen it in cases of shock. Once he had arrived at the scene of an accident after it had happened. A man had skidded into a light pole. It had struck on the passenger side, crushing the man's wife to death. There had been a stack of folded pamphlets in the car, advertisements for the small business they owned. The pamphlets were widely scattered on the wet street. The man had gotten out of the car. His right wrist was grotesquely broken. With his left hand he was slowly, carefully, picking up the pamphlets, one by one. When Mike had gone to him to stop him he had looked up with much the same expression Troy was wearing.

"I guess we never got around to that therapy you were talking about last night, Troy." Mike heard his own voice, curiously jolly, elaborately casual.

" . . . Therapy?"

"You were going to drink yourself back to that moment of truth or whatever you call it."

" . . . Was I?"

"Yes. I guess it didn't work."

" . . . No, I guess it didn't."

"Are you all right?"

" . . . Me? I'm all right. Why?"

"I don't know. You seem listless."

" . . . Hung over, I guess."

"What are the plans for today?"

" . . . Plans?"

"What are we going to do?"

" . . . I don't know."

"Will you join me on the beach?"

" . . . On the beach? No. No, I don't think so. I'm . . . I'm going away." Troy got up, turned rather slowly and walked into the living room, toward the master bedroom. There was a jerkiness about his stride, a lack of coordination, a somnambulistic quality.

"Where are you going?" Mike demanded. Troy did not answer. Mike followed him into the bedroom. Troy took a suitcase out of the storage wall and opened it on Mary's bed. He went to the bureau and began to select things from the top drawer.

"Where are you going?"

"Away from here."

"Why?"

"It's time to get away from here."

"Troy. Troy! Hold it a minute."

Troy put a pile of shirts into the suitcase and straightened up. "You can't stop me."

"What does running away from it solve?"

"You don't understand, Mike."

"I think I've got more of the picture than you have, maybe. You were drunk. And it was her idea, not yours. She set you up for it."

Troy stared at him. The immobility was gone from his face. It twisted in a horrid muscular spasm. "What did we do? Mail out invitations?"

"It was an accident. Shirley and I went to look at the boat."

"Does . . . *she* know you know?"

"Yes. It doesn't upset her much. I tried to talk to her about it. I couldn't reach her."

Troy looked down at his fist. "I thought Jerranna was as low as you could go. I was using Jerranna as a club to beat Mary with. I don't know why. Maybe because she's too damn good. But this — with Debbie Ann — it's too much. I've got to get out of here."

"You afraid it will happen again?"

"She told me a swim would sober me up. She turned her back. I stripped and went in. I swam out a couple of hundred feet, slow. When I stopped she was right next to me, laughing in that damn tiny little voice. She shoved me under. I chased her and caught her. Lots of laughs. Sure I was drunk. But I knew what I was doing. I wasn't blacked out. By the time we came out there wasn't even any attempt to put the clothes back on. We grabbed them up and went right to the boat. I can't tell you how she looked, Mike, naked, soaking wet, laughing in the moonlight. I knew it was as wrong a thing as a man can do. But I didn't give a damn. I told myself it couldn't be a serious thing, the way she kept laughing."

"Are you going away so it won't happen again?"

"No."

"Then why?"

"So I won't kill her. I woke up first, early. I was going to do it then. I put my hand on her throat. It woke her up. I couldn't do it then. Maybe I wouldn't be able to do it the second time, but I'd come closer. And then the next time I could probably do it. I've got to get out."

"Where will you go?"

"I don't know. Over to Jerranna's, maybe."

"What am I supposed to tell Mary?"

"Tell her she's better off. She is. Tell her to get out, like Bunny did."

"It wasn't your fault."

"She's my daughter, Mike."

"Stepdaughter."

"And it was just fine, Mike. Fine last night. Fine again this morning. She's real good." An expression of thoroughly savage mockery changed his face. "Try it any time. It's free. It's on the house. Be my guest."

Mike watched in silence as Troy packed. Maybe it was a good answer. It might be the easiest way for Mary. And of the three of them, she was now the only one worth any consideration.

"How about the land project, Troy?"

"I'll go to the lawyer's office tomorrow and sign my stock over to Mary. Maybe she can salvage something. There isn't anything else . . . to turn over to her. Not a damn thing." He took out his wallet and looked into it. "Got any money?"

Mike checked. "Sixty bucks. Want that?"

"You won't get it back."

"It doesn't matter. Here."

Troy put the money away. He started to shake hands and then pulled his hand back. "There's no damn sense in that little gesture. It doesn't mean anything. I don't want your friendship, Mike. I don't want the obligation."

"Okay. So this is the end of that, too." He hesitated. "Are you going to take a car?"

"No."

"Can I drive you up to Ravenna?"

"No."

"Goodby, Troy."

Troy looked at him and through him and walked out. Mike followed him slowly. Saying he didn't give a damn. Fighting his feeling of involvement. All my life, nibbled to death by lame ducks. Looking into empty people, looking for something I can't describe, finding it sometimes. Buttons told me one time what I would have been if I'd come along ahead of the linotype. One of those old boys wandering around, telling stories to the tribes. Anything with a maximum exposure to people.

So there goes Troy Jamison, walking out of life, coat over his arm, suitcase making the other shoulder sag. Too bitched up to be survival-prone. These are the years when the basic, thousand-percent sons of bitches get along nifty. They flourish. And so, thank God, do those rare ones who are both strong and good. Like Mary. But all the Troys are screwed. Because they're half and half. Oversimplification? The good part can't live with the son of a bitch. And the price of everything is marked up. No bargain basements. No special clearance sales. You pay top dollar every time, and it stings.

There should be a new operation. A bitch-ectomy. Scalpel, clamps, sutures, deep sedation. Whichever aspect is dominant, remove the other one. Then everybody survives. Only two kinds of people. The energetic, enthusiastic, functioning son of a bitch. And the tin Jesuses.

Make a dull world. Cancel the research.

He walked out onto the path. When he was fifteen feet from the road he could see, beyond a monster sea grape, Troy walking south in the sunlight. Sunday afternoon. You don't get tragedy, he thought, without some grotesquerie, some little taint of slapstick. Everybody is his own comedian. The wittle boy packed him wittle bag with him teddy bear and outer-space pistol and runned away.

Through the shimmer of heat he saw the car coming and soon recognized the Porsche, top down, Debbie Ann at the wheel, her hair tamed by a bright scarf.

"Don't stop," he said aloud. "Don't stop, girl!"

He thought for a moment she wouldn't, but she passed Troy and stopped and backed up very competently, then kept backing up, maintaining his pace, evidently speaking to him. Then she increased the speed and stopped twenty yards beyond him and got out

290

and stood waiting for him.

As Troy reached her and stopped and put the suitcase down, Mike began to run. He couldn't remember the last time he had tried to run fast. He had about three hundred yards to go, and he didn't have the build for it. The years had done something to level ground. It all ran uphill. And he felt as if the long fleet stride of youth had shrunk to about eight inches.

He was fifty yards away when Troy hit her. Though sweat had run into his left eye, he saw it clearly. It was not a slap. It was not one of those wild windmill swings of the angry amateur. This had the merciless competence of the professional, despite the fact it was a right-hand lead. Elbow close. Nice timing, starting from heels firmly planted, so the full power of legs and back and shoulders got into it. A straight jolt, upwards, the fist moving maybe ten inches before the point of impact, and with a nice follow-through — happening so quickly she had not the slightest chance to duck or move back or even begin to raise her hands.

It was the noise that made his stomach turn over. You could achieve the same effect if you took a nylon stocking, packed the foot tightly with raw chopped liver, and then swung it three times around your head before slamming it against a brick wall.

Debbie Ann went up and back, a doll slow in the sunlight, landing rump-first across the hood of the Porsche to collapse there, supine, almost motionless for an instant before sliding forward, down the blunt pitch of the hood of the Porsche, making one half turn to thud face down on the sand-and-shell road, in front of the wheels, one arm pinned under her, the other extended over her head, legs sprawled, all of her utterly still.

Mike arrived, gasping for breath. Troy glanced toward him, but not at him. He massaged the knuckles of his right hand. He picked up his suitcase and jacket and walked on, walked south, without looking back.

As Mike knelt beside her, four people were suddenly there. He had not seen them approach. There was an elderly couple in swimming clothes, both of them brown, spindly, white-haired. He remembered seeing them at the Club, but not meeting them. The other was Marg Laybourne and her husband. It had happened almost in front of their house.

"It's Debbie Ann!" Marg yelped. "What's happening? Where is Troy going? What happened to her?"

"I'm a doctor," the spindly brown man said

with quiet authority. "If you'd give me some room, sir . . ."

Mike gladly moved out of the way. The old man knelt in the road, found the pulse in the side of the throat deftly.

"Did the car hit her? Did she fall out of it?" Marg demanded.

The doctor sat back on his haunches. "I'm retired. I'm not licensed to practice in Florida. I would say, however, that in this case it might not be wise to wait for an ambulance to come out from Ravenna. I don't want to move her any more than necessary. I want something we can use as a stretcher, something rigid, a pillow, two blankets and a station wagon. Quickly!"

Marg stopped asking questions and did some effective organizing. After she and her husband had hurried away, the doctor looked up mildly at Mike and said, "You saw him strike her also?"

"Yes."

"The way you were running attracted our attention, and we saw it happen."

"Horrible," the doctor's wife murmured.

"There could be fractured vertebrae. That's why I want to be very careful. And there will be shock. You can see how profusely she's beginning to perspire."

293

Mr. Laybourne arrived with a collapsed army cot. The doctor said it would do splendidly. By the time they had unfolded it and placed it beside her, with the legs still collapsed, Marg Laybourne was backing the big Buick station wagon into position. Three cars had stopped. About twenty people had gathered around, looking avid and nervous, whispering misinformation to each other.

The doctor carefully instructed Mike and Mr. Laybourne as to where to hold her, what to do when he gave the word to roll her onto the cot frame. The doctor handled her head.

"Now," he said, and they eased her onto the cot. Mike gave an involuntary grunt of shock when he saw her face. The whole left side of it was bloodied and crushed in, grotesquely. Dust and shell fragments were stuck to the blood. The other half of her face was a soapy gray, beaded heavily with sweat. Powdered shell and dust clung to her parted lips.

Mike and Mr. Laybourne, plus four volunteers, carefully slid the improvised stretcher into the back of the station wagon. The doctor tucked the two blankets around her. He arranged the pillow in a way to minimize head movement.

"Go gently on the rough road and take corners carefully," the doctor said, instructing

Mr. Laybourne. He turned to Mike. "You, sir, and the lady, might ride in back with her. Go directly to the emergency entrance. If I could go in and use the phone in your home, they will know what to expect. They'll be all set up to treat her quickly for shock."

"Go right ahead. There's a phone near the front entrance, on your left," Marg said.

A young man approached Mike and said, "I know Debbie Ann. The keys are in her car. I'll run it up into the carport. Okay?"

"Thanks a lot."

"What happened to her?"

"She fell."

"Out of the top of that pine tree?"

Mike got in. Traffic on the trail was infuriatingly dense and slow until the continual bellowing of the horn on the Buick attracted the attention of a state highway-patrol car, headed the other way. Within a minute he was behind them, siren keening. Mike pointed at Debbie Ann. As the patrol car passed, Mike yelled, "Ravenna Hospital!" and saw the trooper nod.

The siren opened the traffic ahead of them. Marg, well braced, held Debbie Ann's shoulders. Mike held her by the hips. After one hard swerve when they still managed to hold her immobile, Marg turned and gave Mike a hard, impudent grin, and it astonished the daylights out of him to realize he could probably learn to like this woman. She was idle, silly and mischievous — but she reacted well to a thing like this.

They were prepared for them at the hospital, with the bottle of plasma all rigged and ready.

While Charlie took the car off to the hospital parking lot, Marg and Mike went to the waiting room.

"Wonder if I should phone Mary before we get the whole scoop," he said.

"Phone her, of course, Mr. Rodinsky. She'll want to be here in any case. That child is badly hurt."

"Rodenska."

"Troy did it, didn't he?"

"She fell."

"He's been so strange lately."

"I'll find a phone."

They said they thought Mrs. Jamison was out by the pool. If he would hold on a moment. It was a long moment before she came on the phone.

"Hello? Oh, Mike! I had the feeling it would be Troy. I don't know why. How are things?"

"Mary, I don't know any fancy way to say

this. I'm at Ravenna Hospital. Debbie Ann is hurt. I think you better come right here . . . Mary?"

"I'm still here," she said. "It was that damned car, wasn't it? She drives like a fool. And she's . . . dead."

"She's not dead!" he said angrily. "And it wasn't the car. She — fell and hit her face."

"Fell? Debbie Ann?"

"Yes. They're treating her in the emergency room right now."

"Is Troy with you? Why didn't Troy call me?"

"We can go into all that after you get here. Who's your regular doctor?"

"Sam Scherman, but Debbie Ann hasn't had to see him in years and years. But you better let him know, I guess. I can't understand how she could . . . I guess I should stop talking. I'll be along very soon, Mike."

"Don't worry about it. She'll be okay."

"Is she . . . disfigured, Mike?"

"Temporarily. She — wants you here."

"Tell her I'm on my way, Mike."

He went back to the waiting room. Marg and Charlie looked at him. "How did she take it?" Marg asked.

"Pretty good. She'll come down by cab right away."

"That girl is in bad, bad shape," Charlie said heavily.

Marg leaned forward and lowered her voice. "You don't have to be so secretive, Mr. Rodenska. I'm perfectly aware of the fact you don't like me one bit."

"Now, Marg!" Charlie said.

"It's perfectly true, darling. He made it quite clear the first time we met. Maybe I deserved it. I was feeling bitchy that day. Mr. Rodenska, Charlie and I are certainly aware of the fact that Mary and Troy have been having . . . problems. We call ourselves their friends. We haven't wanted to butt in. We've heard the rumors about another woman. We haven't helped spread those rumors. And we haven't in our own talks about it, taken sides. Maybe a little bit, on Mary's side, but that's only natural. Charlie and I have said that sooner or later either Troy or Mary or even both of them, might call on us for help. And we wouldn't back off just because it could be a messy situation. We would help. Is that clear?"

"Very."

"And so it has gotten messy. He got drunk and smashed the Chrysler. Mary has gone away by herself. We both saw Troy walking down the road, carrying a suitcase. He was walking *away* from Debbie Ann. Not looking back at all. He didn't turn when Charlie yelled at him and he couldn't help hearing him. So it's perfectly obvious that whatever happened to Debbie Ann, he did it. How messy can a situation get? Mary adores Debbie Ann. Personally, forgive the expression, I think she is a spoiled, selfish, tiresome little slut."

"Marg!" Charlie said. "Now, Marg!"

"Hush, darling. You know, Mr. Rodenska, that Mary won't be able to forgive Troy for hurting her so badly, hurting that invaluable daughter of hers. Here we are, perfectly willing to help in any way we can. So don't you think it would make sense to tell us what's going on?"

Mike thought it over. "Yes, I guess it would make sense. Maybe I should. But it isn't my option. How much people know, no matter how close they are, is Mary's business. And I've got a juicy problem of telling her how the girl got hurt. Once she knows the score and has had a chance to think things out, then you ask her. Okay?"

For a few minutes Marg stared at him with indignation and exasperation. And then suddenly she grinned at him. "If I ever *have* to tell somebody a secret, Mike, I'll look you up. It would stay a secret, wouldn't it?"

"I'll tell you one thing, Mrs. Laybourne.

You gave me that last-outpost-of-gracious-living routine, and I figured you for phony through and through."

"So you put on an act too, didn't you?"

"Sure I did. So my opinion is revised. Consider this an apology."

"Thank you. But I certainly don't know why I should feel pleased. I wasn't looking for your good opinion, Mike. And I am, in many respects, a phony. Right, Charlie?"

"You're always right, dear."

A huge young doctor with a bland round face and an eighth of an inch of bright orange brush-cut appeared in the doorway, filling it.

"I'm Doctor Pherson. Which of you belongs with the Hunter woman?"

"Hunter?" Mike said blankly. Then he remembered that was the name Marg had given them, Debbie Ann's married name. The pause gave Marg an opening that she could easily have taken. "We're neighbors and close friends and this man is just a house-guest." But she didn't take it. She waited. "I brought her in," Mike said.

The huge young doctor took him fifty feet up the corridor. "First I'll give you the scoop, and then you'll answer some questions. We just read the wet plates. Shock is under control. She's semi-conscious. She was hurting so bad, I deadened the areas of trauma. Sedation isn't indicated so soon after shock. She's got a cracked vertebra in her neck, a crushed left antrum, the cheekbone mashed back in, and the skin split over it, a simple jaw fracture, one molar knocked clean out and three loosened. There's no skull fracture, but there's indication of a dandy concussion. And I nearly forgot, a fracture of the middle finger of the right hand. The nurse caught that. I was about to miss it. She'll need to be watched close. I've ordered a special. We've fastened the jaw in place temporarily. We'll have to see if she's well enough to work on tomorrow. Who are you and what's the relationship?"

"Mike Rodenska. I'm just a house-guest."

"*Her* house-guest?"

"No. Her parents'. Her mother and her stepfather, that is. He's Troy Jamison."

"Oh. The builder. That place on Riley Key. Sure enough. That answers the question about the room. We've got a private room open right now, which is unusual, and we'll move her there from emergency. Who's their doctor?"

"Dr. Sam Scherman."

"I'll let him know. Where are her people?"

"Her mother should be getting here pretty soon. Will she be able to see her?"

301

"No reason why not, after we move her, but there won't be any conversation going on. Now we come to the bonus question. How did it happen?"

"She fell."

"Is that right?"

"She tripped and fell and . . . hit her face against the bumper guard on her car."

"She was standing by the car?"

"Yes."

"The car wasn't moving?"

"No."

"My friend, you can have a nice little chat with the cops. Your story is feeble. I'll list this one as assault with a deadly weapon and let them worry about the lies you're telling."

"All right," Mike said wearily. "I assume you'll keep this to yourself. Somebody hit her."

"With what? You're doing better."

"With his fist."

Mike received a stare of cold contempt. "Look my friend. I've got more to do than stand around here trying to pry the facts out of you. If you hit her, phone a lawyer. But stop wasting my time."

"I'm telling you the truth, damn it! I saw it happen. He hit her with his fist."

Pherson started to turn away and then

turned back, dubious, skeptical. "You really mean that?"

"I swear it's the truth."

"His fist! Who is this joker? King Kong? Floyd Patterson?"

"Doctor Pherson, if a man is disturbed, if he's on the edge of some sort of a breakdown, can he — be more powerful than he ordinarily would be?"

"How big is this guy?"

"Six two. Maybe close to two hundred pounds. But not in good shape. Forty years old."

Pherson frowned. "When the normal man smacks a woman he almost always instinctively pulls his punch. If a man that big got crazy mad enough . . . and her bone structure is fragile, small . . . you're not kidding me?"

Rodenska, with a trained reporter's skill, told Pherson exactly what he had seen.

Pherson shook his head. "Okay. I believe. But you better get hold of the cops right now and have them pick that boy up. He came awful damn close to killing her with one punch."

"I'd rather not."

"So you *still* want to talk to the law."

"Doctor, this is a family thing. It was her stepfather. Her mother doesn't know that yet. I told you, I'm just a house-guest. I'd really like to leave it up to Mrs. Jamison. Maybe she'll want to sign a complaint. I wouldn't know. But it's her — little problem."

The big doctor whistled softly. "My, my, my!" he said. "Any other witnesses?"

"Two. A retired doctor and his wife. He didn't seem talkative."

"Well, she *did* fall off the front end of that car. That's when she popped the finger. I'll put it down as a fall. I'm going off now, right away. Soon as I arrange the room and phone Sam Scherman. Should I tell Sam the score?"

"He'll believe you quicker than you believed me. And I guess he ought to know."

"Okay. And I'll leave the mother to you."

"Thanks so much."

"Sam will have some ideas about who should work on that face. Is she a pretty girl? It's hard to tell."

"Very pretty."

"They'll watch her close tonight. You couldn't call her critical, but concussions are tricky."

Mike thanked him. Apparently the heavy traffic delayed Mary. Mike was glad it did, because it gave Dr. Scherman a chance to get to the hospital and check on Debbie Ann before Mary arrived. Sam Scherman was in his fifties, an irascible little man who spoke his own brand of shorthand in a quick, light, bitter voice.

"Delivered that girl child," he said to Mike privately. "Third delivery in career. Post partum hemorrhage. Lost Mary, almost. Beautiful baby. Lovely girl. Damn Jamison. Used a rock or a club, clean job. Mary due?"

"Overdue," Mike said, feeling as if he was catching the shorthand disease.

"Jamison?"

"Packed and left."

"Why Marg and Charlie?"

"They helped bring her in. It happened almost in front of their house."

Scherman stared at him thoughtfully. "Man slugs a woman, it isn't politics, cheating at bridge. Emotions. Sex. And Mary away?"

"Doctor, I'd rather not make any guesses about — "

"First I'll settle her down about the girl, tell her we'll get Hanstohm from Tampa, put her face back together. Then with the pressure off, you better tell her who, where, how, why. She'll find out anyway. Gutty woman. Deserves whole score. Keep her away from that damn Marg. Here she is now."

Mary hurried to Sam Scherman, giving Mike the absent glance she would give a stranger. "Sam! Where is she? How is she?

What happened?"

"Come along. Talk on the way up."

Mike went back to the waiting room and told the Laybournes Mary had arrived and had gone up with Scherman to take a look at Debbie Ann. It was fifteen minutes before she came back, accompained by the doctor, arguing with him.

"But I *want* to stay with her, Sam! Really!"

"Nonsense. No danger. Go home. And you people go home."

"But Sam!"

"Maybe tomorrow she needs you. So then you're dead for sleep. What good are you? You got that Placidil left?"

"Yes, there's a few . . . "

"Take one tonight. Come tomorrow with flowers. Smiling. Stop arguing."

Mary permitted herself to be led out to the station wagon. Charlie had set the rear seat up again, refolded the cot. Mike got in back with Mary. She seemed stunned.

As they turned out of the parking lot she said, "But what happened?"

"It was an accident," Mike said. "She took a fall." He waited for Marg to contradict him, but she kept silent.

"Just an accident," Charlie said ponderously.

"Where did she fall?"

"I'll show you how it happened when we get home," Mike said.

"Where's Troy?"

"I'll tell you about that too," he said, and touched her hand with a warning pressure. She looked quickly at him and he saw the sudden comprehension in her eyes — her understanding that whatever it was that he wanted to tell her, he did not want to tell her in front of the Laybournes.

"Poor baby," Mary murmured. "People seem so . . . alone in a hospital."

"She'll mend fast," Mike said. "She's healthy."

When they got back onto the Key one half of a florid sun showed above the steel edge of the Gulf and the water birds were heading for their mangrove homestead. Mary, with warmth, declined Marg and Charlie's offer of further help, and thanked them for all they had done. Durelda's Oscar was waiting for her. Durelda came out to meet them in the yard as the station wagon drove away.

"Miz Mary," she said excitedly, "I was waiting on you. Something bad is going on and I can't find out a thing about it. Some boy brang Miz Debbie Ann's car back and said she got hurt and they was taking her to the hospital so I phoned the hospital and they toll me she was doing well as expected, so with nobody telling me nothing I toll Oscar I'd just wait right here until somebody come to let me know."

"Thanks for waiting, Durelda. I really appreciate it. Debbie Ann had a bad fall and hurt her face, but she's all right now. I'm sorry nobody thought to let you know."

"They said she was lyin' an' bleedin' in the road," Durelda said darkly. "Run over, I wondered. I looked at the little car and there was no blood at all."

"You go on home now. You've had a long wait."

"I can anyway carry your bag inside before I go, Miz Mary. You home for good?"

"I guess so, Durelda."

She started toward the house carrying the suitcase she had taken away from Mike, saying over her shoulder to them as they followed her, "With you gone ever'thing gets messed up around here, nobody telling nobody nothing."

"I should have phoned you, Durelda," Mike said.

"Surely you should," said Durelda.

After Durelda left, Mary stood in the living room looking out toward the Gulf, her back to the room. "Troy packed a bag," she said quietly.

"Yes. He left, Mary."

"For good?"

"That was the impression he gave."

She turned toward him, angrily. "Did you try to stop him? Did you?"

"What do you think?"

"I'm sorry, Mike. How did she fall? What's happening? Sam acted strange. Marg and Charlie acted funny. You better tell me."

"Can I fix you a drink?"

She laughed in a mirthless way. "One of the little niceties of the culture, Mike. People don't say brace yourself. They don't say I hate to tell you this. They ask you if you want a drink. Yes, I want a drink. But if you take more than sixty seconds bringing it to me, I'll go out of my mind."

It was dusk on the terrace. He took the drinks out there. She followed him.

"All right, Mike. I'm sitting. I'm braced. This is a strong drink. Aim and fire."

"Troy drank heavily last night. He didn't get up until about two. As soon as he had some coffee, he packed a bag. I couldn't get much out of him. He didn't want me to give him a ride. Debbie Ann was coming home in the car. She saw him walking with the suitcase. She stopped. Apparently he wouldn't talk to her. So she backed up and got out and waited for him. I started . . . walking toward them. I couldn't hear what was said. And suddenly he . . . hit her."

Her eyes were round and wide in the dusk, the drink motionless halfway to her lips. "He what!"

"He hit her, Mary."

"Couldn't . . . couldn't anybody stop him?"

"He only hit her once. He knocked her onto the hood of the car. She fell off the front end of the car. And he kept on walking."

"This is incredible! Who else knows this? Who saw it?"

He explained about the elderly couple on the beach, about the Laybournes' suspicions, about telling only Pherson and Scherman, and telling Pherson only to keep it from being police business.

"About the police," he said. "That will be your decision, and Debbie Ann's."

"He's sick, Mike. He's so sick."

"I know."

"To just . . . hurt her like that. She's so sweet. She wouldn't hurt anybody. Tell me, Mike. Why would he do a thing like that?"

Now is the time to tell her, he thought. We've got her clubbed to her knees. Now we kick her in the face. Tell her about her sweet little daughter. Come on, Rodenska. Here we go.

"I don't know why he did it, Mary."

"It's so pointless!"

"The fact is that he did it. And she's going to be all right."

"But think of the psychic damage, Mike."

"I'm not going to worry about that."

"Where did he go? Right to that . . . Rowley woman?"

"Probably."

"I shouldn't have gone away, Mike."

"I'll give you that. You're right. You shouldn't have gone away."

They talked, but the talk was meaningless. They had another drink, but there was nothing festive about it. Finally he talked her into letting him fix something for them to eat. He said he knew where things were, said he could scramble the hell out of an egg. He fed the two of them. She helped clean up. She phoned the hospital to check on Debbie Ann, and then went off to bed. Mike went to his room and wrote to his sons. He took a stroll on the beach. There was a moist west wind, a haloed moon. It had been, all in all, one of the very long days. He felt too tired to try to think about anything. After he was in bed he was conscious of the stillness and emptiness of the other guest bedroom. Mary was in the far end of the main house. He wondered if she was sleeping. He hoped so.

ten

The phone started ringing early on Monday morning. The concerned, the curious. There had been a paragraph in the Ravenna paper, so brief and noncommittal that it merely whetted curiosity.

"Mrs. Debbie Ann Hunter of Riley Key, daughter of Mrs. Troy Jamison, was rushed to Ravenna Hospital yesterday afternoon after a serious fall. Her condition is said to be fair."

After taking three calls herself, Mary instructed Durelda to take any others that might come in and tell them Mrs. Jamison was at the hospital.

One call was for Mike. He took it on the wall phone near the kitchen door, and recognized the whispery croaky voice at once as Shirley said, "Mike, that's a private line, isn't it?"

"I think so. Yes."

"So is this one. Mike, the whole Key is buzzing. People are saying Troy put the slug on her. Is she hurt badly?"

313

He gave a capsule report of the injuries.

She gasped and then said, "Mike, I heard another rumor too. They're saying Mary got out because Troy was . . . fooling around with Debbie Ann."

"Nice clean outlook these people got."

"I guess you can't blame them too much. But I thought it would get back to you, and I wouldn't want you to think I . . ."

"I wouldn't have."

"Thank you, Mike. I felt creepy all day yesterday. Spooky, sort of."

"Yesterday was one of my large-size days."

"If there's anything I can do . . ."

"I'll let you know, kid. Thanks for calling. We're going in right now."

It was a little after nine when they arrived at the hospital. Her private room was on the third floor. Sam had already seen her and had left word for Mary that she seemed to be in pretty good shape and he was setting up the operation for the following morning.

"Can Mr. Rodenska see her too?" Mary asked the floor nurse.

"As far as I know," the nurse said.

"Go see her alone," Mike said. "She'd like that better."

"I want you with me. Please."

"Okay."

The door was ajar. Mary tapped. The special nurse let them in, introduced herself, said the patient was feeling a little better, and left, after asking them to stay not more than ten minutes.

Debbie Ann's bed was cranked up a few inches. The left side of her face was shocking. The split skin had been stitched and dressed. But what had been a concavity was now a high mound of dark red discoloration. The eye was pinched shut. The swelling distorted the nose and puffed the left corner of the mouth. Her jaw was taped in place. Her finger was splinted. She wore a clumsy-looking neck brace. One gray-blue eye stared at them, wearily, bitterly.

"Oh, my poor baby!" Mary said. "My poor darling." She pushed a chair close to the bed, sat and took Debbie Ann's left hand in both of hers. "Do you feel just horrible?"

"I feel awful, Mommy." The high-pitched voice was very frail. "I hurt in a hundred places."

Mike stood behind Mary's chair. That single eye was not dulled. It was aware, and wary. Mike suddenly realized the girl had no way of knowing how much he had told Mary, and had good cause for alarm.

"It was a horrid, brutal, unspeakable thing

for him to do. I think he was striking at me through you, darling."

"Have you seen him, Mommy?"

"No, I haven't, dear. And when I do I'm going to tell him just what I think about — all this."

"I stopped because I wanted to talk to him and . . . all of a sudden he had a . . . terrible expression on his face . . . and there was a big kind of white flash, and . . . I woke up here. I thought . . . he'd shot me in the face . . . but the nurse said . . . " She slowly closed her eye.

"Darling! Are you all right?"

The eye opened just as slowly. "I'm all right."

"Why did he hit you? Have you any idea?"

The single eye glanced quickly up at Mike, then looked away. He knew the question in her mind had been answered. He felt his muscles tensing.

"I — don't want to tell you, Mommy. I'm ashamed."

"Ashamed of what? You must tell me."

The girl's voice was halting, remote — her diction impeded by the taped jaw. She had to speak through clenched teeth. "Shirley and I went to the Hutchasons' party Saturday night. Then we went back to the house. We had some drinks. Mike and Troy were there, drinking. We sort of — went right on drinking. Troy was making my drinks. I guess they were strong ones. I lost track. Then we were . . . walking on the beach . . . Troy and me. And he said . . . let's go look at the *Skimmer* in the moonlight. We went below . . . to see if there was any liquor aboard. When . . . he grabbed me I thought it . . . was like a joke. And then . . . I knew it wasn't. I guess I screamed. But Shirley and Mike were playing records. I . . . could hear the music. *Begin the Beguine.* He . . . tore my clothes. They're in . . . the back of my closet . . . on the floor. Before he . . . finally let me go he made me promise I wouldn't tell. He said he'd kill me. By then Mike and Shirley were gone. Yesterday . . . I went for a long ride to think things over . . . and I decided I . . . would tell. But first I wanted to find out . . . if he was sorry or anything. I saw him and he wouldn't talk. So I got out of the car, right in front of him. I said . . . we should both tell you what happened, Mommy. And he . . . hit me. That's why he hit me. I think he . . . thought he killed me." She gave a long gasping sigh through clenched teeth and then made what must have seemed to Mary like a pathetic little attempt at a joke. "If that's what rape is like . . . it's pretty hard to do like they tell you to do — relax and enjoy it."

Mary stood up so suddenly the chair banged back against Mike's knees. She turned blindly, her face like dirty chalk, and plunged toward the doorway. Mike looked at the wide gray-blue eye. In its expression he read smugness, mockery, satisfaction.

"Bitch!" he said softly, and hurried after Mary.

He caught up with her at the hallway desk near the elevators. She had picked up a phone. The floor nurse was objecting. Mary was ignoring her, and requesting an outside line. When she got it, she dialed zero, waited a moment and then said, "Connect me with the police, please."

Mike leaned past her and pushed the cradle down, breaking the connection. She looked at him in complete fury.

"Stop interfering!"

"I want to talk to you first."

"Get away from me!" She pushed at him and dialed zero again.

Mike took a deep breath. As he firmly, forcibly, took the phone out of her hand, he smacked her solidly on the cheek with his left hand, harder than he had intended. It staggered her slightly. The rigidity of outrage left her — her eyes reflecting the sudden comprehension of a person coming out of shock.

"Why did you — "

He hung up the phone and grasped her upper arm firmly enough to cause a little movement of pain across her lips. He pulled her close to him and said, "Do I have any damn reason in the world to lie to you?" He made his face and voice angry.

"No, but — "

"I want to talk to you before you go off like a rocket."

"But he should be — "

"Make your call fifteen minutes from now if you still want to. Where can we talk privately, Nurse?"

"The treatment room is empty. The second doorway on the right."

He walked Mary down the corridor, pushed her in ahead of him, closed the door behind them.

When she turned to face him he could see that she was beginning to be furious again. "I know you're a good friend of Troy's, Mike, but you can't cover up something like — "

"Shut up! You're here to listen, not argue. I'm not protecting Troy. The hell with Troy. I'm keeping you from making a damn fool of yourself — from setting up a public scandal. The girl isn't worth it, Mary. She's lying. And she'll keep right on lying to you in that silly little voice, and if it ever came to the point of a trial, any punk little attorney Troy wanted to hire would tear her testimony to small dirty pieces."

"But — "

"I know what actually happened. Shirley McGuire knows, and Troy knows and Debbie Ann knows. And you haven't the faintest idea what happened or what she's like. I was gutless last night. I should have told you what happened the night before. She didn't pull this act until she made damn sure I hadn't told you."

"How can you sound so hateful about that poor baby — "

"Listen, will you? And keep remembering I'm not grinding an ax for anybody. I'm the innocent bystander people keep shooting at."

So he told her. He knew he couldn't do it delicately, because then she would refuse to believe. It had to be shock treatment. Harsh words. Factual. He put it all in. Her bath-towel routine. Her anecdote about Rob Raines. Her public reputation. Her devious-ness. He had always been able to remember dialogue, the special way people fit words to-gether, so that in repetition it has the distinc-tive flavor of truth. So, after he had told her graphically of his two visits to the *Skimmer III*, he repeated his conversation with Shirley, with Debbie Ann at breakfast, and finally with Troy.

Defiance had gone out of her. She sat in a hospital chair and stared with lowered head at the green tile floor.

"Check it out," he told her. "They talk about a wife or a husband being the last to know. Hell, it's the parent who is the last to know. I've seen them in court. They're terribly confused. They're caught up in something they don't understand. So they say to the judge, but Tommy was always a good boy. Or, Janie was always so sweet and polite to everybody. Debbie Ann doesn't give a damn if she maneuvers you into starting a grubby mess, demanding your own husband be picked up for rape. All she could think about was getting even with Troy for bashing her. She's not your sweet little baby, Mary. I'm sorry. She's a woman, married and divorced, idle, sexy and, I'm afraid, a little vicious. The adoration you've been giving her isn't healthy, for either of you."

He stopped talking. She was motionless except for fingers that plucked at the seam of her skirt.

"Are you all right?"

She raised her head to look up at him. Her face looked dulled, puffy. The lines that bracketed her mouth looked deeper.

"Aren't they going to leave me *anything?* Anything at all?"

She was so much longer with the girl than he thought she would be that he had begun to feel uneasy. It had gotten so hot in the station wagon that he had walked over to the shade of a big fern palm at the corner of the lot.

When he saw her coming, it was a sight that lifted his heart. She took long strides, her head held high, the sun striking the glossiness of her dark hair and the strong planes of her brown face. She moved with a physical articulation which was, at a distance, a youthfulness which dropped her from forty-two to twenty-five. But there was no sense of letdown when she came closer. When, in a woman, full maturity is combined with character and with pride, it creates a special beauty unattainable by the very young. Her strong chin was high, and there was a look around her mouth of a person who has tasted something slightly spoiled.

It's pride, he thought. That damn rare wonderful thing. A proud man will keep getting up. Break both his legs and he'll still give it a try. A proud woman won't whine. She won't give you the stifled sob and sheep-dog routine. She'll square her pretty shoulders and stick those knockers out like a bureau drawer and suck in her tummy, and put a little swing in her hips, and spit right square in your eye.

He fell into step beside her. "I'm sorry I took so long," she said. "I ran into Sam in the elevator. The orthopedic surgeon will operate tomorrow. He's had a look at the X-rays and he thinks he can reconstitute that cheekbone so her face won't be lopsided. The concussion was minor. Results of the lab tests are good."

They got into the car and headed south toward the Key. He sensed she'd report on Debbie Ann when she was damn well ready. And she wasn't damn well ready until two-thirty that afternoon. He was floating a hundred feet from shore when he saw her standing on the beach in skirt and blouse, shading her eyes. He thrashed in, trying valiantly to look less like a stern-wheeler in reverse, and came up the beach toward her, trying to hold his stomach firmly against his backbone.

"I've made all the damn fool phone calls, Mike. I'm going back to the hospital now."

"I can get ready fast."

"No. I'll go in alone." She smiled in a

crooked way. "And finish the job."

"Finish it?" he asked, and thumped water out of his ear with the heel of his hand.

"I still had little tiny doubts, Mike. I had to be sure. So I used one of — her weapons. The lie. I let her think I'd reported Troy to the police. She was delighted. I sat and led her on. I made her embroider her nasty story. She contradicted herself. I looked concerned until my face felt stiff. Then I fell on her. I told her I hadn't called, wouldn't call. I called her a liar. I told her if she wasn't hurt, I'd thrash her. She got defiant. She said she would tell the police. I told her to go ahead. She could go ahead and I would see that Troy had a trial, and I would make certain that you and I and Shirley and Troy testified against her. I told her that Troy would then have a basis for civil action against her and he could very well take away most of that money she's so fond of. Then I got very motherly when she started to cry. My heart went out to her — almost. I told her to stop trying to get even with Troy in any way. I told her she had been very bad — that she had done a monstrous thing — and she should concentrate on getting well. I kissed her on the forehead and left. I found the special and told her Debbie Ann might be quite upset for a while. I was so firm with her,

Mike. So cool with my baby. And so close to breaking down in front of her. But I couldn't let that happen. I know I shocked her terribly. She stared at me with that one pathetic eye as if she'd never seen me before."

"Maybe she never has."

"If she's well enough when I go in, she's going to get some woman talk. Woman-to-woman, not mother-to-daughter."

"You're quite a gal, Mary."

"No, Mike. As long as there are motions I have to go through, I'll go through them just as thoroughly as I can. I don't like any part of it. It's rough to take the veils off your eyes and really look at your own child, and see something that shames you. Can I wish a nasty job on you?"

"Sure."

"See if you can find Troy. Tell him I'm starting divorce action immediately. Tell him about Debbie Ann and what I would have done if you hadn't had the good sense to stop me. It might scare him a little. Tell him that Durelda is packing the rest of his things and if he'll give me an address, I'll have them trucked to a storage warehouse and send him the receipt. Tell him not to come back here on any pretext whatsoever. And tell him I want his stock in Horseshoe Pass Estates signed over to me immed — "

"I forgot to tell you. He said he was going to do that today. At the lawyer's office."

"You can use Debbie Ann's car." She looked at her watch. "I'm running behind schedule. I'll see you back here?"

He watched her walk briskly up the path and across the road, light skirt swinging, red shoes in female cadence.

Efficiency, he said to himself. Pack the stuff. Hire a truck. Get the stock. Pow. The alternative — lie in a darkened room using up a whole box of Kleenex, blaming it all on Everybody Else.

Shelder's Cottages were locked in the hot doze of siesta. Sun turned the crushed, bleached shell to a blinding white. Mike stood, squinting, in front of the porch door to number Five, trying to peer into the interior of the cottage. The Mercury was gone. He had not seen the Mercury in front of Red's B-29 Bar. The inner door was open.

"Troy?" he called. "Jerranna?" He banged on the screen door. He had the feeling that someone in one of the cottages across the way was staring at him. He could feel the icy weight of their intentness on the sweaty nape of his neck. He turned and looked behind him. A slat of a Venetian blind fell back into place.

He shrugged and opened the screen door and walked into the cottage. It was almost as hot inside as it was out in the full glare of sunshine. The couch in the small living room had not been made up. Gray sheets were bunched at the foot, a burned hole as big as a saucer visible. The litter was inclusive — cellophane wrap and empty bottles and empty cans and butts stomped into the green grass rug and a random shoe and a black bra and seahell ashtrays, overflowing; and frayed comic books and movie magazines and girlie magazines; and damp towels; and, taped to the wall, over a lamp with a tilting broken shade, a Playgirl of the Month, in full color, her face emptied by a solicitous grimace, her rump glossy, her breasts improbable — pink junket from a jokester's mold. She looked across the room at him with her color-press eyes, frozen there forever in that meaningless and cynical and never-to-be-fulfilled promise to infinite pimply-faced legions.

The still, heated air was an intricately symphonic construction of aromas. The major themes were the mouldy damp, with a basic old-laundry motif, with a repetitive glissando of perspiration, and the final theme of old-smoke — spilled-beer. Through and above and between this almost Wagnerian ponderousness could be detected the sharp little discords of perfume, marijuana, orange peel, burned food, female, urine and tropic sex.

He had stood in rooms like this one in many places. You looked at where they'd chalked the outline of the body on the floor. You watched them dusting for prints. You marveled at how high the blood had spattered on the wall. You listened to the coarse humor of officials with heavy faces and dead eyes, and if they threw a joke right at you, you laughed it up, because if you could keep on being one of the boys you'd get first crack at the next tawdry little room where animal violence had been done.

But, he reflected, if violence were done here, you wouldn't write a news story that gave the reader the reek of the place, the look of dreadful indifference. LUST MURDER IN RESORT BEACH LOVE NEST.

He moved to the bedroom door. He hoped he was wrong. But he wasn't. The room was a suitable companion to the living room. It was empty. Troy's suitcase stood in a corner. The shirt he had worn yesterday was across the foot of the bed.

This is what he wants, Mike thought. This

is the way he wants it. This can make him content, because it's the proper punishment for all his crimes. He is unworthy in his own eyes, and this is his bed of nails. This is his satisfying torment, his ceremony of purification. Once upon a time I knew a man who killed his wife. He loved her. He killed her unintentionally. He was proud of her. He wanted her as slim as the day he met her. So he hounded her, out of love. So she dieted intelligently and it did not do a bit of good because in maturity she had a natural heaviness, so she dieted unintelligently and that worked and she got down to the hundred and ten pounds he had been harping about, and she looked terrible, but he couldn't see that. And then she could not reverse the process, and she weighed ninety-five when the doctors got a chance to work one of those miracles of medical science on her, but she was beyond the point of being able to use a miracle, and died weighing not much over seventy pounds, and they gave the man hell for permitting his wife to diet herself to death out of vanity. And it took him sixteen months to kill himself. He was a big man. It took him that long to eat himself to death. They had to use a special coffin. And dig a bigger hole than usual.

So is this so entirely different? You can

nasty yourself to death. It's part of the same wish. The death wish is the daughter of guilt. Let every man belly up to the bar and order his own poison.

There were some papers on top of the bureau. He moved over, silently, looked without touching. There was a carbon of a legal document. It was dated today. Notarized today. It transferred seven hundred shares of the Horseshoe Pass Estates Corporation from Dexter Troy Jamison to Mary Kail Dow Jamison, written so as to imply that the certificates, properly endorsed, would accompany the original. There was a stub of red pencil in the bureau-top tray. He turned the letter over and quickly wrote, "Troy — Mary will start proceedings at once. You need expect no police trouble over Debbie Ann. She will require surgery but is in no danger. A warehouse receipt for the rest of your things will be sent to this address. Mary requests you make no attempt to contact her. Mike."

He hesitated, the pencil poised. Stick on a jolly postscript to my old buddy-buddy? Some little gesture of warmth? No, he doesn't want that. He doesn't want the obligation.

He started to walk out of the place, after putting the note in the middle of the sagging double bed, weighing it down with a half pretzel, and was vastly startled to be confronted by an enormous old woman who stood on runover shoes just inside the screen door, blocking the way and dwarfing the porch.

"What you doin' here?"

"Leaving a note for a friend."

"I own this here place. They's payin' for two and sleepin' three. I got toll about somebody movin' in with a suitcase yestiddy, so they owes more, startin' then. You see 'em, you tell 'em."

"I won't see them."

"Don't keer about a thang but gettin' full money."

"I have a feeling they won't be with you long."

"That'll be a good thang, mister, on account I got me too many complaints on them people." She turned like the *U. S. S. America*, grasped the door frame, lowered her weight down the two steps with much grunting, and headed for her cottage.

He followed her slowly, went out to where he had parked the Porsche. The shabby gaudy shacks stood disconsolate in the late afternoon sun. The Wiltin' Hilton, he thought. Bad housekeeping. Nobody has dusted the cabbage-palm fronds. Somebody left some fish in the sun. Come to this retirement paradise, all you senior citizens. (This seems more palatable than 'oldsters.') You've got your savings and you've got that Social Security, so take your choice. Be a guest of Ma Shelder and live right on the water. Or should you prefer to own your own home, the possibilities are infinite. Take Gracious Heights, for example. There you can buy the version of the Retire-a-Days which best suits you. These exquisite cinderblock homes range from $7,777.95 up to $13,333.50, including closing costs, complete with jalousied Florida room, modern kitchen, carport, septic tank and homestead exemption. Gracious Heights is only fifteen minutes from a new modern shopping center. (Clocked by Fangio in a D Jag with a running start.) You will live in the real Florida. (Entirely authentic, eighteen miles back into the scrub lands, flat as a two-dollar tire.) Become an expert on the flora and fauna (Chinch bugs, red bugs, cockroaches, fire ants, coral snakes, nutria, palm rats, buzzards, strangler figs, palmetto, saw grass, scorpions.) Retire the exciting way. (Gracious Heights is under an average six inches of water twice a day during the rainy season.) Or, if you prefer to build, spacious quarter-acre lots available, ten dollars down, ten dollars a month. (A quarter acre is roughly one hundred feet by one hundred feet.) Four more natural lakes ready soon.

Rodenska inserted himself into the Porsche, fumbled it into reverse, backed out and got away from there.

That was Monday. On Tuesday Hanstohm operated on Debbie Ann in the late morning. Sam Scherman observed the operation. He was pleased and optimistic about the eventual results. As Debbie Ann came out of the anesthetic in the recovery room, a nurse waited with wire clippers so as to be able to free her jaw quickly should Debbie Ann become nauseated and thus in danger of strangling. She was moved back to her private room in the late afternoon. Mary saw her and reported to Mike that she seemed very listless and groggy but otherwise all right.

They had dinner alone that night at the Key Club. Mary skillfully parried the questions of the overly curious who stopped at their table. She said there would be talk about the two of them being together — stupid, inventive talk, but she did not give one damn. They drank to that and drove home through a gusty night in the Porsche, with the top down, the radio tuned too loud to a Havana station.

On Wednesday morning Mike drove Mary

to the hospital and waited there for her, and then they drove into town and conferred with the lawyer, vague elderly Morton Stalp, whom Mike had met during the course of his investigation. Stalp kept the books of the Corporation. He explained all that had to be done to change the setup so deeds could be properly signed, and promised to start taking the first steps immediately. From there they went to the sales office on the property and talked to Marvin Hessler.

Hessler was depressed. But he cheered up remarkably when he found that Troy was out, and that things might well improve. They talked a long time. Hessler's ideas seemed valid to Mike. He knew he would have to check them out with expert, disinterested parties before going ahead.

As they were about to leave, Marvin said, "Say, yesterday that old Purdy Elmarr was here, poking all over the place. He didn't want any help at all. Said he was just looking. That's what they all seem to say. But he sure looked a long time."

"Thanks, Marvin," Mike said.

After they were in the car, Mary said, "Trouble?"

"I don't know. Maybe that old man snowed me good. I had the feeling he quit too easy.

He's — hard to figure. He's playing poker every minute. Now I got the feeling I showed him my hole card and while I was doing it, he was palming an ace."

"If he's going to squeeze us, Mike, I won't let you come in with me. I won't permit that."

"He's got you scared?"

"I'm not scared of Purdy or anybody else and you know it. But trying to buck him would be like — trying to stop a train by falling in front of it."

"I'll have to see him again."

"We'll have to see him. Both of us. And tell him Troy is out."

"I'll bet eleven dollars he knew all about that by noon last Monday."

Mary fixed dinner for them Wednesday night. They played cribbage after dinner. She was a resolute competitor, with all the proper desire to win.

The phone rang during the middle of the third game. "Don't stack the cards," she said as she got up.

"Yes?" he heard her say. "Yes, this is she. What? What is that? Oh! Oh, my God!"

He had gotten up quickly at the sound of her voice. He went to her. Her face was so bloodless her deep tan had turned a dirty yellow. She swayed. He pushed her into a chair.

"Debbie Ann?" he asked her.

"No. Troy," she said.

He picked up the dangling receiver.

eleven

The back roads of Florida are narrow, straight and rough. The big produce trucks roar through the night. Back there in the black night are the lonely gas stations, the infrequent shabby motels, the night-time beer joints with their quorum of dusty local cars and pickups. The rare towns are small islands, darkened houses and a brave spattering of neon. The cross-state traveler makes good time at night on the back roads, but there is a sameness to all of it, like crossing a dark sea. The headlights are hypnotic. A raccoon makes a very small thump against a front tire, and an opossum even less. So the cars whine down the roads, falling through the night, the lights picking up the wink of animal eyes and dead beer cans.

And sometimes in the lonely cottages set back in the piney woods, the sleeping people will be awakened by a sound like that of an enormous door being slammed. The first time it is heard it cannot be readily identified. But those who hear it the second time know at once what it means.

This one was only eight miles from the Tamiami Trail, on a big curve on State Road 565 that runs east-west and comes out about four miles below the Ravenna city limits. So there were people to hear it. A few. Not many. Sometimes the sound goes unheard, except by those for whom it is their final sensory experience. This is the up-to-date version of the ancient, illogical wheeze about that tree falling in the middle of the desert.

Anything that kills over thirty thousand people a year, and has killed a million since it first became possible to kill a person in this way unique to our culture, is going to be studied intensively. Of course, on a passenger-mile basis, our highways get safer every year, a fact distasteful to the National Safety Council which sees its function as a continuing effort to keep the daylights scared out of everybody. Give them this. It seems to be working.

At any rate, at such institutions as Cornell University, there are continuing studies of what happens to people who are going from here to there, for no particular reason, too carelessly.

Newton's laws of motion are eminently applicable. And it is interesting to contemplate the idea that were a modern automobile to be reduced to an overall length of three inches, with all parts in perfect scale, the steel foil of the body would be so delicate that it would be impossible to pick it up between thumb and forefinger without denting the sides in, deeply. And were a baby to hammer one with his fist it would flatten like a cream puff, tail fins and all, except for the stubborn hazelnut of the engine. We go fleetly in frail chariots.

The unimaginable energy of a ton and more of one of the delicately realized myths of Detroit traveling at ninety miles an hour must be dispersed in some fashion. Usually it is accomplished by wind friction, road friction, friction of moving parts, savage pressure on brake drums and a long spoor of black rubber, screamed onto pavement. But should something upset the equilibrium, this momentum can also be dispersed by a long end-over-end and sideways roll through tree trunks, power poles, rock gardens, store fronts, school children — whatever objects are immediately available. The effect of this on the passengers who happen to remain with the vehicle is somewhat similar to the effects that might be obtained if you popped them, along with two bushels of scrap iron, into a blown-up model of a piece of laundry equipment and set the dial for Spin-Dry.

But by far the quickest, most startling and most efficient way of dispersing all of this energy is through a truly classic head-on. A perfect head-on is a rare thing. The energy of the two vehicles — which is the product of mass and momentum — must be almost identical. And they must meet perfectly centered, both traveling in a reasonably straight line, with no attempt on the part of either driver to diminish speed before the moment of impact. When this feat is accomplished, and in all cases where the combined speed of the two vehicles had been in excess of a hundred miles an hour, no one has ever survived. The momentum of each vehicle is totally dispersed by the act of absorbing the energy of the other vehicle. It has been computed that when each vehicle is traveling at ninety miles an hour the impact is just a little bit less than were a single vehicle, in free fall, to strike an utterly unyielding surface. The state of free fall is achieved when any object has attained its maximum rate of fall. To state it another way, if an automobile were strapped to the belly of a big jet and released at forty thousand feet and fell, nose first, onto an enormous block of tool steel, the inhabitants of that vehicle would provide the medical people with much the same set of interesting distortions and jellied phenomena as can be observed after a classic head-on at a combined speed of one-eighty plus.

At twelve minutes after eight on that Wednesday evening in spring, a five-year-old Mercury and a nine-year-old DeSoto slammed that enormous door on a long and very mild curve on State Road 565 about twelve miles southeast by east of the City of Ravenna, Florida

And in that instant of finality, in the construction of that sound audible in the still night over two miles away, seven brains, hearts, livers, spleens, burst like rotten fruit which had clung too long to the branch of a high tree.

The experts of the State Highway Patrol did their best to reconstruct it. There were no skid marks to measure, so speed could be but roughly estimated. The green Mercury had been heading west at an estimated ninety plus. For the driver, the long curve was to his right, so he should have remained in the lane on the inside of the curve. But the high speed even on such a gentle curve had induced a factor of centrifugal force which had carried him out so that he was straddling the double yellow line at the point of impact. On the other hand the DeSoto had probably been traveling at such a high rate of speed that the driver could not keep it in the lane on the outside of the curve without losing control. So he had drifted in, cutting the curve, and had been straddling the center line at the point of impact.

The two vehicles struck with such force that they both rebounded from the impact and came to rest, smoking, still aimed at each other, the DeSoto with its rear wheels in a shallow ditch on the south side of the road, the Mercury on the shoulder on the north side. By then, of course, the trade names of the vehicles were academic, the use of them a matter of convenience. As in all classic head-ons, most of the passengers remained with the vehicles. Directness of impact made the windshield the only exit route, a quick journey available only to the passenger beside the driver. The driver, with the steering column through his chest, and the motor in his lap, tends to remain in place. Also, in the classic head-on, there is a grotesque lack of damage to the rear half of each vehicle. From the midpoint forward, they were compacted, unrecognizable junk. From the midpoint to the tail lights, they were quite obviously automobiles, but even in the undamaged rear it was possible to detect startling evidence as to the force of impact. Tail light lenses were collapsed in upon themselves. Gas tanks mashed forward. Rear bumper braces compressed. Rear window glass hurled forward into the car. Dense objects in trunk compartments were hurled forward through the trunk compartment wall into the car's interior. When the vehicles stopped with that ultimate abruptness, every loose or weakly braced object, every bit of bone, blood and tissue, strove mightily to continue forward at the unabated pace of approximately one hundred and thirty-five feet per second. This is approximately the initial velocity of a three-hundred-yard drive by Snead, and the initial impact flattens the dense ball to almost one half its normal diameter.

A man was hurled through the windshield of the DeSoto, a woman through the windshield of the Mercury. In delicate irony, after each vehicle had come to rest, the ripped and broken bodies of those ejected two each lay closer to the car in which they had not been riding. This momentarily confused the investigation until one trooper noted in the floodlight glare that a body can make skid marks, in blood.

Moments after the impact the DeSoto caught fire, and it burned briskly for over ten minutes before foam smothered the flames. By then there were four state patrol cars, two county cars, three ambulances, two wreckers and a fire engine at the scene, as well as approximately fifty spectators who had parked their cars along the shoulders. The red dome lights winked. The bright floods cast heavy shifting shadows. Men took flash photos. Other men stretched tape measures along the pavement and made computations. Another man was on the radio, relaying the Oklahoma and New York plate numbers to the message center to speed identification of the bodies. Newspaper reporters and photographers had arrived. The coroner arrived, stared, shrugged and went home. Troopers were sending the curious on their way — in lesser quantity than they were arriving — as the bodies were being loaded to be taken to the Police Morgue in Ravenna in the basement of the lab wing of the hospital. The first probable identification was made at the scene. A trooper, holding his breath, gingerly worked a wallet out of a hip pocket in the Mercury. The hip pocket was not where one would expect to find it. In fact, the hip was not where it should have been.

He held the identification cards to the light, then called his superior over. "Local guy, it looks like. Address on Riley Key."

"Troy Jamison. Troy Jamison. I heard that name before. A builder. Or maybe he peddles real estate."

"Line up forty guys around here and twenty of them peddle real estate."

"Don't get wise with me, Russ. Tell Harry to call this name and address and phone in and tell them to start checking. They all loaded? Okay, you wrecker guys! Hook up and roll 'em."

Ten minutes later the long curve was once again empty and dark and silent. The infrequent car went by, taking the long curve unaware of the insignificant stains of blood, the discarded film wrappers.

The process of identification continued. It was a full twenty hours before the four occupants of the DeSoto were identified. Had one of them not been thrown clear it could have taken longer. They were all male, all in their middle twenties, all Puerto Rican, all migratory workers. The Mercury was not as difficult. After a Mr. Rodenska at the Jamison home came on the phone and was given a description of the car he suggested the other two occupants might be a man and woman living at the Shelder Cottages on Ravenna Key. He gave the woman's name as Miss Jerranna Rowley, and he knew the man only as Birdy. His physical descriptions and estimates of age matched the bodies well enough to warrant sending a team out to number Five. The number of the Oklahoma plates matched the nickel-notebook records maintained by Mrs. Shelder. The team reported back in, when they brought back all personal possessions from the cottage for official storage, that they had been unable to find any papers indicating blood relatives who could be contacted. As it so happened, Mr. Rodenska was then at the morgue, having brought Mrs. Jamison in to make the necessary official identification of her husband.

Fortunately for Mrs. Jamison, of the seven victims only Mr. Jamison had escaped extensive facial abrasions and lacerations. His face was distorted however, as though it were being viewed through a flawed pane of glass. A sheet covered the more serious damage. From the position of the body in the wreck it seemed possible that Jamison had been asleep in the rear seat at the moment of impact.

Rodenska brought the woman in and held her by the arm. She looked at the dead face. The lieutenant thought her face looked just as dead as his.

"Is there any special way I say this?" she asked calmly. "Any sort of legal formula?"

"No. Is that your husband?"

"Yes."

"Thank you, Mrs. Jamison. That's all we need. You can have your funeral director pick up the remains at any time."

She turned away and Rodenska took her out. He took her to the car. She got in. "Are you all right?"

"Yes."

"They want me to go back in there."

"Why?"

"I don't know. I won't let them keep me long."

He went back in. The lieutenant said, "I can only ask you to do this and you can say no. But can you try to give me a tentative on the other two? I'll tell you they aren't pretty."

"I'll give it a try."

"Thanks. They're back in here."

The bodies lay stripped on the zinc slabs, side by side. He looked at a faded rose on a slack and ruptured biceps. And at the woman's pale brown hair, long neck, meatiness of thigh.

"I'm positive," he said. "Birdy and the Rowley woman."

"Thanks," the lieutenant said. As he walked back out with Mike he sighed and said, "We'll check through the plates back with the Oklahoma people, and we'll check the prints through the F.B.I. files, but on that pair I got a hunch it'll end up no known relatives. There's money enough on them to bury them and some left over, and so that'll be stuck in escrow and their junk warehoused, and seven thousand years from now it'll be turned over to the state."

They had reached the outside door. Mike could see Mary sitting in the station wagon under the street light.

"They were all afternoon in a crummy joint ten miles east of where it happened, getting boiled. How come a guy like Jamison was running around with a pair like that?"

"I don't know."

"I knew you didn't know. I'll bet his wife couldn't figure it. I bet even he didn't know. You run into that every once in a while. A prominent man, he has to go off and get his kicks running around with trash. Funny thing when a man has everything."

"Correction. He had almost everything. And with some people that's exactly the same as having nothing."

"What?"

"I better get her home, Lieutenant."

"Sure. Thanks for helping out."

He drove her back to the Key. She stood under the kitchen lights. "I think my personal timing is going to be just about right, Mike."

"What do you mean?"

"I'm going to cry my eyes out. It's just so far away from me, hanging over me like a — glacier. It's getting closer and there's going to be just enough time to get to bed before it falls on me. I'm going to let it rip. I'm going to bellow like a herd of sheep. That doesn't sound right. A flock of sheep. And I guess they bleat, don't they? But that's a word with no dignity." She took a step closer and kissed him lightly and quickly on the mouth and stepped back. "I've got to stop thanking you and thanking you. It's getting to be a dull routine. Good night, Mike."

In the morning, when phone calls and callers threatened to drive them out of their mind, Mike, with sudden inspiration, got hold of Shirley McGuire who said she would be happy to run interference. The morning paper gave the accident page one treatment, with a grimly specific shot of the accident scene. Mike read the coverage and decided it was both pedestrian and unnecessarily windy.

For the first time in a long, long time he had the quick strong wish that he had directed the coverage: pics, captions, makeup and copy.

At a little after eleven there was a lull, and the three of them, Shirley, Mike and Mary, had coffee on the screened terrace. Mary had been very subdued and quiet, without acting dangerously depressed.

"You've been a help, both of you," Mary said to Mike and Shirley McGuire, "and I'm grateful. But all of this isn't your problem. Mike, why don't you have Durelda fix a lunch, and you two take Debbie Ann's little car, and go a long way away and try to forget all this for a little while. You could drive to Marco. There's a wonderful beach there. . . . "

Mike glanced at Shirley and saw the quick flicker of interest and anticipation in her dark eyes.

He turned toward Mary and said, "Thanks. But there's too much to do. Red tape. Legal stuff. Checking account. Lock box. Wills. I can help with that stuff, Mary."

"I did it before. I know the routines. I can do it again."

Mary stood up as the phone started to ring. Mike said, "No reason to do it alone when I'm here to help. And . . . you've got to tell Debbie Ann what's happened, Mary. I think I should be with you."

"I can tell her, Mike," Mary said, and turned to go to the phone, but just as she turned away he saw a look of dread, and he knew he could not leave her.

"They say it's a lovely, lovely beach at Marco," Shirley McGuire said.

"And we'll have a fine picnic, girl. Some other time. Okay?"

Finally, remembering that look of dread, Mike got Mary alone and told her he was perfectly willing to go and tell Debbie Ann by himself, that perhaps it would be better that way. Mary argued, but there was little force in her argument.

So it was agreed that he would go and tell Debbie Ann, provided Sam Scherman said it was all right to tell her, and provided some fool nurse hadn't given her the morning paper — if she was well enough to read it.

Mike located Sam making his morning rounds. He said Debbie Ann was well enough to be told, that in fact he had debated telling her himself and had decided it would be easier for her coming from her mother. No, Debbie Ann did not know. The special had used her head and commandeered the free paper for the hospitalized before Debbie Ann had seen it.

So Rodenska squared his shoulders, pulled his stomach in and marched to Debbie Ann's bedside. Her color was much better. The left side of her face was heavily bandaged. Her hair was combed. She had been cranked up into a half-sitting position. The special went out and closed the door behind her.

"What are *you* doing here?" The locked jaw put a hiss in her speech, an odd tonal quality. "Where's Mommy? Why isn't she here?"

"She sent me to visit the sick."

"This goddamn neck brace is driving me out of my mind. They fixed it so I can't breathe through the left side of my nose. And they took out a perfectly good tooth, a perfect tooth right in front, goddamn them, so I can suck the foul goop they give me through a straw. So the last thing I want to look at this morning out of this one eye is you, you dirty snitch bastard! Go away, for God's sake!"

"Anybody could tell you're vastly improved."

"How the hell did you all of a sudden make her start hating me? You're pretty damn smart, Rodenska. You sold her the whole story. Thanks so much. You destroyed her love for me. God, I hate you!"

"Not her love, kiddo. Just her liking for you, and respect for you, and pride in you.

Love goes on. You don't turn that kind off."

"How comforting can you get?"

"I didn't tell her anything until I had to. Then I had to do it the hard way, to keep her from charging Troy with rape."

"Is that so bad?"

"It wouldn't have stood up. There wouldn't have been a conviction."

"I don't care about that. I wanted them to pick him up and take him to a little room and beat the living hell out of him. That's what they do to rapists."

"Only on television. Except when they're the wrong color."

"Oh. Anyway, somehow he's going to pay. Even if I have to hire people to do it. I want his face smashed the way he smashed mine. And crack his neck and break a finger, just like what happened to me. He didn't have to hit me!"

"What did you say to him?"

"He wouldn't answer me. He just kept walking. It made me mad. So I stopped and got out. He told me to get out of his way. I asked him where he was going and he said just as far from me as he could get. So I just said he didn't have to worry about it ever happening again. He didn't have to run from temptation, I told him. Because just once was plenty for me. I said it was pretty dull merchandise, probably because he was so damn old. Then he hit me. When you see him, you tell him I'll get even sooner or later. That's all you're good for — telling people every damn thing you know. It makes you feel important. You stick your nose in other people's lives because it makes you feel like a big shot. Get the hell out of here! I get sick looking at you and they keep warning me I shouldn't throw up."

"I can't tell him, princess. I can't tell him a thing."

"Why? Did he really go away? I thought it was just an act."

"He did just what he said he was going to do. He got just as far away from you as he could get. And you'll never get even."

"You think."

"I know. I can't give you this between the eyes, because there is only one eye. And I'm just bastard enough to be able to get a little bit of enjoyment out of this. He's stone cold dead, baby. It happened last night. Automobile accident. Head on. He's one of seven deceased. He didn't precisely kill himself, and you didn't precisely murder him. Let's just say that if you had had the decency or the desire to keep your legs crossed, he'd be alive. And you wouldn't be in here."

The eye snapped shut. He saw her sudden pallor, the clenching of her good fist, the spasm of her throat — and he went running for the nurse. She came on the double, snatched up the wire cutters and hovered over Debbie Ann.

"Are you going to be sick dear?"

"I . . . don't know."

"If you get absolutely sure you're going to be, nod your head yes and then spread your lips back out of the way."

They waited in tension and silence for thirty seconds. Just as Mike realized her color was coming back, Debbie Ann said, "I'm not going to be sick."

"Good for you, dear. I think you better go, sir."

"Stay here, Mike!"

"She's upset, sir."

"Upset, *hell!*" Debbie Ann snarled. "I'll be more upset if I don't hear more about this. Now get out of here, please, Parkins, and let us talk."

The nurse hesitated. "I'll be right outside the door. Don't be too long, sir."

When the door shut Debbie Ann said, "Mommy wasn't involved in it, of course?"

"No."

"Was he with that woman?"

"Yes."

"And she was killed too?"

"Nobody could have gotten out of that one."

"How is Mommy taking it?"

"Pretty well. She identified him. She's pretty . . . subdued today, but she's making the funeral arrangements herself."

"Does . . . does she blame me, Mike?"

"She hasn't said."

"Do you think she will?"

"She knows the situation was bad. And she can't help knowing you made a bad situation a hell of a lot worse. You slept with her man when he was sick, mixed-up and vulnerable. You gave him a guilt he couldn't live with. I don't see how she can ever think of you again as her sweet little lovable baby. You asked me. I told you. But you didn't have to ask. You know all that."

"Oh, God!"

"There's an old-timey idea still in force. Whatever you take, they get stubborn and make you pay for it."

"I should have been with him last night, Mike. That would have made it a hell of a lot neater. I wish I'd been with him."

"Don't tell me! Am I hearing right? Debbie Ann expressing remorse? Regret? Guilt, even?"

"Don't pound on me, please."

"Or maybe it's just an act. You want to soften me up for some reason. So you make with the tragedy-jazz. Remember? You're the golden girl. You can do anything in the wide world you want to do and it's right because it's you that does it. Everybody in the world is a slob except the infinitely desirable Debbie Ann."

"What are you trying to *do* to me? My God, I hate myself enough without you — "

"Not enough. Not yet. But you're moving in the right direction. Remember I told you about looking in the mirror. You haven't yet. But maybe it's possible."

"Who were . . . the other people killed?"

"Stop changing the subject. Ask the nurse for the morning paper after I leave, which is going to be just about now. You got a lot of time alone. Play this game. Be somebody else, looking at Debbie Ann, getting to know her. What would this somebody else think?"

"I don't want to know."

"Yes, you do."

"I don't!"

"Do me this," he ordered. "Give it a try. You got all day." He held his left hand out. The single eye had a baleful stare.

"Bastard!" she said.

357

"Coward!" he said, and did not take his hand away.

Finally she reached across her body with her uninjured left hand and took his. "Okay. But I have a feeling I'm not going to enjoy it."

"Who said it would be a pleasure?" he said, and walked out.

He went back to the house. When he had a chance to speak to Mary alone he said, "She could grow up, that girl. A little delayed, but not impossible."

"How did she take it?"

"It jolted her. It knocked her off balance. While she was on a tilt, I jolted her another couple of times. The modern style of handling Sleeping Beauty. No kiss. A boot in the tail. Maybe she sits up and looks around. Maybe she goes back to sleep. It's anybody's guess."

"Maybe I kept her asleep so long, treating her like a little child."

"Don't treat her that way any more."

"How could I?"

"Treat her with love. Love isn't for reward and punishment. Respect is what you give and take away, not love."

"Mike, Mike," she said, the tears starting to come.

"If you can cry again, good. Go do so."

She tried to smile, and fled. He roamed the

house restlessly for a little while, and then went over and basked on the beach. He swam a little — with great fury and determination. He walked and found a shark's tooth, black as the eyes of McGuire. He summoned up specific memories of Buttons, and braced himself for the big wave. It came, and it blinded him, but did not nudge him off his feet.

Mike Rodenska. A chunky brown man on a lot of beach, balding, thoughtful, and alone — relighting the hoarded half of a cigar.

He sat down. A pale gray crab came out of his sand-hole home and squatted, motionless, staring at Rodenska.

"What do you need?" Mike asked him. "You got a hole there. You got a hard shell, and all the beach you can use. You know your trouble, my friend? You're over-privileged. You got it too good. Go back in the hole and count your money."

He flapped his hand. The crab darted back into his hole. Mike lay back and went to sleep.

epilogue

The wide beach is there, unchanging. A storm nibbles some of it away. Another storm replaces it. And the wild things are there, watchful, hungry — generation after generation, yet always the same. Man is but a guest on the beach. He changes nothing, and is soon gone.

A little over a week after Troy's funeral, Mike Rodenska and Mary Jamison sat on Purdy Elmarr's front porch, cautious, watchful.

Purdy was saying, "Like I told you, I kept thinking on how Corey Haas could just set quiet and make out real fine on his piece of that corporation, and you two ain't rough enough to squeeze hard enough to squeeze him out, and him doing so good isn't in the plans I got for him, and I pledged you I'd help out with that deal, and if a man's going to help it's only natural he gets a piece of it. So I just squoze Corey out."

"You said you bought him out," Mike said.

"That I did. But Corey's never stayed as liquid as he should, and when all of a sudden he started needing fast money here and there for this and that, he sold cheap."

"I guess that . . . makes us partners," Mary said.

Purdy grinned at her. "You two don't look like you'd heard any kinda good news. I'll want some say in how we run it, sure. And you're wondering now I got my foot in the door, maybe I'll squeeze you a little. Keep right on a-wondering. It'll keep you on your toes."

"I guess we don't have too much choice," Mike said.

"You spoken a true word right there. I'm in to stay. I'm taking a real interest," Purdy said.

"And my lawyer will check every piece of paper," Mike said.

"You'd be a damn fool if he didn't. Now you come along and look at a brand new colt came into the world yesterday. Pretty thing. Wobbly on his laigs."

"I'm telling you, Purdy Elmarr, if Mike should lose money on . . ."

"Now you hush up, Mary Kail. We're through with money talk for the day."

Ten months later, after all lots were sold out in Area One of Horseshoe Pass Estates, Area Two was opened for sale, prior to completion of the final portion of the roads and sea walls. The public response was most encouraging to the officers and directors of the corporation.

A week after Area Two was opened, a letter arrived from Thomas Arthur Rodenska to his father.

Micky and I have been looking at those pictures you sent a thousand times I bet. And we can't hardly wait to fly down Easter. Last summer was sure a keen deal, being in Florida, but like you said in your letter to Micky it's one thing renting a place and another thing having your *own*. Are you sure the house will be done by the time we come down? Will it be ready to live in even? We have been having big fat arguments about what the surprise is. Finally I figure the way Micky does. In one picture you can see just left of the house a sort of thing that could maybe be the end of a dock. Could the surprise be a boat? Could it be a sailboat? I know you won't tell because you never do, but I am asking anyway. If it *is* a boat, will it be there when we get there? There is one thing you should know about next summer anyhow, even if it is a boat. We have talked it over, what you said about good times and all that in *my* letter, and it is best for you to know we are going to get jobs next summer. That means we will not have so much time for the sailboat, so if it was there for Easter we wouldn't have anything else to do and we would get a lot of good use out of it. You said you had everything sent down and that means all our junk from home and a lot of that is kid stuff. So it was too bad to spend the expense of sending it down but we can sort it down there for give away and throw away and keep. We can probably do that at night when it is too dark for anyone but foolish reckless people to be out in a sailboat.

A little over a year after Troy's funeral, Mary Jamison received the first letter in three months from Debbie Ann. It was mailed from Los Angeles. The address was the same, but the tone of the letter was new. It was a very long letter, and Mary Jamison went over it many times.

Part of it read:

I don't know if this is of crashing importance to anybody but me, but somehow I have let myself get all worked up and earnest about a Project. I am sorry not to have written in so very long, but now that things have sort of simmered down for me, I might do better. After I bored the Scotts to death in Carmel, and bored Nancy Ann to distraction in La Jolla, I looked up June Treadway in L. A. I don't think you ever met her. I am a real pro at moving in with people and staying practically forever. I located her through her parents. She had a marriage that went blah, and she rooms with a girl in an apartment so roomy they could fit me in. But they both work, so it was very empty daytimes, and you can really get bloody bored just shopping and beaching and seeing movies and having daytime dates with the tiresome men they seem to have a lot of out here. June does social work for the City and County of Los Angeles. Case investigation. I always thought social workers were a joke, a very tired sad joke. But June told me such weird things I got interested. I can see that if I try to give you the whole history this letter is going to take forever. Here is the current picture. I am employed. How about *that?* I got sneaked onto the payroll as a trainee, and I can't do any casework all by myself, and the pay is pitiful. I am taking night courses at U.S.C. and putting billions of frightening miles on the Jag I bought just before I left Florida. I can barely find time to eat and sleep, and I haven't had my hair done in a century, but I love it, and I keep wondering when it will suddenly wear off and I will be my usual aimless self.

I am dating one guy only, name of George Pickner, who is exactly one day older than I am, a fact he brings up whenever possible. He is a graduate student, hacking away at his doctorate in Sociology and teaching on a fellowship. My instructor. That's how we met. Anyway, he is such a nice guy that I finally tried to drive him to cover by giving him the whole dreary emotional history and tawdry escapades in the life of Deborah Ann. It gave the poor dear a rocky evening, but he has bounced back by convincing himself I am a New Woman. This he cannot sell me. I have told him to stay braced because all of this is only one of my temporary enthusiasms and it will no doubt wear off suddenly when least expected. Enough of that.

The clipping about Rob Raines being disbarred was unexpectedly depressing. Very hard on him and Dee too, I would imagine. Say hello to Mike for me. . . .

A year and a half after Troy Jamison's death, Mr. Michael Rodenska, President of the Horseshoe Pass Estates Corporation, before leaving on his honeymoon, made a public announcement that he was retiring from the land-development business, had bought into the Ravenna *Journal-Record* and, after his return, would take an active hand in the operation of the paper.

Two weeks later Mike Rodenska and his bride were baking themselves into a happy, lazy stupor under a Mediterranean sun, on a private hotel beach on the Costa Brava — protected from a chilly wind by a canvas windbreak.

"Florida beaches are much, much nicer," the bride said drowsily.

"Shaddap! This one is cheaper. So Marco is better, but this one is cheaper. I love you, but you complain too much."

"He makes more money than he ever saw before, so he goes looking for a cheap beach! How about that!"

"Listen. It's romantic here. You know. Spain. Castanets. Bull fights. Shut up and enjoy it, please."

She sighed. "That's what's so nice about honeymoons. All the sweet talk!"

"You take my first honeymoon," Mike said, "I was highly nervous. Now I'm an elderly sophisticate. I take it in stride. Nonchalant."

"I guess I've *never* had a better time," the bride said.

"I appreciate the endorsement, lady."

She jabbed him with an elbow. "Fatuous type!"

"Nothing exceeds like excess."

"I'll ignore that, dear. I like the way we talk, that's what I mean. All the laughs. There's nothing wrong with anything."

"Just one thing wrong," Mike said. "How come we run into so many punk kids on their silly, fumbling little honeymoons. They don't know the score. They think they're really living. When they notice me at all, I'm just sort of the background, a dreary old poop trying to get cultured up. If they knew I was on *my* honeymoon, they'd laugh themselves into convulsions."

"I'm not exactly what you'd call a teen-ager," the bride said.

"You are, thank God, beyond the age of pubescence, woman. And from here to here, you are as young as . . ."

"Unhand me, sire! This is a public beach!"

"A private beach. Tell me one thing, Mary. Why were you trying to marry me off to Shirley? It gave me the jumps."

"She would have been good for you, darling."

"As good as you?"

"Hell no! But . . . I'm nearly forty-five. I feel eighteen. Silly, tingly, happy. Is that right?"

"You feel like that? Then maybe you can remember something in the room that you forgot, like. Maybe your lighter. So I could come along, help you hunt for it."

She looked at him solemnly, owlishly. "I *don't* have my lighter. My beach bag is right here, and maybe it's in the beach bag, but that would be too efficient, to look there first, wouldn't it? So I'd say the only thing to do is go look in the room first."

Mike was suddenly on his feet, grinning, paw extended to her. "So let's *go!*"

And so this is the second and final fadeout

— like hand-in-hand into the sunset — this Rodenska family, picking itself up off the grainy Spanish sand, picking up the tools of beaching, hurrying a little because when you stand up into the wind, it is hardly a pleasure.

Above the shallow beach are the rocks, and a path that winds up through the rocks, and beyond that what passes in Spain for a paved highway, and beyond the highway the self-conscious confection of a new hotel, like a wedding cake sitting in a quarry.

So the woman goes first on the narrowness of path, and turns to laugh and say something to the stocky brown man following her so closely. They are observed there in the lemon sunlight by but one couple, a lean long-married pair of English tourists from Maida Vale, snug in hairy garments, sitting on rocks. They turn simultaneous heads to stare with the iciness of heraldic griffins, narrow nostrils widening in displeasure.

The man thinks, "Wherever those American types come, they contrive to spoil it for us, totally."

The woman thinks, "She is hardly a young girl, not by decades, but that figure, my word! By what nasty magic do those types manage it?"

They have reached the top of the path. The

woman turns to speak and smile again, and in response the man, with his free hand, claps her a jolly one on the haunch. The two narrow heads of the observers snap back into position and two pair of gray eyes stare toward Africa.

"Low types," the man murmurs.

"Totally," she replies.

THORNDIKE PRESS HOPES you have enjoyed this Large Print book. All our Large Print titles are designed for the easiest reading, and all our books are made to last. Other Thorndike Press Large Print books are available at your library, through selected bookstores, or directly from the publisher. For more information about current and upcoming titles, please call us, toll free, at 1-800-223-6121, or mail your name and address to:

THORNDIKE PRESS
P. O. BOX 159
THORNDIKE, MAINE 04986

There is no obligation, of course.